Over the last fe to help deal with my ...., when I'm going to sleep at night, I picture myself driving the carriage that meets up with the headless horseman, the one from that old '80s movie *The Legends of Sleepy Hollow*. I hand over my sorrow, in a tidily wrapped up package, to the man with no head and stand to watch as the horse rears up onto its hind legs and eventually gallops off into the fog, taking the package and my grief with it. This allows me to feel empty, not peaceful by any means, but empty enough to close my eyes and let the darkness take over. If I'm lucky, I can clock a few hours of sleep. Sleep is where I'm most comfortable nowadays. Where there's nothing to remember, no pain surrounding my heart, no sorrow, just that sweet vacancy of being.

There are times when I wake up in the morning, that blissful time when I'm neither asleep nor awake, just hovering somewhere in the middle when I feel closest to Lenny. Like if I reach my arm out, he'll be there, on the other side of the bed, warm and ready for me to snuggle into. This moment of bliss always, of course, comes to a crashing halt the moment realization hits, Lenny is still dead. Those split seconds when I could have reached out and touched him are gone, vanished, causing my heart to break all over again.

The Club

by

Jacquline Kang

The Club

Cover Art by *Kristian Norris*

The Wild Rose Press, Inc.
PO Box 708
Adams Basin, NY 14410-0708
Visit us at www.thewildrosepress.com

Publishing History
First Mainstream Mystery Edition, 2020
Print ISBN 978-1-5092-2857-7
Digital ISBN 978-1-5092-2858-4

Published in the United States of America

Dedication

To my children, Austin, Olivia, and Emma.
You can do anything you put your mind to.

Acknowledgments

I want to take this opportunity to thank my editor, Ally Robertson, for being so kind to a nervous writer and for giving me the guidance so I could grow into an author. To everyone at Wild Rose Press, a resounding thank you for all you do; the production side of creating a masterpiece is no joke!

To my friend Namrata Bachwani, whose support in writing and life has been invaluable to me, thank you for teaching me to believe in myself and what a true friend is.

To the PEPS ladies—Stephanie Vanterpool, Winona Hugo, and Christine Harper—thank you for your never-ending encouragement, the date night cocktails, and for becoming my "other family."

To my P.K. mom tribe—Jayme Kennedy, Anne Rethke, Ezra Tanyeri, and Clancy Marschner—thank you for reading the early phases and still believing in me.

To my writing family—Heidi Jenkins, Matthew Wheeler, and Carl Lee—I am forever indebted to you for all the writing advice. I'm so thankful we have each other to muddle through this together.

To my real family—Alex, Austin, Olivia, Emma, Sungsoo, Ungdap, and all the rest—you are my heart and soul, and I couldn't do this, let alone the rest of life, without you!

Chapter 1

Over the last few months, I've learned little tricks to help deal with my grief. Like this one for example: when I'm going to sleep at night, I picture myself driving the carriage that meets up with the headless horseman, the one from that old '80s movie *The Legends of Sleepy Hollow*. I hand over my sorrow, in a tidily wrapped package, to the man with no head and stand to watch as the horse rears up onto its hind legs and eventually gallops off into the fog, taking the package and my grief with it. This allows me to feel empty—not peaceful by any means, but empty enough to close my eyes and let the darkness take over. If I'm lucky, I can clock a few hours of sleep. Sleep is where I'm most comfortable nowadays. Where there's nothing to remember, no pain surrounding my heart, no sorrow, just that sweet vacancy of being.

There are times when I wake up in the morning, that blissful time when I'm neither asleep nor awake, just hovering somewhere in the middle, when I feel closest to Lenny. Like if I reach my arm out, he'll be there, on the other side of the bed, warm and ready for me to snuggle into. This moment of bliss always, of course, comes to a crashing halt the moment realization hits: Lenny is still dead. Those split seconds when I could have reached out and touched him are gone, vanished, causing my heart to break all over again. It's

1

been getting harder and harder to persuade myself to get out of bed. If I stay too long, I will have missed my chance of escaping my own thoughts, destructive things, which usually lead to a day spent under the covers, tears permanently etching my cheeks.

The luxury of wallowing in my own misery hasn't really been an option lately, as nausea creeps up on me in the morning. The waves of hot and cold, propelling me through the cold autumnal air saturating my bedroom, to the white porcelain bowl on the other side of the en-suite bathroom. I've been getting better at making it all the way to the toilet before the contents of my stomach are emptied all over the floor. I've already resolved to replace the beige area rug in the near future.

The dry heaves are the worst part. I never realized, before now, that a person can keep vomiting even when the contents of their stomach are entirely gone.

Today, in particular, is a glorious heaving day. After what feels like an eternity on my knees, gripping the toilet, I wipe the sweat from my brow and lay my head on the cool ceramic tub. The vomiting has stopped, and I feel the familiar surge of relief that it's over for now. Content to rest in a heap on the heated floor of the bathroom, I loll my head to the side, so I'm staring at the ceiling and try to recover. It takes me a good five minutes before I can get my legs to support my body again. I stand and step into the shower, eager to wash away the morning's drama.

Showered, blow-dried, and dressed in The Club uniform of a fitted white polo shirt and sea-foam blue track pants with a white stripe running down the side, I head into the kitchen. Surrounded by two walls of full-length windows, I feel like a lone fish in my own concrete, steel, and glass fishbowl. I pass the limestone counter on the kitchen island and reach for the handle of the Bosch refrigerator, ready to make toast and a banana smoothie—the only things palatable to me these days. Standing in front of the fridge, I'm bombarded, as I am every day since Lenny died, with memories of our happiness. Our idyllic images jump off the pictures, held in place by tiny heart magnets, and slap me in the face. I absorb the assault, letting it seep into my subconscious, then open the door for the carton of soymilk.

Grabbing a handful of frozen blueberries and a banana to throw into the blender, I start the positive self-talk my therapist taught me during our last session. She insisted that if I start my day with confidence the rest of my daily mundane tasks will be able to fall into place. I will be able to make it through the next twenty-four hours without wanting to curl up into a little ball on the sidewalk. I'm starting to think I need to look for a new therapist.

"I am a person of quality, I deserve to be loved, I am strong," I recite aloud, my voice echoing in the empty condo. Pausing, I let the silence surround me again before finishing with the most important mantra, "Today will be a good day." There have been days when I've repeated this mantra over and over again, to the point of actually convincing myself that "Today will be a good day." I've walked out the door with keys in hand, headed down to the parking garage of One Main, gotten into my white Range Rover, and even driven out of the heart of Old Bellevue, traveling the three short miles to The Club with this firmly etched in my brain. Creating my own "conscious confidence," as my shrink calls it, all the way into The Club.

Entering The Club is just like entering an amusement theme park; all the employees—or 'cast members'—of The Club must arrive through the back doors, weaving our way through the laundry room, where spa robes, work-out towels, and massage table sheets are all being prepped for the day. A smell of detergent and starch mixed with bleach lingers in the air and follows us through to the compressor and boiler room. Personal trainers, spa practitioners, and other staff mingle around trying to have conversations above the hiss and grinding of the machines. It's here you'll find lockers for the personnel who aren't lucky enough to have their own offices on the inside.

Keeping my head lowered, I dodge a few employees, only smiling and tossing a wave when my name is called. I stop at the door that opens into the back hallways of The Club and take stock of what I see in the mirror. Also like at an amusement theme park, all cast members are required to be "stage ready." The life-size cartoon poster, erected right next to the mirror, depicting a perfectly groomed employee with a cheesy smile plastered across her face, makes me want to vomit again. My own dark circles and pale skin are assured to displease the management. Pulling at the waistband of my track pants, I suck in my stomach, tuck my drab mousy blond hair behind an ear, and press on. The maze of hallways tucked into the back of The Club are narrow and brightly lit. I stay close to the wall until I reach my own office. Another glass bowl for me to flounder in.

On a good day, I get to close the door to the rest of The Club. Shutting out the chipper chit-chat happening on just the other side of the walls. Content to be surrounded by nothing more than my file cabinets and piles of paper, where I'm able to concentrate on the accounts at hand, focusing my attention on the computer screen, blocking out reality for the next eight hours.

Today is not that day.

I haven't sat down for more than five minutes before there's a knock on my door.

I don't even bother with an answer. I know the door will open on its own, no invitation needed.

The space in my already minimal office is instantly diminished as she enters, standing perfectly groomed, waiting for my acknowledgment.

"Ireland." It's a statement not a question.

"Yes?" I barely look up, keeping my fingers moving on the keyboard.

"Did you get the accounts receivable for September?"

"I left the report on your desk last night, right before heading home." I keep typing.

"Fine, I'll check it and let you know if I have any questions." The sound of a tiny bell chiming resonates from her pocket. Instinctively my eyes leave the computer screen and glance in the direction of the interruption. Taking out her phone, she holds up one finger, indicating I need to wait for her while she takes the call.

"Yes?" she barks into the mouthpiece of the slim, gold phone.

Without acknowledging me, she walks out of my office into the hallway, closing the door behind her. With the click of the lock, I finally turn my full attention on her, watching her through the glass, an expression of clear discontent stretched across her face. Her mouth moves in tight little lines, making it impossible to decipher what she's saying. Moments later she's abandoned the conversation and taken to slamming her fingers against the screen of the innocent phone. Apparently relaying a text message with about as much finesse as a bodybuilder lifting a hundred-and-fifty-pound weight above his head. I'm sure the text is full of shouty capitals and "!!!" in order to convey the message with the correct sense of urgency.

I bet she misses the day when she could just snap her phone shut with a flick of her wrist, in essence dismissing the poor soul on the other end of the conversation with a single action. As it is, she's reduced to settling for the correct emoji to display the magnitude of each particular situation. Mind you, there's always a situation.

Through the glass door, I continue watching as she slips her phone back into her pocket and returns to my office.

"Like I was saying, I'll review the numbers, but of course, I'll expect you to have answers to my questions."

"Of course," I answer.

Her eyes drift to my left hand, which is still poised over the keyboard. I feel the heat from her searing gaze bore into my ring finger, where my engagement ring still holds its place of honor. I refuse to follow her gaze to my hand, instead I continue looking her in the eye, bracing myself for what she's likely to throw at me next.

Avoiding the elephant in the room, she draws her

eyes up to meet mine.

"You know, Ireland, as a representative of this company you are expected to arrive polished and ready for work. I expect you to take the time to be presentable." She flicks her wrist in my direction. "Start with the hair."

I reach up and finger my limp locks. I haven't given them much thought since Lenny died. There was no need; the person I would have been making an effort for was no longer present. It seemed like a waste of time and energy to worry about my appearance when there was such a lack of audience.

"Yes, of course, I'll try to do it during my lunch hour." Yet again, lunch was going to have to be eaten at my desk, the piles of papers my only companion. I'm used to having that precious time, when most people socialize or take a walk, taken up by some errand deemed urgent, or a chore needing immediate attention. Why should today be any different?

"Don't try. Do." She pauses and looks down at her watch. "And I expect my employees to be on time when they come to work." Turning on her heel she walks out the door, as always, having the final word.

"Of course, Mother. Anything you say. It was nice talking to you too." My words fall against the closed door, in the same manner they did most of my childhood.

Reluctantly I pick up the phone and dial the extension for the salon. After the arrangements are settled for a cut and blow dry, I turn my attention back to the computer.

My earlier reserve that "Today will be a good day" has followed Mother right out the door. I lean back in my chair and struggle to get my motivation back. I give my temples a quick massage and sit back up, determined to get back into the groove. I scroll through my e-mails, trashing the spam and mentally categorizing the remaining messages by priority. There are e-mails from the manager of the food department, with the subject line: "Dining Budget," one from the Aquatics Department with the subject line: "Maintenance Budget" and one from our tax accountant with the subject line: "Deadline approaching!" Farther down the list is one from Collette with the subject line: "Men!" and one from Mel Evans with the subject line: "Seating."

It's the last one on the list that gives me pause. I've been avoiding contact from Mel Evans for over a week now. The mere mention of his name causes my throat to tighten and my pulse to accelerate. I've put off responding now for so long it has become more than just uncomfortable, it was erring on the side of pathetic. My inability to come up with an appropriate response to his messages has rendered me virtually immobile.

My thumb caresses the mouse as I move the cursor, hovering over the e-mail. Just a quick click and the message will spring to life in front of me. I can face it head on. I should face it head on, get it over with right here, right now. But instead, being the coward I am, I give a quick flick of the wrist and click on the one from Collette. I feel the shame seep in slowly, like it's a dirty dishrag left on the counter, spoiling the marble top under it. With a sigh, I start reading.

From: ColletteJ@gatesfoundation.org
To: IrelandJ@Belletrio.com
Subject: Men!

Hey Sis,

How you doing? Never mind, already know the answer to that one. Look, if you need me to come over any time just call and I'm there, you know that right?

Anyways, I was getting ready for work this morning and Greg walks into the room to see if I could pick up the girls from school today. They have early release.

He was supposed to be picking them up, but apparently he had something come up. He is so oblivious to the fact that I might actually have something to do while I'm at work! When we agreed that he would be the stay at home parent I thought it meant that he would actually be doing some of the activities required of parenting! I didn't know it meant that he would be jetting off to the gym or whatever it is he's wasting time doing in the middle of the day. I don't know what part of me working full time he's not understanding, I just don't get it! Am I missing something here?

Sorry to vent, talk soon.

Love,

C

Oh, domestic bliss! When Collette scored a considerable promotion working for the Bill and Melinda Gates Foundation earlier this year, she and Greg had had many heated discussions, most of which focused on Greg quitting his burnout job at Microsoft and becoming a stay-at-home dad. It was obviously going to take some time to iron out the details of their new arrangement.

I pick up the phone next to the computer and speed dial Collette's work number.

"You got my message?" she asks without bothering to say Hello.

"I did. Sounds like you need to talk things out with Greg, set some ground rules for how things are going to work so you both know what to expect," I reply, also dismissing any unnecessary greetings.

"But, in the meantime, want me to pick up the girls today? I would love a distraction, and you know they're always good for that. Besides I haven't seen my nieces for a while," I say, hoping this will make up for my lack of recent attention.

"Really? That would be a Godsend! Thank you! I'll call the girls' school and let them know their aunt will be picking them up. You can take them to the park or something and then meet Greg back at the house around four."

"Sure, sounds like a plan. Maybe I'll throw some ice cream in there as well," I say, already refocusing my attention on the computer screen.

"They'd love that. You really are too good to me!" Collette professes.

I let out a laugh in the form of a grunt. "You're right, I am too good to you. All right, get back to work. I've got this, and I'll see you tonight." I put the phone back in its receiver and feel my lips cracking from my involuntary smile. I focus on relaxing the muscles in my face and returning to the work on the screen in front of me. It's still there, the e-mail from Mel Evans, the one with the subject line: "Seating." You'd think such a harmless subject line wouldn't evoke fear in a person's heart, and yet, with trembling hands, I have to force myself to click on the e-mail and start reading.

From: MelE@Evansenterprises.com

To: IrelandJ@Belletrio.com
Subject: Seating
Hello Dear,

How have you been? Sheila and I have been hoping you would return our phone calls or e-mails. I can only imagine how hard this time must be for you. Lenny's mother and I have been devastated by the loss of him as well. There are no words to express the grief one feels when they lose their son. It goes against the natural order of things, children are not supposed to die before their parents. They are supposed to put us in the ground, not the other way around. It's been hard around here, but knowing we have the strength of each other to lean on makes it slightly more bearable. I hope you know that we still see you as family. We want you to feel that you can lean on us for strength and support. Something like this is never easy, but if we have each other, we might just make it through.

I know our son loved you very much and we have grown to love you as well. Please, don't shut us out at a time like this. Lenny would have wanted to make sure you were ok. I need to make sure you are ok.

The memorial service is set for this Saturday at Bellevue Presbyterian Church for two o'clock. I sent you an email about it earlier but have yet to hear back from you. The front two pews will be reserved for family, to us you are family, and we would like you to sit with us.

I will keep my eye out for you.
Much Love,
Mel Evans

Damn it, I knew I shouldn't have read his e-mail at work. I reach for a tissue while trying to ignore how my heart feels. Like it's in a vise grip, being squeezed until my breath comes out in short little gasps. In and out. Just breathe, I coach myself. The panic that was building starts to subside as I take deep breaths in from my nose and out through my mouth, just like the therapist taught me. I close my eyes and try to figure out how I'm going to respond.

I rack my brain but can't come up with a single thing that could possibly suffice as an appropriate reply to my dead fiancé's family. Maybe, 'Hey there, sorry I didn't call sooner, I've been spending my days and nights lying in the fetal position wondering what the hell I'm going to do now.' No, that's definitely not going to work. The service is tomorrow, and I still haven't let them know if I'm coming or not. Possibly a simple, 'I'll be there. I've been thinking of you too.' Too weak, but beyond true. I've pretty much spent this last month doing nothing but thinking of Lenny's family.

I cross my arms on my desk and let my head drop. The effort to come up with a response has suddenly left me drained of all energy.

Gutted, depressed, sad, grief-stricken—I've heard them all, with suggestions from other people as to how I might be living through my grief, like they have a better idea of what I should be feeling than me.

I've somehow been interned into a club all its own, one of grieving widows and people who have lost those closest to them.

All of a sudden, I'm expected to act or appear a certain way, but really the only thing I feel is hollow. An empty cavity of a person walking around in a swell of people who are full. Full of joy, full of companionship, full of family, full of all the things that have been taken from me.

Chapter 2

"Well, you look like shit." A plastic cup containing some mysterious green liquid is set down on the desktop just inches from where I'm still resting my head. "Drink up, buttercup."

Jenna plops down in the chair across from my desk and proceeds to disregard her manners, kicking her bare feet up and letting them come to rest on the corner of my desk. From my point of view, I can see her recently painted toenails, a deep turquoise that reminds me of tropical water. I adjust my head, my gaze following her feet up to her toned, yoga pants-clad legs, finally resting on the face that has always brought me solace.

To the rest of the world I look wrecked, but to Jenna, I'm still just me. I know this by the patient grin on her face as she sits, waiting for me to compose myself.

"Tough day?" she quips.

"Not the best so far," I admit, finally pulling myself up to a sitting position, smoothing my hair as I go.

"Why don't you tell your dear old friend all about it." She takes a long sip from the straw stuck in her own cup holding the same green liquid that's in mine.

I push her bare feet off my desk, feeling a sense of satisfaction when I hear them smack against the floor. "Don't you ever wear shoes?"

"As the resident yoga instructor, I'm not required to wear shoes."

"That's gross. I thought you didn't wear shoes in class. If you walk around The Club without shoes, you're going to end up with athlete's foot or something worse, like a wart."

Rolling her eyes at me, she points to the floor, where a pair of discarded flip-flops sit waiting for her to slip her tiny toes back into. "Don't worry, I've got it covered."

"Well, that's a slight relief."

"All right, I've known you forever, and you have that look. What's going on?"

The comfort of her words makes my eyes prickle like tears might be welling up any minute. I blink them away and silently thank the heavens they delivered Jenna to The Club. She had wafted in here almost six years ago, on a breeze of lavender and honey, when The Club was in need of a new yoga instructor. Like a breath of fresh air, she had taken up residence in the studio, quickly becoming a favorite of all the members. Being close to the same age, Jenna and I had instantly attached ourselves to each other. Despite Mother's warning of "getting too close to the help" we had stayed friends ever since.

"Oh nothing, you know, just reading e-mails from Mel."

"Uh-oh, what'd it say?"

I sigh deeply. "Oh, you know, just some stuff about how they still think of me like family, how they love me, funeral details, nothing big." I swallow the lump in my throat and beg the tears to stay buried deep where they belong.

"Damn. That sucks," she says, not even having to ask why I'm so upset. She was there that day; she knew firsthand how hard it's been for me. "Have you written them back yet?"

"No, I haven't. Honestly, I don't know what I'm going to say. I feel like I shouldn't be bothering them right now. Mel and Sheila have been through so much already. I feel like just writing to them will remind them of all they've already lost, don't you think?"

"No, I don't. What Mel said is true. They think of you as family."

I stare at an imaginary spot on the wall.

"Look, I think you need to come with me, meditate on it for a while before you write back. I've got a class in ten minutes." She gets up out of the chair, virtually bending her body in half with some side-stretch thing. "I think it would be good for you to get some stress out."

"I'd love to," I lie. "But I can't today. I told Collette I'd pick up the girls from school."

"Why? I thought she landed herself a stay-at-home hubby to do the menial work, like picking up the kids."

"For someone who's supposed to be a feminist, that's a very dated way of looking at their situation," I say as she shrugs her shoulders. I decide not to press the issue and instead try to remember if Collette had mentioned the reason in the e-mail. "I guess he asked her last minute. She has a meeting, so I volunteered to get them."

"She's so lucky to have you, always rushing to help out."

The tone of her voice indicated she indeed thought Collette was lucky, but also that I was a pushover.

"You know I would do anything for those girls." I reply, ignoring her tone.

"I know. Those little snots are cute, I'll give you that." Turning on her heel, she heads toward the door. "Love you, Chica, have a better day. I'll try to stop by later to see how you're doing."

"Thanks, and for this." I raise the green drink and take a sip, trying not to screw my face up while I pull at the straw.

"No probs, drink all of that, no wasting! Catch you later." And just like that, she was gone.

****

"Ugh," I bemoan at the interruption of the phone ringing. I was just getting into the flow of getting some real work done—after wasting my lunch hour at the salon—so a disruption has me literally grinding my teeth together. I flick my eyes in the direction of the caller ID.

Mother.

It takes a few seconds of debating, which will be worse, answering or ignoring, before I finally snatch the receiver off the base, groaning inwardly.

"Yes, Mother?"

"I need you in my office."

"Now?" I ask as I steal a quick glance at the clock hanging above my desk. "I'm scheduled to collect Molly and Maggie from school in twenty minutes," *And I still have a ton of stuff to get done*, I don't bother saying out loud.

"Yes, now." She pauses. "You do work for me, not Collette. Or am I mistaken?"

"No, you're not mistaken. Of course, I work for you. It's just, Collette needed my help today. So, I figured…" I trail off, feeling as though I didn't need to state the obvious. The obvious being Collette is her daughter, and family should be there for each other. But even if I spell it out, she won't get it.

"You figured what? That you would take the place of that slacker husband of hers? Can't Greg be bothered to pick up his own children? I thought he was supposed to be some trophy father or something, the one doing all the heavy lifting for the family."

This time the sigh is audible, I can't help myself.

"I'm not sure where he is today, Mother. All I know is Collette needs help picking up the girls, so I told her I'd do it. Which is why I need to leave in twenty minutes."

This time it's Mother's turn to sigh. "Then you better get up here!" The other end of the line clicks to silence before I get the chance to say anything else.

I click the speakerphone off while my eyes travel to the picture box frame hanging on my wall. Inside it is a short little straw. I focus on the straw and remind myself why I put up with this daily abuse.

Gathering up my papers and locking the door behind me, I start the trek to Mother's office located two floors above mine. It really isn't any surprise that my own office is tucked into the recesses of the back hallways, away from the glamour of The Club. It always takes me at least a few minutes before I even reach the reception, where the elevator waits to whisk me up to the top floor.

Passing the exercise studios on my right, with their all-glass wall partitions, I catch a glimpse of the tight little bodies, bouncing up and down in rhythm to the pumped-up aerobics music. Reminding me of yet another thing I've avoided since my tailspin into darkness. I reach down and pinch my side. There is no denying the extra inch of tissue trapped between my fingers. Mother would certainly not approve of this either.

Tracy, the instructor, shouting at the ladies to "bend and reach, bend and reach," catches my eye through the glass, waves, and blows a kiss in my direction before continuing her verbal assault on the sweat-dripping bodies.

I wave back, acknowledging her with a smile as hints of citrus and cucumber tickle my nose. Unlike the employee entrance, Mother was adamant that The Club should not smell like the sweaty gym down the street. In order to mask the smell of bodies working and sweat dripping, The Club pours a small fortune into the air system, pumping the citrus/cucumber elixir out twenty-four hours a day.

At the reception desk, a new girl I haven't noticed before is cooing into the phone in her sweetest voice, "Thank you for calling The Club, where bodies are shaped, and lives are transformed."

I nod in her direction and gaze upon the image in front of me.

"It's like it was plucked from the streets of London/Paris/Milan/New York," is the phrase heard repeatedly in the reception, as women gawk at the elaborate white tile mosaic flanking the reception desk, the soft sound of water trickling down from the orchids and glass spheres dangling from the ceiling. It's like nothing they've ever seen before and quite frankly probably won't ever see again.

I continue through the expansive receiving room to

the bank of elevators on the opposite wall.

Once inside, I push the button for the top floor and wait as the doors close. Startled by the life-size poster of Mother and The Club logo plastered on the inside of the closing elevator doors, I take an involuntary step in retreat, until my back is pressed against the rail.

Across from me is Mother's vision of the modern metropolitan woman. Or in other words, what every member of The Club should strive to be like: Polished and poised and always #livingmybestlife and representing #TheClub motto.

My mother is the one and only Cynthia Jacobson, owner and founder of Belle Trio—or simply, The Club, to those who are fortunate enough to be members—the most exclusive women-only club in the Pacific Northwest.

Starting out twenty-seven years ago, Belle Trio was a simple corner establishment providing only the essential services such as facials, manicures, and massages. But Mother was smart with her money and with her dream. Slowly and steadily she grew the eight-hundred-square-foot spa into a forty-five-thousand-square-foot retreat boasting its own gym, spa, wellness center, restaurant and smoothie bar.

They say the more you nurture something, the better it will be. Which is why I seek weekly therapy sessions, while The Club has grown to be a little piece of heaven, dropped down in the middle of downtown Bellevue.

The glass roof atrium located on the top floor, mere steps away from Mother's office, is where you'll find political figures, Seahawks' wives, CEOs, CFOs, socialites, and the occasional celebrity, all networking and rubbing shoulders while lounging by the indoor heated pool.

Recently, The Club was awarded the prestige of being featured in numerous women's and travel magazines. With the increase of media attention and corresponding new ad campaigns, The Club memberships applications were growning at the same rate as Mother's ego and drive for success.

My current position as the accountant to The Club makes it my job to manage all of said VIPs' membership accounts. Along with balancing the P&L, processing payroll and numerous other tasks Mother requires of me, often last minute and without warning. I frequently work late into the night making sure every penny is accounted for and every member's account is accurate.

When the elevator pings, letting me know we've reached the top floor, I pause a minute to collect myself. I've worked at The Club for seven years now, and over the years I've developed a misplaced sense of pride in these halls, occasionally—and falsely— believing that all Mother's hard work is a direct reflection of everything I've given up in order for Mother to build her empire.

Knowing Mother is probably on the phone, I knock softly when I reach her office and then continue through the door without waiting for a reply. She'd be annoyed if I wasted any of her precious time hanging around on the other side, waiting for her to let me in.

I enter quietly, knowing better than to disturb her phone conversation. I cross the expansive space, finally reaching the white leather chair that faces her pristine desk. I steal another quick glance at the clock before I sit down.

Mother turns from the floor-to-ceiling window where she's been standing and holds up her finger, indicating for the second time today that I am to wait while she finishes her conversation.

Mother claims the seed of The Club was planted in her head the second she found out our father was in a car accident. Suddenly finding herself alone and pregnant with Collette and me, she knew she had to come up with a way to provide for her family. Apparently, the thought of being a single parent gave her all the motivation she needed. She decided right at that moment she would do everything in her power to provide for the two of us. To make us proud. Or so went the story she told us as children, when she bothered telling us stories at all. In actuality, I think she was just terrified of the aspect of raising twin girls on her own, and The Club became her excuse to spend as much time as possible away from us.

I shake my head to rid the thoughts and reach down to get the papers out, preparing for the questions she likely has for me on the numbers this month.

"Yes, yes. Execute that next week, and we should touch base on the rest of the details soon after." She waits for the response on the other end of the line.

"Yes, I got it, okay, bye." She hangs up and sets her cell phone on the edge of her desk. She sits in her own white leather captain's chair, opposite me, crossing her legs at the ankle under the desk, and smooths any nonexistent wrinkles out of her pencil skirt. With a few flicks of her wrist, she brings up her computer screen.

She studies me, and I wonder if she is deciding if my hair is now acceptable or not. But instead of acknowledging any difference in my appearance, she plows straight ahead with business.

"I was just on the phone with Loraine. She wants us to amend some things before we submit the taxes this year."

I poise my pen, ready to take notes on the changes our accounting firm wants done, hoping if I take the information down on paper I can get out of here quickly and pick the girls up on time.

"There's a list of uncategorized expenses on the credit card receipts. Go through those and categorize them. Loraine needs to know the totals for the write-offs."

"Okay, I can do that." I jot down the first item on my notepad.

"Itemize gross pay for the whole club. Divide it, so I have the pay for the Spa and Salon versus the Gym and Studio staff."

"Okay." I keep my pen moving as she speaks.

"Change the dates on the travel expenses for my trip to Paris from this June to June of last year. Specifically the private jet and car rentals."

My eyebrows draw together on the last request.

"I'm not sure I can do that. We've already closed out last year. Why do you need that done?"

She sighs. "Ireland, when are you going to learn?" She leans back in her chair and glares at me over her reading glasses. "You've been here, what, for seven years now? And yet you're not any closer to understanding how this Club operates than when you started."

"Actually, I wanted to talk to you about that. Don't you think it's time that I try out a different position?

Maybe one in management? I think I'm ready, and I could learn so much more."

"How could you possibly work in management when you can't even handle the simple tasks I'm asking of you in accounting? This is not the right time for you to make a move. I've been watching, and you haven't been able to concentrate at all since Lenny. When you can get yourself together and prove your worthiness in this company, we can have another conversation."

I can feel my heart rate starting to accelerate at the impending argument I'm about to deliver, but before I can respond in defense of myself, she stands up and crosses the room to hold the door open.

"That's all. I'm going to need those changes back to me by the end of the day tomorrow."

It takes me a split second before I start to collect my papers and pens, hugging it all to my chest, in an effort to make a hasty exit. "Not a problem, I'll have them for you," I mumble on my way out the door. I don't bother to say goodbye. I know she won't care anyway.

Chapter 3

"Auntie Ireland!"

I smile as two uniform-clad cuties bound into the back seat of the Range Rover, throwing their backpacks on the floor and kicking the back seat with their playground-encrusted shoes. I check to make sure they are belted in their seats before merging out of the pickup line and back into traffic, leaving the school parking lot behind.

"Hey girls, how was school?" I glance in the rearview mirror at the two curly-haired angels smiling back at me. I mentally kick myself for virtually abandoning them these last few weeks. Seeing them again instantly reminds me how Molly and Maggie— five and six respectively—have always been the light in my life. I've missed those rosy cheeks, the ones that just so happen to have today's art project evident all over them, glitter and paint illuminating their little faces.

"Good," they say in unison.

Maggie, taking over the conversation in her usual dominant way—she takes after Collette—starts asking questions in rapid fire. "Why are you picking us up today, Auntie Ireland? Where's Dad? What are we going to do?"

"I'm not sure what your dad is up to," I answer truthfully. "But I thought I'd pick you up today and maybe"—I pause for dramatic effect—"take you to the park. What do you think about that?" I ask, knowing the answer before I even ask the question.

"Yeah!" The squeals from the back seat come as a severe threat to my eardrums.

"Park! Park! Park!" Molly chants in her sing-songy voice.

It's a short drive from the school to the park. We get there in record time, and I find a parking spot next to the playground. The instant I've turned the engine off, the girls are dashing down the hill, their arms waving and hair flying in their haste to get to the Wee Saw, their favorite structure at Bellevue Park. It's a seesaw type of apparatus that seats four people and has a space in the center. Kids will virtually fall over each other for the chance to stand and "surf" in this coveted center position.

I help the girls, getting them organized in the chairs and making sure they're playing nicely with the two other kids already on the contraption. Once settled, I shuffle over to the bench and take my place with the other mothers, fathers, and nannies—close enough to jump up and rescue any play gone wrong, far enough away to not be labeled a helicopter parent or, in my case, helicopter auntie.

I smile as I watch the girls squeal with laughter, yelling directions to one another, determined to rock the Wee-Saw as hard as they can, trying to knock off the person in the middle.

I see Collette in each of their faces, and I try to remember a time when she and I had fun in a park like this. I know I shouldn't be as shocked as I am when I can't come up with a single instance. But growing up in our household, children were supposed to be seen and not heard; we were expected to appear in perfect white dresses, hair done in bows, only allowed to play outside when it suited Mother, and it rarely suited Mother.

Back then, if anyone had asked me, "Who is the most important person in your life?" I would have, without hesitation, answered, "My sister." Collette and I were glued to each other most of our lives. Mother was more of a shadow, floating in and out when it suited her. In grade school when we would draw pictures of our family in art, I would always come home with the same picture. Collette and I holding hands, standing in front of a house with empty windows. My second-grade teacher had once suggested that I add my parents into the picture, to which I responded by adding a single stick figure in the window. Even at that age, I knew enough to draw a cell phone in her hand.

I look over at Molly and Maggie, now pumping up and down on the Wee Saw, and realize Collette was able to break free of our childhood, raising her girls in an entirely different way.

I remember being so nervous to hold the girls when they were first brought home from the hospital. They were so tiny and fragile, I was certain I would hurt them somehow. But the instant Collette laid Molly in my arms, I knew I would love these girls for eternity. I would protect them from anything life would throw at them. I would make sure they never felt at a loss for love. I also knew that I wanted what Collette and Greg had, a family of my own, a child to love.

A wave of heat rips through my body at the exact same moment I realize my own dream of a husband, two kids, and the picket fence is gone. All my hopes, smashed, along with the wreckage of that airplane.

The tightness in my chest, now a familiar feeling, grips me as the bile starts to rise in my throat. I struggle to get my equilibrium back and remember what my therapist taught me to do in these situations.

In-out, in-out. Nose-mouth, nose-mouth. "Slow deep breaths." I coach myself, for the second time that day. The heat starts to dissipate in my face and the tingling leaves my fingers as I continue to breathe slowly and deliberately.

"Ouch!" Molly's voice interrupts my methodic breathing, immediately followed by a howl and sobbing. I look up and see Maggie running over to me as fast as her little six-year-old legs will take her.

"Auntie Ireland come quick! Molly's hurt!" Maggie takes my hand in her chubby one, pulling me to my feet, immediately erasing the feeling of any nausea.

"What happened?" I ask Maggie as we speed across the spongy tarmac of the playground to where the girls were just playing. We stop in front of a set of slides, where Molly is huddled, crying and bleeding from somewhere I have yet to ascertain.

Oh, this is just perfect! What a great auntie I am. "Sure, sis, I'll watch your kids for the afternoon. Let me just make sure I return them to you battered and bleeding!" Collette was going to flip.

I bend down next to Molly and pull her into my arms, smoothing her hair and shushing her cries. "It's okay, it's okay. Auntie's here. What happened?" I ask again, using a soothing voice in the hopes she'll calm down.

Molly hiccups into my shoulder. "That boy pushed

me down the slide when I wasn't ready to go. I fell and hit my face on the ground."

I lift her chin so that her face is peering up at me and notice that she is, in fact, bleeding right above her left eye. The skin is split, and there is a large black bruise starting to form.

I take a tissue out of my purse and dab at the blood, careful not to cause her any more pain.

I look around for the boy she was just pointing at, wanting to know who's behind my niece's playground assault.

I stand up, carrying Molly with me, and approach the little boy. Looking at him, he isn't so little, he must be at least ten, and he's built like he has linebackers for parents.

"Excuse me, did you push this little girl down the slide?" I ask him.

He looks at me with nonchalance and shrugs his shoulders. "She wouldn't go down. She was holding up the line." He points over his shoulder to where there is indeed a queue of children waiting for their turn to go down the slide.

"That is no excuse to push her," I chastise the boy. "She ended up getting hurt." I point to the spot over her eye that isn't bleeding now but will definitely be a shiner tomorrow.

Molly sniffs to prove my point.

"Excuse me, are you talking to my son?" a large voice booms from behind me.

I turn around and am confronted with the afore-mentioned linebacker of a parent. With broad shoulders, the boy's dad, who is at least six feet tall, towers over me as he approaches.

I'm momentarily intimidated, but one glance at Molly gives me the courage to square my shoulders and brush aside any feelings of inadequacy.

"Yes, I'm sorry to say that your little boy pushed my niece down the slide, and she ended up getting hurt." I point to her eye again.

"Look, lady, I don't know who you think you are, but you don't need to be reprimanding my son. He's a child. Children play."

Gob-smacked, I can feel the heat rise from my core to my face, lighting my cheeks on fire. "Excuse me? I was not *reprimanding* your child. I was simply trying to explain to him how he pushed my niece and she got hurt!" I don't understand why this father is so adamant that I can't point out the obvious to his son. The obvious being that he needed to be more careful on the playground.

"If she—your niece, did you say?—can't get down the slide on her own, then you shouldn't let her up there in the first place," he retorts.

"And if your son can't play nicely on a playground maybe he shouldn't be here in the first place, either!"

I'm floored. My free hand involuntary clenches into a fist, I have to force myself to relax it again. I look around to see if there are any other parents close by listening to our exchange. Anyone who can add a few words of wisdom to this convoluted conversation. But all the parents are either tending to their own children or on their cell phones, oblivious to our confrontation.

I grab Maggie by the hand and adjust Molly higher onto my hip. "Come on, girls, we don't need to play with people who can't play nicely." I shoot the dad a look I hope conveys my irritation and walk away.

"The audacity of some people," I mutter under my breath.

"What's audacity?" Molly asks as we make our way back to the Range Rover.

"It's just a grown-up word for people who think they know everything." I water down my explanation so the six-year-old can understand it.

I buckle them back into their seats, check Molly's eye one more time, and head for Collette's house, just down the street, in Medina.

"Why do we have to go, Auntie Ireland? I wasn't done playing." Maggie whines from her seat in the back.

"I know, pretty girl. I'm sorry we had to leave early, but Molly needs to be cleaned up, and I don't have any Band-Aids with me. Can we go to your home and get one? I know, how about I play with you for a while after we take care of Molly?" I offer as a consolation.

Maggie bounces up and down, apparently happy with the plan. "Yeah, we can dress in our princess costumes and have a zoo tea party."

I smile at her in the rearview mirror. I love how a five- and six-year-old can take any dire situation and turn it around just by the mention of make-believe and tea parties.

****

Collette and Greg live in the heart of Medina. Unlike some of the sizable houses in the area that can set you back a cool five or ten million, theirs is a small rambler set on a seven-thousand-square-foot lot. It was actually Mother who found the house. Insisting her future grandchildren be able to attend school in the best school district, she hadn't left Collette and Greg a choice in the matter when she plopped down the earnest money, selling it as their "wedding gift." Mother sealed the deal by paying for the house a week later. And she hasn't let them forget it since. It isn't the biggest or most beautiful house in the neighborhood by far, but it has turned out to be the perfect one for their family of four.

After they moved in, they painted the outside of the house a navy blue, with white trim and shutters. It was the perfect complement to the neighborhood. Greg built the white picket fence himself, and Collette, in a rare Martha Stewart moment, planted an extensive garden around the lavish lawn.

"Daddy's home!" Maggie squeals, noticing Greg's silver Audi parked in the garage, the garage door still open.

As soon as I stop the engine, the two of them bound out of the car and race into the house through the garage, pushing each other out of the way to be the first through the door.

I gather their backpacks and my purse and head into the house after them. Once inside, I drop their things in the mudroom and make my way to the kitchen, located at the back of the house, following the sounds of chatter.

Ahead of me, the girls veer into the hallway that houses their rooms. I hear talk of gowns and tiaras and preparing for the tea party.

I smile to myself and continue into the kitchen where I find Greg, sitting at the kitchen table. Today, he's channeling his inner urban hippie, dressed in a fitted black V-neck and black jeans. He has a complementary black leather bracelet fastened around his wrist. The bracelet simultaneously blends and stands out against his dark arm hair.

"Hey there," I say, grabbing an apple from the fruit bowl on the kitchen island. "Back already?"

"Geez, Ireland. You nearly scared the crap out of me," Greg says, jumping in his seat.

"Sorry, I thought for sure you'd hear us. The entourage and I weren't exactly quiet."

Recovering, Greg chuckles and closes his laptop and stands up. "So, you're already back?"

"Our trip to the park got cut short." I rub my heel against the gray-colored hardwood floors, but before I can explain any more, Molly and Maggie speed through the door into the kitchen dressed head to toe in princess costumes.

They proceed to dance around their dad, talking a mile a minute about what happened at the park and how Molly got a boo-boo and needed a Band-Aid.

"That's quite a story!" Greg says when they have finished and scoops Molly up to give her eye a get-better kiss. I always marvel at how a parent knows the mere action of just kissing a cut or scrape will make it feel better. I also marvel at how my mother never got that particular memo. If Collette or I ever got hurt, all we would hear was, "Get up. Winners don't cry," or "I'm sure you're not that hurt." Nope, there was definitely no boo-boo kissing in *our* past.

"I was such a brave girl, Daddy! Auntie Ireland said so!" Molly professes to her dad while he places her back on the floor.

Greg turns to me. "Sounds like Auntie Ireland could have used some back-up on the playground today."

I giggle in spite of myself. "Yup, I was getting ready for battle, that's for sure! No one messes with my niece and gets away with it." I lean down to tickle Molly who squeals and runs away.

"Well, I for one am glad you headed home instead of trying to take down the bully at the playground. No good ever comes of picking a fight out there." He winks at me and grins. "Feel like staying for dinner? Least we could do for saving our little girl from the big bad wolf."

I think about what I have planned tonight and come up with the cold realization that the only thing waiting for me is a dark apartment with reminders of Lenny at every turn. Delaying my return to solitude does sound appealing. "Sure, I'll stay for a bit. What can I help with?"

"I'll tell you what. If you can keep the girls occupied while I make dinner, that would be a help in itself."

I turn to Molly and Maggie, who are looking at me with expectant faces. "Looks like it's a royal tea party for us!"

Both girls bounce up and down and clap their hands together.

"Come this way, Auntie Ireland!" Maggie says, grabbing my hand and dragging me off my perch on the bar stool.

"I'll call when dinner is ready," Greg calls after us as I'm propelled down the hall by two little Tasmanian devils.

I spend the next hour with a feather boa wrapped around my neck and a princess crown on my head, playing tea party with the girls, alternating between pouring the tea, making the tea, and serving the tea. I've come to learn the girls take their tea parties very seriously. They explain how the tea is made, by magical fairy dust. How to serve the tea, like a princess. And how to drink the tea, with your pinkie finger sticking out and making a loud slurping noise.

I'm poised with my pinkie finger in the air when we hear the engine of Collette's BMW pulling into the drive. As is par for the course, I'm no competition for the arrival of their mother. I'm abandoned with the empty teacups as the girls flee the room, excited to greet Collette.

I pull myself up from the tiny table and chairs we were playing at, unwrap the boa from my neck, and follow the girls to greet Collette in the hallway.

"Hey there." I stick my hand out to take her coat and handbag. She hands them over readily so she can bend down and hug her girls.

"Hi!" she says while taking each girl into her arms and hugging them. She pauses after catching a glimpse of Molly and shoots me a look over her forehead. "What happened to you?" she asks, her voice soft and motherly.

"I got pushed down the slide, and Auntie Ireland yelled at the man," Molly explains while grabbing her mom's hand and dragging her down the hallway into the kitchen, chatting the whole way.

I dump Collette's belongings on the hall tree and take Maggie's hand as we follow behind them.

By the time we catch up, Molly has relayed the whole story to her mom.

"Well, it sounds like Auntie Ireland had it all

covered. I'm just glad it wasn't any worse." Collette shoots me another glance above Molly's head before she takes Molly in both her hands and looks closer at the injury. "Looks like it will heal just fine. It should be all better soon, just in time for picture day in two weeks." She kisses the spot right above Molly's eye, careful to not brush against the injury itself and props Molly on one of the bar stools next to the kitchen counter.

I thank my lucky stars that picture day is so far away. The last thing I need is to have my weakness in babysitting duties recorded in Molly's kindergarten school photos.

Collette walks around the kitchen island to the stove, where Greg is mixing something red in a big pot. The unmistakable aroma of garlic and onions fills the kitchen and makes my salivary glands start to work overtime.

Collette stops and gives Greg a quick peck on the cheek before reaching into the white cabinets above his head and pulling out a stack of plates.

Molly and Maggie take the opportunity of their mother's back to them to run back down the hallway, presumably to continue their tea party.

"How was your day?" I ask from across the counter, eager to switch the subject away from my inadequate babysitting skills.

Collette walks back around the island and hands me the white ceramic plates, then returns for the silverware.

"Long. I had meetings all day. I get so frustrated with my team sometimes. Everyone has something to say, so we end up talking in circles. I just want to see some progress. Is it too much to ask for a little cooperation? I know we have to go through all the correct channels and follow the law, but man, it drives me crazy, the bureaucracy we have to go through, just to do some good in the world!"

She stops at the counter and picks up the bottle of wine. Pouring herself a glass, she holds the bottle up to me. "Want some?"

"Not right now, thanks." I decline, not wanting to try my luck with the nausea gods at this particular moment.

"Anyways, enough about work. Let's talk about something else."

I stare at her blankly, realizing I currently have very few topics in my back pocket available for conversation. My whole existence has been taken up with the mere effort of simply making it through the day. I haven't kept up with current events or even Hollywood drama. I couldn't possibly have a coherent conversation about politics or world affairs if I wanted to right now.

And I inherently know Collette won't want to hear about my own day at the office. There is a reason she changed the conversation and didn't bother to ask about my day. Ever since I started working for Mother, Collette has been careful to steer clear of any discussion that would bring to light the luck she encountered that day we drew straws. I can never tell if Collette harbors a feeling of guilt or if she merely doesn't want to acknowledge the life I gave up so she could be free to live hers. Either way, we've never spoken about it after that day. Our relationship has never really recovered from that point, causing it to be more on edge, her careful not to ask, and me careful not to tell about what life is really like working for our mother.

Sensing the lull in the conversation, Collette takes the opportunity to address Greg, who is still standing at the stove. "How was your day, honey?"

Greg looks up from his stirring. "Oh, me? It was fine." He reaches down to change the temperature of the stove.

"What were you doing all day? I think I'm not the only one who wants to know why you couldn't pick up the girls from school today," she says, making an obviously passive-aggressive move by referencing me in the conversation.

Greg wipes his hands on his red apron and moves to the kitchen island to pour more wine into his own glass. "You know, I was at the gym yesterday and ran into an old colleague. He just started a new job at Google. We got to talking, and he suggested having lunch today. I thought it would be a good opportunity to find out about the company, see if they were hiring and all that." He takes a sip of the wine. "As it turned out, he just wanted to catch up and kick back a few beers. No leads to report." Greg leans against the counter.

"What do you mean 'to see if they were hiring and all that'?" Collette makes finger quotes in the air after she has put the final place setting at the table. "I thought we agreed you would stay home with the girls for at least a year while I adjust to this new position."

"Yes, we did." Greg's response is drawn out. "I was just checking to see what's out there."

"But we talked about this." Collette's voice rises an octave.

Greg sets his wine glass down and walks around

the counter to where Collette is standing by the round dining table. Being six foot two, he easily lays his arm around her shoulders and draws her into him.

"I know. But sweetheart, I'm starting to go out of my mind here. Every day is the same routine. Wake up, make lunches, drop off the girls, go to the gym." Greg flexes his free arm and kisses his muscular bicep, lightening the mood. "Pick up the girls, make dinner. I miss the office. I miss the clicking of my brain trying to solve problems. I'm trying to resist, but the itch to go back gets stronger every day. I need more in my day than play dates and meal planning."

Collette's eyes narrow. "But we discussed this." She swears under her breath and twists out from beneath his arm, turning toward the window that now has a spattering of raindrops trickling down it.

"I think we need to discuss it some more," Greg says, standing where she left him.

"It's too late to discuss it more," Collette retorts.

"I don't think it is. There has to be a solution. Can't we just try and work it out?"

My head ping-pongs back and forth between the two. In all the years Collette and Greg have been married, this is the first time I've seen them really argue.

I'm sure they have—what married couple doesn't?—but Collette is a master of disguise. Ever able to cover things up, making it all look good for appearance's sake. I'm sure it's come from years of being told to "not make a scene" from Mother, but this is the first time I've seen a crack in the armor.

Collette, noticing my interest in the conversation, turns to Greg and says, "We'll finish this later."

Then, turning to me with a smile plastered on her face, she says, "Let's call the girls. Dinner's ready."

Chapter 4

The first thing I do when I walk through the door of my condo is peel off my soaking raincoat and hang it up on the hook next to the side table. I drop my keys into the glass bowl sitting atop the hall table. The sound of metal hitting glass reverberates off the walls, bringing my attention to the stark difference between the silence of my condo and the constant buzz of Collette's house. Doing my best to block out the emptiness, I walk through the kitchen without bothering to turn the lights on. The streetlights cast enough of a glow through my windows that I can see where I'm going, and having lived in this condo for over seven years, I could navigate my way around the whole two thousand square feet blindfolded if I needed to.

When I originally volunteered to pick the girls up from school earlier today, I didn't have any ulterior motives, I just wanted to help out, but the longer I stayed at Collette's house, the more I dreaded coming back home. After spending so many weeks isolating myself, shut up in my bedroom, it felt like someone had shocked me with a defibrillator. The realization that other people were carrying on, living their own lives, was a revelation of sorts, but in a good way.

So subconsciously, or maybe consciously if I'm being honest with myself, I had dragged out my stay there as long as was appropriate on a school night.

Soaking up every chaotic detail of their busy household. Listening to the kids shrieking and Collette and Greg quietly arguing. I had secretly enjoyed every minute of it. But when it finally became apparent I was outstaying my welcome, I begrudgingly packed up my things and left, dreading coming back to this condo, enclosed in nothing but my memories and silence.

Still not bothering to turn on any lights, I sit on the side of my bed, sinking into the down comforter. The exhaustion that seems to envelop me every time I'm in this place starts to creep in. I sit up straighter in an effort to fight it off when a picture of Lenny and me catches my eye. I reach over and pick it up, wiping off the dust. I haven't cleaned in here for so long, I honestly can't remember the last time I dusted anything.

I turn it over twice in my hand and stare at the two of us, happy on the back of a friend's boat. Oblivious to the realization that we are in fact mortal, and there is no guarantee of the future.

"I would give anything to have an argument with you, Lenny. About anything, I'd even settle for one about who was going to be the homemaker and who was expected to watch the kids, like Collette and Greg were just arguing about." Now I'm talking to pictures. I wonder if my shrink will officially mark my file as being a crazy woman. I flop back on the bed and stare at the ceiling, hugging the frame to my chest. Tired of fighting the loneliness, I let it filter in. Slowly, it envelops me like a wet blanket, cold and clammy. I resign myself to the uncomfortable feeling, like a tanker truck crashing into the recesses of my mind, and I let the memories flow like oil on the pavement.

****

"Hey Ireland, your phone is dancing across the counter! Better come grab this thing before it cha-cha's its way to the floor!" Jenna yells at me from across the kitchen.

"Grab it for me!" I call back as I hand to Collette the dishes I was just clearing from the table. Jenna, Greg, Collette, and I were just finishing an early dinner at the condo, and I was expecting Lenny to call me when he landed. Because most of the dinner conversation had revolved around wedding planning and honeymoon destinations, I was excited to talk with Lenny. I didn't want to miss his call.

I see Jenna grab my phone and put it to her ear.

"Mmm, hold on a second," she says into the mouthpiece. "It's Alexandrea," she explains, handing me the phone as I come into the kitchen. Lenny's assistant was in the habit of calling to let me know when Lenny was running behind. Alex was Lenny's calendar, stopwatch, and notification center all rolled into one taskmaster of an assistant.

"Hey, Alex," I start.

"Ireland," she cuts me off before I have a chance to continue. "Have you seen the news yet?" Her words come out in a rush.

"No, why?' The tone of her voice has the hair on my arm standing at attention.

"Turn on your TV to King 5. A plane has gone down."

"What do you mean 'gone down'?" My tone is more accusatory than I mean it to be.

"I'm not sure yet. They just had on a clip announcing a news story. Look, I don't want to cause any undue stress, but Lenny was supposed to land about half an hour ago. They lost contact with his plane, and I haven't been able to reach him."

Cause me undue stress? Well, that was too late. She should have waited to call if she wanted to save me from unnecessary stress.

I click the flat screen above the fireplace to life and wait while a commercial for some toilet paper with a bear wiping his butt finishes so we can get on with the inevitable.

"Breaking news this evening," the reporter starts. "Just outside of Paine Field we are getting reports that a private twin-engine jet has crashed and burst into flames. The information we've received so far indicates no survivors have been recovered from this tragic event. It is believed the plane was carrying a total of five people—two passengers, the pilot, and two additional crew members." The reporter pauses to check her side pocket for incoming information. "It has now been confirmed that all passengers have perished in tonight's tragedy."

I can't breathe. I listen to the reporter ramble on about how weather and an inexperienced pilot are most likely to blame. I tune her out as she drones on. My eyes are still transfixed on the screen, but I can't seem to concentrate on her words. Everyone has started trickling into the room, and I can now sense them behind me, watching the TV.

I feel the adrenaline starting to surge through my body. Tearing my eyes from the scene, I look down and am surprised to see the phone still in my hand. I put it to my ear. "Alex?" I whisper.

"I'm still here. Ireland"—she hesitates—"I'm

getting in contact with the authorities now to find out the identification of the plane and those on board. I need you to sit tight. I'll call you back as soon as I know anything. Try not to worry until we know more, okay?"

I must have been mutely nodding my head because I hear Alex say, "Okay?"

"Yes, of course, right. Just, please, call me as soon as you know anything."

My knees feel weak, like they're going to buckle under me at any moment. I sit down on the couch keeping the phone to my ear and my eyes on the TV screen, searching for something in the pictures that are being shown that might provide a clue. Something, anything that might give me the answers.

"I promise." There's a click and then silence. I keep the phone to my ear for a minute before I notice the line has gone dead. I drop it into my lap like it's burnt my hand.

"Ireland, you're as white as a sheet. What's going on?" Jenna is by my side, sitting next to me on the couch.

"That was Alex."

"I know."

"Uh-huh, she calls me when Lenny's running behind, which is nice because then I'm not kept waiting for him." I can hear myself rambling, not getting to the point, but Jenna just sits and waits patiently.

"They lost contact with his plane about half an hour ago…" I turn to the TV to let it explain the rest.

It only takes Jenna a few seconds to make the connection. She clasps her hand over her mouth, stifling her sharp intake of breath.

Greg comes around the couch and touches my shoulder, sending a jolt through my body. "I'm sure he's okay. It can't be Lenny. Watch, I bet he comes through that door any minute."

My gaze slides to the door, like I'm anticipating what Greg is saying will actually happen. Lenny was going to walk through the door any minute, and this would all just be a big misunderstanding.

"Why don't you just try to call him?" Collette suggests.

"Yeah, okay, I can do that." My hand trembles as I pick the phone back up and touch the speed dial for his number, crushing the phone to my ear as I wait for Lenny to pick up.

It goes straight to voicemail. "Voicemail," I squeak out.

Jenna comes around to sit on the side of the coffee table separating the couch from the TV. "I'm sure it went to voicemail because he's still on the plane. Maybe they had to re-route because of the crash. I bet all the planes have to be redirected now."

There's a murmur of agreement amongst everyone as we turn our attention back to the screen. It's switched now from in the studio to live at the scene. A woman, dressed in a yellow rain jacket, is giving details of what they think happened while directing the camera to yet another close up of the wreckage.

Trying to fight the feeling of helplessness, I get up and go to the kitchen, pour myself another glass of wine, and somehow manage to down it in one long swallow.

As I replace the wine glass on the counter, I realize everyone is looking at me. Silent, no one daring to speak or question my immediate consumption of alcohol.

"Alex told me not to worry yet, she's going to get in touch with the authorities. She said she'll call back as soon as they know anything," I say, addressing the whole room. Willing myself to calm down. To push down the panic rising higher every second.

"She's right," Collette pipes in. "we can't borrow problems right now, we need to wait until we have more information."

I pick up a picture of Lenny and me from the side table. It was taken just a few months ago on a friend's boat. Our skin bronzed from a summer spent outdoors, laughing at each other, our noses only inches apart, unaware of the camera pointed in our direction.

We are all lost in our own thoughts when the buzzer for downstairs rings, causing the whole room to jump a little.

"It's him!" Jenna exclaims.

I push the buzzer on the intercom with a pit in my stomach, because I know what Jenna does not.

Lenny has a key.

I press the intercom. "Hello?" I try my best to sound casual.

"Hello, ma'am. My name is Officer Coby, I'm looking for an Ireland Jacobson?"

"Yes, that's me."

"I hate to bother you, but I was hoping I could come up and have a word with you."

"Of course." I can literally feel the pulse on my wrist as I press the buzzer, letting Officer Coby up.

Time moves excruciatingly slowly as I wait for him to arrive at my door. At the slightest hint of a knock, I open it immediately.

Officer Coby is dressed in uniform, holding his hat in one hand.

"Evening." He greets me.

"Evening," I repeat, noticing the "good" being left out.

"May I?" He gestures to the entranceway.

I move aside and let him in.

"Miss Ireland, I've been in contact with a Miss Alexandrea Lean this evening." He holds his hat in both his hands and looks at the floor. It's the moment he breaks eye contact with me that I know. "It would seem that you both are in connection to a Leonard Evans." He pauses to let me confirm this information.

"Yes, I'm his fiancée, and she is his assistant," I clarify, still holding out hope that if I let this conversation play out, it will have a different ending. I refuse to believe it until he says the words.

"Yes, yes," he repeats, seeming to be at a momentary loss for words. "Well, again I'm sorry to bother you tonight, but I've been working with the Snohomish precinct concerning a plane crash on Paine Field."

"Yes, we've heard of the incident." I gesture to the people in the living room, who are now starting to trickle into the hallway to hear our conversation.

"Yes, well at eight thirty this evening, a private jet, Flight 456, was scheduled to land at Paine Field. We are still working out the details. The FAA will conduct an investigation into the crash, most likely due to the weather."

I wish he would stop rambling and get to the point. I can hear the blood rushing through my ears, but I

"Are you okay?"

I nod yes, and she pats my hand and moves it back to her death grip on Mel's. She resumes paying rapt attention to the preacher. Eating up every encouraging word he says.

"I would like to open the podium to the congregation, friends and family alike, anyone who might like to say a few words." The preacher relinquishes the microphone and stands to the side of the podium, patiently waiting for someone to make the first move.

Terror grips me when the preacher looks my direction.

There is no way I could give a speech right now. I would turn into a sobbing pile of snot, and even though it would be for Lenny, the idea of crumbling in front of a hundred strangers makes me want to shrivel up and hide under the pew I'm sitting on.

There's a rustle to the far left corner of the congregation, and immediately, a rush of relief floods through my body, as Lenny's friend from college, Barry, makes his way up front.

Barry approaches the podium and, like most amateur speakers, taps on the mic, causing a screeching sound to echo through the halls of the Bellevue Presbyterian Church.

"First off, I would like to thank you all for the opportunity to say a few words about my dear friend Lenny. I wrote a few things down because I didn't want to miss anything." He reaches in his jacket pocket and takes out a folded piece of paper. He unfolds it, lays it flat on the podium, and smooths it down with his oversized hands.

"Lenny and I met freshman year when he literally fell through the door of our dorm room." Barry makes a falling motion like he's tripping. "He was hands down the geekiest kid in the hall. After I helped him off the floor and dusted him off, I thought to myself, 'This is great! Next to him, I'm a stud. I'll be the one getting all the girls.'"

There's a tittering of polite laughter from the audience.

"As the years went by, Lenny came through for me, over and over again, helping me with my schoolwork and coaching me on my study skills. As repayment, I taught him how to do his hair and how to look cool in the gym."

Laughter from the congregation again.

"Try as I might, I couldn't shake Lenny. We became inseparable, staying together for all four years of undergraduate school. Eventually, we became a mixture of each other. I learned how to pass a class on my own, with a good grade even, and he learned how to be suave, popular, and how to get the girl." He winks at me, and I smile up at him, feeling my cheeks stretch.

"Mel and Sheila, you taught him he could be anything he wanted to be. You didn't set any limits on him, and in return, he flourished into the young man we are all so in love with."

"Lenny was the best son, brother, and friend any one of us could have asked for. He was destined for great things, and he was on his way to achieving them. Lenny made it look easy when he aced his architecture exams, and he made it look easy when he started his own business and turned it into a successful urban development company. He made it look easy to love his family, and he made it look easy when he stole the heart of his dream girl. Lenny was going to make the rest of his life look easy, this I was sure of. Sadly, he did not get the chance to finish his easy ride down here on solid ground." Barry pauses, wipes the tears from his eyes and clears his throat before continuing.

"I believe Lenny can hear us now, that he is busy up there making things easy for the rest of us down here. I know he will look over all of us from above. And when we need him most, he will still be here for us. So, with love in my heart, I say to Lenny, 'Be well, my friend. Take it easy up there, and when we meet again, we will take it easy together."

My eyes well up again, and before I can stop them, tears are spilling down my cheeks, leaving big wet blotches on my navy-blue silk dress.

There's a creaking of the pew behind me as a handkerchief is laid on my shoulder. "Wipe your tears and sit up straight. People are watching," Mother whispers.

I take the fabric and dab my eyes obligingly.

Barry steps down from the podium and comes over to the family pew, shaking Mel's hand and kissing Sheila and Violet on the cheeks before turning to me, taking my hand in his and placing a kiss on my knuckles.

"You were his girl. He waited a long time to find you. I know he will always look after you, either here or up there," he whispers so only I can hear him before he lets my hand go, pointing up with his own.

"Thank you," is all I can squeak out, the tears choking my throat and making it hard to breathe, let alone speak.

Barry returns to his seat in the corner, and the preacher closes the service with the Lord's Prayer. The family is excused first, and the rest of the congregation follows us out of the nave, into the open entrance of the church.

I stand united with Lenny's family as guests come and kiss us, offering their condolences. We smile and say, "Thank you for coming," and I'm struck by how easy it is to pretend I belong with them.

After most of the guests file out of the church sanctuary, Mother approaches, ready to give her condolences to Mel and Sheila.

"It was a lovely ceremony. I'm so sorry for your loss," she says, grasping Sheila's hand in her own.

"Thank you. I know how hard it's been on us. It must be hard on you as well, and on Ireland." Sheila looks at me even though she's still holding on to Mother's hand. I smile and look away.

"Yes, well, I've been keeping her busy. I believe it's best she stays engaged with reality, so she doesn't dwell on it too much, don't you think?"

My breath catches and I cough-choke.

"I'm sure that can help. But I also think it helps to keep his memory alive." Sheila responds with the class I have come to expect from her. "I believe the only way we can move on is if we embrace the memory of Lenny and accept that even though he is no longer with us in physical form, he will always be with us in spirit. At least that's what has helped Mel and me get through these last few weeks."

Really, the composure this woman exhibits so soon after the death of her own son astounds me. The thought that Lenny could still be with me in any sense causes a sensation of warmth to travel through my body and take hold in my heart.

"If that's what helps you," Mother deadpans. "I just wish Lenny had had the presence of mind to update his will. You know, to reflect his intent to marry Ireland."

I gasp, "Mother!" I seethe through clenched teeth.

She turns to me. "What?" She sneers. "With the lack of progress you've been making at The Club, I don't see you taking on a role that will be paying you anything close to what Lenny could have provided for you. You don't think you get special treatment just because you're the daughter of the owner, do you?"

I feel the heat starting in my belly, rapidly rushing to my cheeks. "I don't think this is the time or the place to discuss this is what I think," I whisper.

"Let me tell you a little secret. An accountant's income is not going to provide the kind of lifestyle you're accustomed to. I approved of you marrying Lenny because I knew he could provide for you. I guess you're just going to have to get used to living on a budget until you can prove your worthiness at The Club."

I can't believe we are having this conversation right here, right now, in front of Lenny's parents, at Lenny's funeral.

I feel the bile rising in my throat.

Mel, who has been standing idly by until this point, decides to join the conversation. "Anything Ireland needs, she can ask for. Sheila and I consider her family, married or not."

"No, Mr. Evans, that's too much, really. I'll be fine on my own." I put my hands up to refuse the offer being made.

"You'd do better to re-think that, young lady," Mother advises.

"Anything, really. Please let us know. We want to know you're okay. Lenny would have wanted it."

"Really, I'll be fine," I attempt to protest again, but this is all I can say. I run over to the corner and heave my breakfast into a trash can. Once I'm finished, I pull out the handkerchief Mother gave me earlier and wipe my mouth on it now, not even bothering to worry about the possible stains I was leaving behind on the white linen.

I feel eyes boring into the back of my head. I'm sure the whole congregation has turned to see what the commotion I've just caused is all about. I've managed to make a spectacle in front of everyone.

Taking a deep breath, I straighten myself and with shaky hands smooth down my dress. Once I'm steady on my feet, and with as much confidence as I can muster, I turn around and walk past the Evans family, the rest of the congregation and Mother, heading straight for the front doors of the church.

The cold air hits my lungs the second I'm outside. Hungrily I take in big gasps and lean against the railing. Slowly sinking down onto a nearby bench, I rest my elbows on my knees and stare at the ring Lenny gave me on the day he asked me to be his wife. A spectacular, 2.5 carat, cushion-cut diamond ring. Twirling it around my finger, I let the weight of it press against my hand.

I hear the door behind me open and close.

I don't bother to look over my shoulder. I am too mortified to acknowledge anybody right now.

A hand enters my line of vision, offering me a tiny package containing a red-and-white mint.

I look up and give a weak smile.

"I'm so sorry about that," I say as I gratefully take the mint and pop it into my mouth. I swirl the peppermint candy around on my tongue, the putrid taste evaporating by the second.

"It's okay, sweetheart, these things affect people in different ways. Your way is just a bit more…visual." Mel sympathizes with me.

I reward him with a smile and pat the bench next to me.

"You should keep it." He points to my hand. "The ring, I mean." He lowers down and falls a short distance backward so that we are sitting side by side. He pats his thighs and sighs.

"It was a lovely memorial," I offer lamely.

"It was."

"I'm sorry I didn't say anything, it's just…"

"No need for an apology, dear. I know."

"Thanks."

"He loved you very much, I know because he told me." I glance at him, and he gives me a one-sided smile.

"I loved him too. Still do."

"Which is why you need to keep that ring. Lenny would have wanted it. I remember when he came to me and told me he was going to ask you to marry him. He was nervous, you know?"

I can feel my cheeks turn up in a smile because we both know Lenny never got nervous.

"It's true. I think it might have been one of the only times I've seen him like that. All in a tizzy about how he was going to do it. He was so certain you were the one. He kept saying he couldn't let you get away." He chuckles.

"Not possible. Lenny was never nervous."

"That's where you're wrong. Lenny got plenty nervous. he just knew how to hide it."

"Right," I say, accepting his fatherly advice. I mentally take notes and file them away. I sigh remembering the weekend Lenny proposed to me.

I close my eyes and can still smell the sea air. I can picture Lenny, so clearly, on bended knee, asking me to be his wife, on the shores of Friday Harbor. I can almost feel his lips, soft and pillowy against mine as I repeated the word "Yes" over and over, promising my life to his.

Chapter 6

When I open my eyes, I find I'm alone again, sitting on the bench in front of the church.

I make sure no one is watching me, take a deep breath, let it out, and start talking, whispering really, to Lenny.

"Hey, babe," I start, then pause, feeling awkward. "Why did you have to go and leave me? Barry said you would look over me and make things easy. Well, *things* haven't been easy so far." I feel the anger rising as I continue. "How do you expect me to just get on with my life? It seems damn near impossible without you."

I hang my head down and cover my face with my hands, trying to hold back the tears.

The door opens behind me. I turn around, expecting to see Mel again, and instead am surprised to see Mother, staring down at me.

"For God's sake, get yourself together, Ireland. You can't sit out here all afternoon. People are expecting you to—"

"To what, Mother?" I challenge her. "To smile and shake their hands like I'm running for office or something? This is my fiancé's funeral. Why can't I be allowed to have a moment?" I shake my head and catch my breath.

"Here's what I don't understand," I continue, not letting her talk yet. "You went through this when you were my age," I say, referring to the year she went through the same heartache when our father died in a car accident. Mother had only been five months pregnant with Collette and me. We never even had a chance to meet him.

I look at the ground. "How long did it take? To start feeling normal again?"

"I was pregnant. I didn't have the luxury of time. I had to figure out how to provide for you girls. How to survive," she shoots back.

I twist my head up to look at her as she attempts to stare me down. "Did it harden your heart so much that you can't find it in yourself to give me some sympathy? Is it too full circle for you? You'd think you could put yourself in my shoes for a minute, and I don't know..." I pause, searching for what I need from her. "Hug me? Provide a little warmth or at the very least compassion for what I'm going through?" I stand up from the bench so that we're facing each other.

I wait for her response while she takes me in. I feel like she's looking at me for the first time, scanning me from head to toe. I concentrate, so I don't fidget under her scrutiny.

I think I see a semblance of empathy in her eyes as they finally meet mine, and a hopefulness builds in my heart. She blinks, and just as fast as it appeared, it's gone. Her eyes are hard again.

"Ireland, it would do you some good to toughen up a bit."

I don't think it would have hurt any less had she actually slapped me across the cheek. She had just made it crystal clear. Sympathy was something I was going to have to find elsewhere. I should have already known she was never going to be my friend or my shoulder to cry on.

I square my shoulders and, without another word, turn on my heel and walk back into the church, leaving Mother alone, standing on the stairs.

Still embarrassed from earlier, I walk through the crowd with my head down, doing my best to avoid eye contact, not wanting to talk to anyone.

Unfortunately, being the fiancé of the deceased is like having a target on my back. Every guest I walk by wants to offer their condolences. The more forward people hug me with a sad look in their eyes.

I pause at each encounter long enough to be polite and then move on, each attempt to connect failing to permeate my skin, their words muffled, like the teacher from the Snoopy movies I used to watch as a kid.

I inch my way through the crowd, doing my best to make my way from the middle of the room to the edge where I see Collette and Jenna chatting in a corner. Like a homing pigeon, I am desperate to make it to the safety of my two best friends.

I scan the crowd as I go and see Violet and Barry standing with Mel and Sheila by a podium. There is a projector on top that Barry is fiddling with. Violet is standing on her tiptoes, doing her best to help him. The juxtaposition of their two bodies next to each other is almost comical. Him, an easy two hundred pounds of muscle and brawn. Her, a petite little thing in a black pencil skirt, probably the very same one she uses for days in court. Even though Barry is easily twice the size of Violet, I'm confident she could take him down with the slice of her tongue, reducing him to a scared puppy with its tail between its legs, like I've seen her do with lesser subjects in the courtroom.

Barry steps aside for Violet so she can fiddle with the projector. A moment later music starts playing, and the lyrics to "Dancing with The Angels" by Monk & Neagle fill the room. The screen on the other end becomes illuminated, and I find myself transfixed by pictures of Lenny. A montage of his life's best moments. Baby pictures of him and Violet, the whole family on the beach, Lenny in a tux with a single rose pinned to the lapel, standing in a crowd of pimply teenagers, college graduation, standing by a shiny car with a bow on it. All of them, images of happiness. It takes me a minute before I realize I'm staring at a picture of my own face. The glowing skin and broad smile are not recognizable to me anymore. It's the same picture as the one in my condo, the one of Lenny and me on the boat. My breath catches in my throat. The next picture is one of us after Lenny proposed. We had goofy grins on our faces, and Lenny is holding out my left hand to the camera.

I'm rooted to my spot in the middle of the room. I can feel people looking at me, waiting to see my reaction. I wish I were wearing a baseball cap, so I could pull the brim down and obscure my face. Instead, I bite my lip and will myself to breath.

The slideshow comes to a close, and people start milling around again. I hear people whispering, "I just feel so awful for her," "what do you think she'll do now," and "what a tragic love story" as they pass by me.

I block them out and resume my pursuit of Collette and Jenna.

"Ireland?"

I turn in the direction of the voice and find myself looking down on a thin man wearing round spectacles, Harry Potter style. He looks familiar, but I can't place him.

"Ireland?" he repeats.

"Yes?"

"I'm so sorry for your loss," he says and extends his hand.

I take it in mine and am surprised at the loose grip of his handshake. "Thank you," I reply lamely.

"It was a lovely service."

"Yes, it was, Mr...?"

"I'm sorry, Mike. Mike Toberouski."

"Yes, Mike, it was a lovely service. I'm sorry, but have we met before?"

"Oh, my apologies. No, we haven't officially met. I was assigned Lenny's story at the *Times*, and I've been working on the investigation of the accident. I recently learned of your relationship with Lenny, and I wanted to offer my condolences."

"Thank you, Mr. Toberouski. I appreciate it," I say, resuming my scan of the crowd for Violet and Collette.

"These last few days must have been very hard on you."

I nod, turning my attention back to Mike. I have a feeling there is more coming.

"You know, I was fascinated by the similarities between the most recent events and what supposedly happened to your own mother all those years ago."

"Do you now? I suppose, being in your line of work, you might find the similarities fascinating. I personally find them tragic."

"Oh, yes. I agree. Very tragic, indeed. What are the

chances that a mother and daughter both, would lose their fiancés before they could walk down the aisle?"

I'm silent. I'm having a hard time figuring out where this conversation is going.

"You know, what I find most interesting is that I can't find any record of the accident your mother spoke about in her last interview. The accident, she claims, took your father's life before you and your sister were born."

I don't know if it's from the exhaustion of the day or if I'm genuinely missing something, but I feel like the part of my brain that's supposed to alert me to danger is desperately trying to fire but is failing miserably.

I can't think of any intelligent things to say, so I remain silent.

"Has your mother ever shared with you about your father's passing?" Mike presses.

"No more than what she shared in her interview. I'm sure you can see how it is a difficult subject for us to discuss."

I just want to be rid of Mike Toberouski for now. He is starting to make me uncomfortable.

"Yes, of course. Especially at a time like this." I watch as his eyes light up. I turn to look over my shoulder and follow his gaze to Mother.

"Well, it's been a pleasure speaking with you, Ireland. Again, my deepest sympathies." He lays his hand on my shoulder, giving it a squeeze. I take a reflexive step back from his invasion of my personal space, giving him an opening to brush past me, making a beeline for Mother.

I watch as Mike extends the same weak handshake

to Mother as he approaches her. Her eyebrows knit together as he engages her in a conversation.

I'm still watching them from across the room when I'm interrupted by a group of Lenny's employees from his architectural firm. "Ireland, we wanted to offer our condolences," a petite woman with curly brown hair says, as she gestures to her surrounding colleagues. "Please let us know if there is anything we can do."

"Thank you, I'm sure I'll be fine," I lie. "But thank you for the support," I say as I keep my eye on the conversation Mother and Mike are still having.

"I hate to bring this up now, but you don't happen to know what's going to happen to the firm, do you?" she asks.

"Um, what?" I turn my gaze to meet curly hair. "I'm not sure. You'll have to speak to Mel about that. My understanding was they ran the company together." I stare at her blankly, not sure why she thought I would know the answer to such a question. "I wasn't involved with any of the firm's business decisions."

"Um, yeah, okay," she mutters. "Again, sorry for your loss," she says, and the group of them melt back into the crowd, leaving me blissfully alone to go find Jenna and Collette.

I spot them, still in the corner, and start weaving my way through the now thinning crowd. I can feel my shoulders start to relax at the anticipation of being with Collette and Jenna, when a hand touches my shoulder, holding me back.

Good God, can't a girl get a break around here? It's becoming too much to take.

I glance down at the hand that is holding me back and follow it to Violet's angelic face. I instantly feel my hackles lie down again.

Mel and Sheila had named their only daughter appropriately. She was soft and delicate like a flower, and there was something about her face that was bright and open. I had seen her use this to her advantage in the courtroom when she had someone on the stand. Gaining their trust by merely looking into their eyes and playing the understanding lawyer. Then attacking when they least expected it. Luckily I was never on the receiving end of Violet's attacks.

"Hey," she says with her quiet, husky voice. "I just wanted to see how you're doing. It's been a lot to take in today." She looks like she's barely hanging on herself. The whites of her eyes are more of a pink and the skin underneath a deep blue.

"I'm fine," I lie.

She gives me a sheepish grin. "Yeah, we're all fine." She does the finger quotes around the word "fine" and rolls her eyes.

"I know, but really, what am I supposed to say?" I ask rhetorically.

"I get it. We can't possibly say, 'I would rather just fall into a deep dark hole in the ground than be here.' That probably wouldn't leave much in the way of conversation."

"Nope, but at least we would be left alone."

Violet gives me a devilish grin. "Wouldn't that be nice." Leaning into me she whispers, "I was so looking forward to being your sister-in-law. I can't believe we went from wedding planning to this, in a matter of weeks."

I nod. "I know."

"Do you think we can still get together? Maybe

grab a coffee or something?"

"Sure, of course."

"It's just…I don't have a brother anymore." She chokes on the last word and takes a minute to recover. "Just, please, promise me you'll still think of us as part of your family."

"I promise," I say, the lie tasting bad on my tongue even as I say it.

Chapter 7

They say when you fall asleep your sense of smell is the first sense you lose, and that when you wake up, it's the last one you gain back.

So when I open one eye in the darkness, I'm not sure I can trust the sweet smell that's wafting up my nostrils.

I've no idea what time it is. I turned my alarm clock to face the wall sometime the day before to stop the continual taunt of time ticking away.

My feet ache as I lift my body off the bed. I can feel them spread out, a lattice of muscles and tendons readjusting to the weight they haven't had to support in the previous hours.

I do a quick stretch with my head to shake off the stiffness and lift my arms up to the ceiling. I can feel each vertebrae separating. With a deep inhale of breath, I feel slightly refreshed.

But as soon as I feel it, the pleasure is washed away by a crushing feeling of guilt. How can I allow myself to feel pleasure when Lenny never will?

I almost sit back down on the bed, but the curious smell of baked goods touches my nostrils again, and I remember what roused me in the first place.

I open the door and follow the direction of the smell down the short hallway, into the kitchen, and there, working in the dark, save for one light above the stove, is Mother.

I rub my eyes to make sure I'm seeing right.

What in God's name is she doing in my condo? Especially after what she said yesterday.

I search the recesses of my brain, but I can't come up with a single logical explanation.

I watch her in the soft light. Her motions are smooth as she works without making a sound. Her movements are relaxed and fluid.

I stare at her in awe. I so rarely see her without a cell phone in her hand, perfectly groomed, barking commands at someone. Yet here she is, in my kitchen at who knows what hour, baking.

Even though her movements are smooth and precise, her hair is all ruffled, like she uncharacteristically ran her hand through it. There's a small line of white flour on her left cheek.

She looks up in my direction. The glow of the stove light is the only light in the condo. She has to blink to adjust her eyes to the darkness.

I stand perfectly still, not quite knowing what my role is in this situation. I can't remember a single time we made cookies together. I'm at a loss of what to do.

She picks up a towel and wipes her hands off, replacing it on the kitchen counter. She moves slowly, coming around the corner of the bar toward me. Keeping eye contact, like she's afraid of scaring away a wild animal.

When she's almost in front of me, she reaches out and takes my hand. The sensation of her skin on mine sends a jolt up my spine, causing me to take an involuntary step forward.

"Come sit here." She pulls out one of the bar

stools. I sit and tuck my knees under the counter.

"I'll make some tea," she says as she walks back to the stove and reaches for the cabinet.

"Milk," I correct.

"Excuse me?" she says

"We're having cookies, right? We need milk," I explain.

The corners of her mouth turn up for only a fraction of a second.

"Milk it is." She closes the cabinet and heads to the refrigerator.

The timer goes off on the oven, and she puts the milk down in front of me with two glasses before turning back to take the cookies out.

She sets them down on the stove to cool and turns back to me.

"So...cookies?" I ask.

She pulls out the stool next to mine and sits down.

"Peace offering."

I look at her out of the corner of my eye. When was the last time she ever made a peace offering? I'm not buying it. Too many years of disappointment have caused me to be suspicious of these kinds of situations.

I shrug my shoulders in response.

She changes tactics. "How about one of my famous chocolaty, chocolate chunk cookies?"

"What makes them so famous? If I recall correctly, you've never made a cookie in your life. In fact, I'm not sure you've ever eaten one."

"Well, for starters, they have real butter in them." She pointedly ignores my snide comment.

When I turn to look at her, there is a look of mischief in her eyes.

I let out a laugh, a real laugh.

I clap a hand over my mouth, embarrassed by the sudden outburst. My eyes feel prickly, and before I can stop it, tears are spilling down my face.

Mother leans over and wraps me in her arms.

This unaccustomed warmth from Mother causes a dam to break, and my body shakes from the cathartic sobs that pour out of me.

We stay this way for a long time as I sob. Mother alternates between rubbing my back awkwardly and hugging me. It must have been the longest we've ever had bodily contact, but it's the comfort I've been dying for.

When the last tear finally makes its way down my check, Mother gathers some of the cookies on a tray with the two milk glasses. "Come, I have something I need to tell you."

She motions to the purple couch, next to the window, that faces the fireplace. She flips the switch, igniting the fire, sits down, and pats the seat next to her.

I grab the cashmere throw on the back of the chair and sit down.

She picks up a cookie and hands it to me.

I take it and study it.

"It's okay. I didn't poison it. You can eat it."

I take a bite and let the chewy goodness roll around on my tongue before swallowing it and picking up the glass of milk.

"Ireland, there is something I need to talk to you about."

"Okay," I say, waiting patiently.

"Do you remember Mike from yesterday?"

I'm momentarily stumped, racking my memory of

yesterday, but finally settle on the reporter. "Yes."

"What did he talk with you about?" she asks.

"Nothing much. He said he was covering the story on Lenny's accident. He mentioned his interest in the similarities of our stories."

Mother turns from her spot on the couch and looks out the window. I follow her gaze. It's pitch black out, the cloud cover not allowing a single star to shine through. The only light is the amber glow from the streets below. The wind is picking up again; there will be another wave of rain soon.

She turns back, and her eyes search my face like she is looking for answers of her own.

"I have something to tell you. Something I was never planning on telling you, or your sister, but it looks like Mike isn't willing to give me an option on this." She flips her hand in the air, like what she's about to tell me isn't that big a scoop and that Mike should just let it rest.

I stay silent, not sure where she's going with this.

"He made it quite clear this afternoon that he had his story and he was preparing to run with it. I've requested he give me twenty-four hours before he runs it so I could talk with you first."

"Okay."

She shifts on her side of the couch, squaring her shoulders and straightening her back. Instantly the mood of the room changes. She starts slowly, searching for the right words.

"When I was in college, I had a boyfriend. Do you remember me mentioning Randy?"

"I guess, in passing," I say.

"He was my boyfriend, for about three years. He

was the love of my life. I thought I was going to marry him. I had all these plans in my head about how we would graduate from college, get married, start a little family. The only thing I didn't plan on was Randy not sharing my same dreams of starting a life together. When we entered our senior year of college, I opened up and told him about the future I saw for the two of us. All starry-eyed and innocent, I expected him to share my ideas for a happily ever after." She stares at a spot on the carpet.

Straightening up further, she clears her throat and continues, "But he didn't. He wanted to explore the world, and he wanted to do it alone. He didn't think he could get the same experience out of it if he had someone he felt responsible for with him. Those were his exact words."

"That must have hurt," I say, trying to follow where she's going.

"I flipped out, we had a massive fight, and we broke up. A few days later I was chatting with my business professor. He was young and handsome and happened to be only a few years older than the class he was teaching. I told him about the breakup and how heartbroken I was. He must have felt sorry for me because he invited me to have coffee with him after class the next day," she says.

"We met that next day. He was so thoughtful and encouraging that when it was time for us to leave the cafe, I invited him back to my place to listen to records, and he accepted. He was so attentive. I felt safe with him. I wanted to feel *wanted* after what Randy had done. One thing led to another, and we slept together." She looks up at me, and I wonder if this is the end of her story, but she continues, looking me in the eye as she says the next part.

"I didn't find out about the pregnancy until three weeks after we had been together, roughly the same time he dumped me and I found out he was married."

"Oh," I breathe.

"I debated telling him, I really did. But in the end, I was so mad at him for not telling me he was married and for dumping me, that I didn't. The most awful part was that even though I was mad at him, I still had feelings for him. I cared enough about him to not want to ruin his marriage or endanger his career. If the college had found out he had sex with a student, he would have lost his job like that." She snaps her fingers, causing me to twitch.

"But I wasn't just worried about him. I was young and afraid of what was going to happen to me too. I had gotten this far in school, and I just needed one more quarter to graduate. I didn't know if I could get into trouble for being with my professor. I was terrified of being a single mother, but I was more terrified of being a single mother with no education. So, I kept quiet, finished my degree, walked with my class for graduation, and left town. I never looked back, I only looked forward. I had something to live for. Failure wasn't an option, so I moved to Seattle, finding work as a spa manager in a hotel my friend worked at, until I gave birth to the two of you."

My throat tightens as I realize this is the real story of what happened to our father, not the abridged version Mother has told Collette and me our whole lives.

"I knew it was wrong to not tell him, but as time passed, I grew more and more certain that I couldn't go back, I couldn't tell him. It was just too late."

She finally stops talking, and I know she wants me to say something, but I can't cut through the thoughts that keep coming at me, like rapid gunfire. Pop, pop, pop. Emotions I can't even name swirl through me while I struggle to make sense of it all.

"Now it's your turn to respond." Mother's commanding words bring me back to the room.

"I don't know what to say."

"Since you are at such a loss for words, how about I give you a suggestion."

I remain silent, allowing her to continue.

"How about you start by saying thank you."

I balk at her statement. "Thank you? For what, exactly?"

"For telling you. I could have taken this to my grave."

I laugh out loud, but it's not like the bubbling laugh we had just shared over the cookies. No, even to my own ears, this is a cruel laugh, one that leaves nothing to the imagination as to how absurd I think this statement is.

"I'm sorry, you want me to thank you for finally telling me that I have a father who is still alive? You want *me* to thank *you*? For lying to Collette and me for our entire lives?" I laugh again. It's beyond my comprehension how she can be so ambivalent about all this.

"I can't believe I was actually starting to trust you. You came into my house, baked cookies, let me cry on your shoulder." I motion behind me to the kitchen. "I thought this was really going to be the beginning. The start of a relationship between you and me. I should have known. You've never cared about Collette and me. All these years you've made us have Christmas at The Club, never at home like a real family. You never came to our sports games to cheer us on, you never kissed a boo-boo or brushed our hair." I shake my head at her and get off the couch, not able to stand being near her for one more second, the fire building in my veins.

"All these years we could have had a parent who actually loved us. Someone to pick us up from school, someone to eat hamburgers with. What about holidays!" My mind is swirling with all the possible ways my life could have been different with a father or a parent who actually gave a damn about his children.

"You don't know if he would have done all those things. He could have shut you out, closed the door in your face, our face."

"You never gave him the opportunity to decide for himself!" I seethe at her, recoiling from the exertion of my own anger. "You never gave us the opportunity to have him in our lives." I stand up, trying to compose myself. "You were the parent who had the ability to shape our lives. If you didn't feel up to the challenge, why didn't you give someone else the opportunity?"

"What's that supposed to mean? Not up to the challenge? I've never backed away from a challenge. I've built an empire from nothing, all by myself. I raised you and Collette without the help of a man or family."

"Raised us? More like we raised ourselves," I say.

"You really are a spoiled child," she retorts. "How do you think all this is provided for?" She waves her arm around the condo, the one that she helped pay for.

"I've slaved to provide for you girls, and all you

can do is complain about how I wasn't the perfect mother, how I was so busy working all the time. Well, you're damn right I was working. How else was there going to be food on the table when you were growing up?"

"It could have been different if you had told him," I say, registering that I still didn't even know his name. "We could have had someone watch us while you were working. You didn't have to do it alone. You didn't give him a chance to be in our lives. You always pride yourself on being independent and doing it yourself, but you can ask for help. People might surprise you sometimes."

She narrows her eyes at me. "I've never been surprised by someone in a good way. When I found myself pregnant, out of wedlock, and by a man who was married, my family wrote me off. You want to talk about surprises? Well, that one sure knocked me off my feet."

"Who leaves their pregnant daughter to fend for herself?" I honestly didn't know if I believed anything that came out of her mouth anymore.

"Very strict Catholics who expected perfection from their only daughter, that's who. In their eyes I had committed the biggest sin possible. They couldn't forgive me, and I couldn't believe it." She pauses with a faraway look. I look closer into her eyes, waiting for a tear, but they stay steadfastly dry. She blinks a few times and continues, "But I'll tell you what it did for me. It taught me to work hard and survive on my own. I rely on myself to get through, and it's about time that you did the same. It's time for you to toughen up, Ireland. No more looking to me for a handout. You need to start figuring out your life like I had to figure mine out."

I stare at her with my mouth agape. She is writing me off, just like her parents did to her, kicking her when she was down, and now she is doing the same to me. How can she not see she is repeating the same cycle?

I try my best to come up with a response, but I can't. All of this has left me exhausted, like a rock is literally sitting on my heart. I sigh and do the only thing I can think of that will make this better. Walking over to the side table by the front door, I pick up her handbag and keys and hold them out to her.

"It's time for you to go now."

Chapter 8

By my third glass of wine, not only are my thoughts swirling in my head, but my head itself is swirling. I need to take a break from the red juice if I'm going to piece anything together tonight.

I don't know if it's the alcohol that I started pouring the second Mother walked out the door, or if it's the shock taking over, but I have an intense feeling that I am outside my own body looking down from above. I wonder if this is what the view is like for Lenny.

The numbness that has enveloped me is keeping me from making any sense of the situation. I force myself to think slowly, like a child putting a puzzle together, one piece at a time.

I have a father. One that is alive. One that doesn't know about Collette or me. I don't know his name. I don't know what he looks like. Does he look like us? Is he still married? Does he have any children—besides Collette and me? Where does he live? How old is he?

My attempt at logical reasoning is quickly taken over by all the questions rolling around inside my head. I wander over to the couch and sit down, letting the questions take over. I wonder if he would have wanted to know about Collette and me. Would he have been there for us, or would he have shut the door in Mother's face, like she assumed he would?

All these questions, and yet I have no answers. I need to talk to someone about all of this, and there is only one person I know who can help me figure it out.

I pick up the phone on the coffee table and hit the speed dial.

"Do you know what time it is?" comes her hoarse voice, thick with sleep and irritation.

"I know, and before you bite my head off, I need to tell you something." I rush to get the words out.

"What? What couldn't wait until the morning? Are you having a hard time? You know, because of Lenny?" Her voice softens a touch.

"No, it's not that. Mother just left," I try, in the way of explanation, but the alcohol is playing tricks with my logic.

I can hear Greg in the background asking Collette who she's talking to, his voice gruff. There's static as she covers the phone, I can hear mumbling through the line. "Hold on a second. I'm going into the other room."

I wait. I can hear shuffling as she gets out of bed and goes down the hallway. "What was she doing there so late?" comes the obvious question when she's back on the line.

I take a deep breath and realize, before it's too late, that this is not the way to drop a bombshell like this on Collette.

"Let's just say she came over to tell me a bedtime story."

There's a snort at the other end of the phone. "Yeah, right. When was the last time she did that?"

"Never." We answer in unison.

"Look, I'm sorry I bothered you so late," I say,

doing my best to backtrack this conversation. "You should go back to bed. But can you meet me tomorrow for breakfast at Gilbert's? I can explain everything then."

"You honestly expect me to go back to sleep after you wake me up in the middle of the night, tell me Mother was there to 'tell you a bedtime story' and that she just left? She obviously did or said something that upset you. Why else would you call me at such a God-forsaken hour? C'mon, what's up?"

I know it's not fair, and I feel awful that I've called her up at the spur of the moment for my own selfish needs, but now that I have her on the phone, I know I can't tell her this way. We need to be together, to hash this one out, sister to sister, and it probably wouldn't hurt if I was sober when we did it.

"I know, I'm sorry I called. Really, I just needed to hear your voice. Let's talk tomorrow, please?"

Collette sighs loudly through the phone. "Fine, I'll go back to bed. What time should we meet?"

"Is nine too early?" I'm hoping I'll be able to slip into an alcohol-induced snooze for at least a few hours, but I'm doubtful I'll be able to.

"No, I'll be there," she answers.

"Thanks, C. See you tomorrow."

"Yeah, all right, get some rest, will ya?" she says, already yawning.

"I'll try. You too. Good night," I slur.

"Night."

I hear the click of her hanging up, and I toss my phone on the couch and wander into the bedroom. I grab the picture of Lenny and me as I pass the dresser and hold it limply by my side as I make my way to the foot of the bed. I flop face down into a sea of comforter and pillows, groaning as my head starts to spin like it does when I twirl Maggie and Molly around at the park.

I flip over onto my back and stare at the ceiling. "Hey, babe," I slur out loud. I wait for a minute. It's not like he's going to answer me back, so I keep going. "I miss you something awful. Barry said you would be up there looking out for me and making things easy. Ha! What a great job you've done so far! If you were here, I'd be so mad at you." I lift my hand—the one not gripping the picture frame—and point at the sky, like I'm telling someone off, and then let it drop, covering my eyes, shutting out the streetlight.

The rest of my words come out garbled as I talk through my arm. "I wish you were still here. You would know what to do. You would probably sit me down and talk it all out with me. You'd have a chart with a logical thought process about what to do next. A column of pros and cons." I hiccup. "But without you, I have no idea what to do next." I feel exhausted from the whole day—Lenny's funeral, Mother waking me up in the middle of the night, and the realization that I have a father. It was all too much to deal with at once. I stop talking to Lenny and let my body become heavy. I try a trick my therapist taught me, which is to start at my feet and tense and relax every muscle in succession, one at a time, working from the bottom to the top until I've flexed and released each muscle in my body.

I've only made it to my calf muscles before a rapid onset of sleepiness takes hold.

The last image in my head is of Lenny, smiling at me. Standing with him is another man, and even though he is a stranger, he is familiar to me. I drift off to sleep with the comfortable feeling that I'm being watched over.

****

My phone rings at nine o'clock on the dot. Collette, always the punctual one, is right on time. And why wouldn't she be? She wasn't the one playing Russian roulette with her liver last night.

I pick up the phone, doing my best to ignore the pounding behind my right temple.

"I'm here," Collette says, not waiting for my greeting. "Downstairs. I'll wait for you."

"Down in a minute," I mumble into the phone while I take a quick glance in the mirror. I've managed to wash my face and sweep my hair into a high ponytail. Going for comfort over style, I'm dressed in my gray tunic sweater over some black yoga pants. Hoping to come off looking shabby chic—but knowing I probably look just plain shabby—I grab my keys and a jacket and head out the door to meet Collette on the sidewalk of Main Street.

Gilbert's on Main is just a few doors down from my condo, which makes it the most convenient and, luckily, the most delicious place for breakfast in the whole neighborhood.

I pull my jacket closed against the wind as I approach Collette, who is standing on the sidewalk with her shoulders hunched over her phone. I pause a moment, looking her up and down. Even just standing on the sidewalk her beauty never fails to astound me.

I catch the reflection of myself in the store window and can't help but compare my own reflection to the vision of Collette standing just a few feet away.

Being twins, Collette and I have always been

lumped together in the attractive category. But I've always been aware of the differences between the two of us. I might have the same body and bone structure as Collette, but when you put us side by side, Collette is the real stunner. A regular Helen of Troy in a Herve Leger dress, able to literally stop traffic just crossing the street. I've seen it happen with my own eyes. I'm certain she could just as quickly start a war with the simple heave of her breasts or the flick of her hair.

She looks up as I approach. "Well, you look like you've had a rough night."

"Gee, thanks," I deadpan, not failing to notice how stylish Collette is in her black cigarette pants and white silk top. "I didn't get much sleep," I offer.

"That much I know. Remember calling me in the middle of the night, or were you too drunk by that point?"

"I wasn't drunk," I shoot back, "and you would have been drinking too, after what happened."

"Fine, so tell me what happened, enough with the secret innuendos and rendezvous."

A couple holding hands come toward us on the sidewalk, and we move closer to the bank of boutique shops lining Main Street to let them pass.

"It's too complicated to go over out here. Let's go inside. I'll tell you over breakfast," I say, knowing I'm just delaying the inevitable.

We walk into Gilbert's through the side door and get in line. The bistro itself has an airiness that comes from the tall, open-air ceiling and grand south-facing windows. With a cornucopia of random books lining the windowsill—Hollywood, a Celebration, Carnegie Hall, Madeline, Thailand, a beautiful cookbook—it's the kind of place you come for a cup of coffee but stay for hours.

When we reach the front of the line, I order the egg white scramble with spinach, Havarti cheese, and Roma tomatoes and add a toasted poppy seed bagel, cream cheese and raspberry jam on the side.

"That's a lot of food for someone who's hungover," Collette comments.

I ignore her jab and pay for my order, take my number, and stand to the side of the line and wait for Collette. She orders a black coffee and an everything bagel with cream cheese and jam. After she's paid, we take a seat at one of the little wooden tables next to the window. In the middle of the table are fresh-cut dahlias housed in an ice cream parfait glass masquerading as a vase. They look particularly perky to me this morning, taunting me with their cheery colors. "Look," they say, "we have purpose and joy still left in us. How about you?"

I sigh inwardly, knowing the answer, and lift my eyes to the yellow painted tapestry on the wall behind Collette.

Placing her white utilitarian coffee cup on the table, Collette wraps her hands around it and shivers. "It's always so cold in here. I don't understand why they can't just close the doors."

I look over Collette's shoulder to the open door and just shrug. "Maybe they just want to make sure people know they're open," I guess out loud.

"It would be just as easy to put a sign on the door that says Open and then crank up the temperature in here. I don't think it's asking too much to have it at least be over sixty-five degrees!" she complains and takes a sip of her coffee, the steam making little swirls in the air next to her nose.

I glance at the table to our right, where a mother and her young daughter are also trying to keep warm. The mother keeps placing the girl's jacket over her shoulders, and the girl keeps shrugging it off. They are having an animated conversation in what I think is Hindi as the mother tries again to cover the girl.

"How's Molly's eye doing?" I ask, remembering my niece and our outing just a few days earlier.

"She has a shiner, but it's getting better. She's been telling everyone in the neighborhood how her Auntie Ireland defended her against some big bully."

I laugh. "I'll always have her back. She's my girl."

Collette chuckles and then stops. After a pause she says, "So."

"So?" I question in return.

"Come on. I'm dying over here. You call me in the middle of the night all upset and tipsy, and then you won't even give me a hint of what happened? Enough already. What is going on?"

Another interruption prevents me from recounting the horrid details of last night as our food arrives at the table. Grateful for the extra minutes to collect my thoughts, I take a bite of the scramble and wait for the waitress to take her leave. I usually love this dish, the sharpness of the Havarti cheese combined with the sweetness of the Roma tomatoes is my favorite, but today it lacks flavor. Tasting dull and heavy, the food sits like a lump in my throat. I reach for the water to help wash it down.

"Mother came over last night," I start after I swallow.

"So you so drunkenly recalled last night." Collette takes a big bite of her bagel and chews. I envy her for a second, blissfully unaware I was about to change her life with my next sentence.

"I thought she was coming over to try and make amends. To try and…" I shrug my shoulders. "I don't know, just be a mom."

"When was the last time that ever happened?" Collette snorts.

"I know, I should have known she was up to something the second I saw her baking cookies in my kitchen."

Collette stops chewing. "She was doing what?"

"Cookies, in my kitchen."

"No flippin' way! I don't believe you." She narrows her eyes at me.

"Trust me, I thought the exact same thing when I saw her there." I pause, contemplating last night. "And in hindsight, I should have trusted that initial reaction. But it was like all my wishes were being answered. Mother was making an effort. Or so I thought." How could I have been so naive? "I was so wrong."

"Well, if it makes you feel any better, I've always been wrong when it comes to Mother." Collette shrugs her shoulders and takes another bite.

"That makes two of us," I say.

We smile at each other, and it gives me the courage to continue. "You know how Mother always told us our dad's name was Randy?"

"Sure, but that's all she'd tell us. Except that he died before we were born. And, of course, how hard life was for her." Collette rolls her eyes dramatically.

"Right, well, apparently, that's not exactly how the

story goes." I bite my lower lip, trying to decide how best to move forward.

"What do you mean?" She puts her bagel back down on the plate and leans into our conversation.

"When Mother came over last night, she wasn't there to offer condolences, or to try to relate to me. It was more like she was there to explain why she *couldn't* relate to me."

"I don't follow you."

I take a deep breath and plunge into the deep end. "Randy isn't our dad," I say and then hold my breath.

"Come again?" Collette says, tipping her head to the side.

"When she was in college, she did date a guy named Randy, but they broke up. Apparently, she was heartbroken and devastated, so when her professor asked her to coffee, she took him up on the offer. One thing led to the next, and they had sex," I say and lay my hands on the table with the palms facing up like it explained everything.

Collette's eyes become squinty. "So you're saying that Randy wasn't our father, but her professor was?"

"Yes."

"Does that mean her professor was the one who died?"

I realize I'm not doing a good job of explaining everything. She still isn't catching on. I take another deep breath and try again. "No, the college professor never died. Mother just told us that our father died and that our father was Randy. No one actually died." I wait for this part to sink in.

"So what you're saying is…"

"That our dad is still alive and is out there

somewhere."

"And we've been lied to our whole lives?" Collette says slowly, finally catching on. She's started shaking. She grabs hold of her coffee mug to try and steady her hands.

"That's not all of it," I say, waiting for her to focus on me again. "Here's the real kicker. He doesn't even know about us."

Her eyes grow to the size of saucers, and before she can say anything else, I quickly fill her in on all the details from last night. When I'm done, tears are streaming down her face, and her whole body is shaking. I reach over and grab her arm to help steady her.

"I just can't believe it." Is all she can whisper through her tears.

I watch as the tears stream down her face, and I can feel my own starting to prickle behind my eyes. I blink quickly, trying to keep them at bay. The few mouthfuls of food I had consumed earlier are now threatening to make their way back up my esophagus. I take a deep breath and close my eyes for a second, willing the food to stay put.

When I open them, I find myself staring into an identical pair of eyes, and without being told, I can feel the heartbreak consuming my other half.

We sit in silence for a few minutes, Collette staring blankly at the tabletop, running her fingers in rhythmic circles over the sanded wood.

When the tears have dried up, and she looks like she can concentrate on what I'm saying, I start talking again.

"After I hung up with you last night, thanks to the

wine I was able to fall asleep, but not for very long. I ended up waking up after just a couple of hours. Of course, all the same questions that I didn't get answers to last night kept swirling through my head. I just keep thinking about what Mother said last night. She said this was the only time she was going to talk about it with me. In fact, the only reason she told me about it at all is because of the reporter digging up information for his story. She knew Mike was going to run the story and she wanted to tell us before we found out another way. I think she was more worried that another reporter would ask us questions that we wouldn't have the answers to. She was more worried about our interaction with the reporters than with how this would affect our lives. The more I think about it, the more I'm sure she would have carried that secret to her grave."

Collette drops her head into her hands and rubs her temples. "This is so much to take in, I can't think straight right now."

I remove my hand from her arm and lay it back on the table. "I know, I'm still numb from it all myself." I pause, not sure if I should say what I want to say next or if I should wait for Collette to have more time to comprehend everything. I decide to risk it and say, "But the more I think about it, the more I want to know. And there's only one way I can think of to get those answers. I want to try and find him." I pause and search her face, waiting for her response. If we did this, we would have to do it together. We've always been a package deal. I couldn't introduce myself to our father, if I could even find him, without having her by my side.

We sit in silence for a few minutes, and I'm afraid I've pushed her too hard, too fast. Finally, Collette pulls herself back up to a sitting position and says, "You know, all my life you've been my other half. I might be married to Greg, and I adore him with all my heart, but you are my person, you always have been. You're my identity. Without you, I'm only half of a picture. If you really want to go find out who this guy is, then I'll go along with you."

"I just want some answers, or at least to try and get some. Don't you?" I ask.

"I don't know. I think so. It's just so new. I need more time to let it sink in."

"That's fair."

"But, in the meantime, we're going to need a plan."

Chapter 9

It's becoming more and more apparent to me the perverse dedication I have to this Club. Despite my natural instinct to run as far and as fast as I can in the opposite direction of Mother, I have managed to arrive in my office at eight o'clock on the dot.

Resigning myself to another day spent behind closed doors, I pull out my desk chair and fire up the computer. With at least an hour to kill before Collette is scheduled to arrive, I figure I'll do my best to get some work done.

Starting with e-mails, I focus my attention on the most pressing. A new hire needs to change something on her W-2 form, a few members have questions about their bills, and a spa employee has a question about how to start a health savings account.

I scroll down the list and notice another e-mail, this one from Mel Evans with the heading, "Nice seeing you." Ugh, I thought I was done with e-mails from the Evans after this weekend. Just looking at his name takes me back to the service, and that is not a memory I want to relive right now. I skip over his e-mail and continue down the list, promising to come back to it when I have more courage. I'm just about to dive into the e-mail from the new hire when there's a knock on the door.

I look up in time to see Jenna sneak in from the hallway.

"Hey!" She takes the seat across from me and places another green juice on my desk. What is it with her and this darn green juice?

"Drink that." She points to the green sludge.

"Sure, maybe in a little bit."

"I don't understand how you can work at the swankiest health club in town, and yet you won't *drink the juice*." She puts her fingers up in quotation marks as she says, "the juice."

"It's green," I say like that explains it.

"It's good, I promise. Just try it."

"Fine," I say, taking the straw to my mouth and taking a sip.

I hate admitting it to her, but it's actually good, really good. It tastes like pineapples and oranges. Tropical, and not at all like mud or grass, like I was expecting.

"Well?" She wiggles her eyebrows at me.

"Fine," I resign. "You win. It's really good." I take another swig.

"You're welcome. What would you do without me?" she says, literally patting herself on the back, right in front of me.

"You're too much." I giggle.

"Well, someone's gotta keep an eye on you. How are you doing anyway? The funeral kind of turned into a shit show, huh?" Ever the poet, this one.

"The service was nice. It's just what happened after the service that sucked." I shrug my shoulders.

"Yes, the service was nice. I can only imagine how much you must miss him."

Her kind words start the sting of tears on the back of my eyelids. I blink them away.

"I haven't even told you what happened later that night," I say, deliberately guiding the conversation away from Lenny. I'm not in the position to go down memory lane right now.

"Hit me." Jenna leans back in the chair, getting comfortable.

"It's a long story, are you sure you have time?" I look at the clock, conscious of her class schedule.

She glances up at the wall. "No problem, I just got done with the seven a.m. class, and I don't have another one until nine. Talk fast, and we'll be fine."

I take another drink of the juice and quickly fill her in on the details of the last twenty-four hours. Telling her as much as I can remember, starting from waking up to the smell of cookies and finishing with the breakfast I had with Collette yesterday.

The conversation is peppered with a lot of "What?' and "You can't be serious!" from Jenna. To which I assure her I am completely serious.

"Well, crap! I can't believe your mother is such a..." She trails off.

"Bitch," I provide. "I know."

"Ireland, how can you handle all this? Lenny's funeral, your Mother's deceitfulness, and now you have a dad? It's too much for anyone to go through!"

I contemplate what she's saying for a few minutes.

"You know," I start slowly, trying to manifest the right words for how I'm feeling. "I think I'm numb, but not just can't-feel-a-pinch-on-the-skin numb. Like, *really* numb."

Jenna nods her head slowly in understanding. "That would be the least I would expect."

"It's like I've gotten so used to being shocked that

I'm walking around on a constant edge. I don't trust anyone I talk to anymore to not cause me to have a panic attack. I feel like the best I can do for myself right now is to lock myself in my office and not talk to anyone."

"I can understand why you would feel that way, but I'm not sure that's the healthiest solution," Jenna counters.

"There isn't anything else I can do. I'm stuck here, and I have to keep plugging through. Life isn't going to grant me a timeout just because I can't deal with it all." I throw my hands up and let them land back on the desk with a thud.

"That's not true. There is something you can do. Have you thought about finding him? Your dad, I mean?"

I pause and think about what Jenna is asking. "Actually, Collette and I talked about that yesterday. It's so hard to know what to do. He doesn't even know we exist. To him, he just had a one-night stand. A quick fling with a student twenty-something years ago. I mean, does he even remember her?"

Jenna snorts. "She's kind of hard to forget."

I crack a smile. "That she is." I pause. "But, really think about it. How would you react, finding out you had long-lost twin daughters? Daughters you knew nothing about? Would you want anything to do with them, or would you turn your back and tell them to get the hell off your property?"

"I don't know. But neither do you. The only way you'll find out is if you go find him. What have you got to lose? All I see here is an opportunity, a chance to start something new. Who knows, you could end up with a great relationship, someone who really cares about you. He could be nothing like your mother. You don't know until you try."

I want to defend Mother against Jenna's implications, but I can't come up with a single thing that deserves being defended. She's right. What is there to lose?

I'm deep in thought when Jenna and I hear, "Hey, bendy Barbie. You're in my chair."

We look up to see Collette standing in my doorway. She's dressed for the office, in a burgundy pantsuit and heels. She's apparently planning on heading to work after our meeting.

Jenna glances at her watch and stands up. With a grand gesture, she waves Collette into the room to take her chair. "I have to leave anyway. There are people in need of my Zen expertise."

I hear Jenna whisper to Collette as they brush past each other, "She told me. Are you doing okay?"

Collette gives a quick nod and says, "I'm doing okay. Better than yesterday, at least."

Jenna stops on her way out the door and looks back at the both of us. "I take it back. If the two of you walked into my life unannounced, claiming to be my daughters, I would look to the heavens and thank my lucky stars. I say do it. Find him, show him how fabulous you two are. Because, really, you both are nothing short of incredible." She skips out the door, leaving her words to sink in on their own.

She really is the best friend a girl could ask for.

Collette takes the space in the chair Jenna just vacated and looks around my office. I realize that she hasn't been in here for over a year, she so rarely comes to visit me at work. I follow her eyes as she takes in all the pictures on my walls and notice she stops on the picture box, the one containing the short straw.

I watch her swallow, and heat rises in my own face.

It was never my lifelong dream to work for Mother or The Club. In fact, looking back, I never really had a lifelong dream to begin with. Growing up there was only room for one dream in our household. The Club took up every dinner conversation, every holiday plan, every moment. Any aspirations Collette or I might have had as children were quickly dismissed as childish and unworthy of further exploration. Which made it virtually impossible to discover our own personal interests.

So when Mother sat Collette and me down on the eve of our graduation from the University of Washington—both with Bachelors of Science in Communications—for a motivational talk, I should have known she had ulterior motives.

After droning on for what seemed like forever about "our generation, the millennials" as the ones who are narcissistic, lazy, and spoiled, she had finally gotten to the point. "You both need to get rid of any delusional work expectations. You will not simply be awarded for a job for just showing up. Which is why you must come work for me."

Collette and I had sat, dumbfounded, neither one of us ready to accept that fate.

"I have worked tirelessly to build this business. It's what provides for the lifestyle you have grown accustomed to, and now it's your turn to work here. You must learn every inch and aspect of this business so that, when the time comes, you can carry on the legacy I have created."

Not knowing what to say or how to react, I had turned to Collette, only to see my own terror reflected in her eyes. We sat in stunned silence until Mother got up from her chair and declared, "Well, that takes care of that," and simply left the room. No discussion, no entertaining any other options. Our fate was sealed in a matter of minutes.

The second she was out the door and out of earshot, Collette turned to me, literally begging me to take her spot at The Club.

"If at least one of us does this, then she might let the other one go. Ireland, I can't work for Mother, I'll die."

"And you think it will be so much better for me?" I snapped back.

"You've always been able to handle her better. You know how to make her happy."

I snorted. "That's the biggest load of crap, and you know it!"

Collette was silent for a moment. "Let's draw straws," she said so quietly I had to ask her to repeat herself.

"Draw straws," she repeated with more resolve. "Shortest straw works for Mother, and the other one gets to do whatever they want."

"That's absurd!" I retorted.

"Maybe, but it's the only fair way to do this."

With visions of drawing the long straw strong in my mind, I had stupidly agreed to the terms of Collette's proposed solution.

And that was how my fate was sealed. I framed the

damn straw and hung it in my office the second I moved in. To remind myself to make better decisions, and of everything I gave up that day.

I watch as the color returns to Collette's face. Without giving anything away or commenting on the picture frame, she turns to face me head on. "Ready?"

"Yeah, I think so." I return her stare, waiting for more.

Not catching on to my hesitation, she starts to stand, pushing herself up out of the chair. "I was thinking last night, and I realized that I haven't even spoken to Mother about this. This will be the first time she's told me herself."

"I know, that thought crossed my mind too," I say, allowing the conversation to drift away from the straw. "I wonder what her take will be?"

"Knowing her, she'll have some kind of excuse," she says with a cheeky smile and turns her eyes back to meet mine.

"Probably. Let's go find out what that is." I put my computer to sleep and make sure the password protection is on before walking around the side of my desk, joining Collette at the doorway.

"No time like the present. Let's do this."

****

The ping of the elevator sounds, depositing Collette and me at the entrance to the atrium pool. Collette takes a step forward, stops, sighs, and says, "I always forget how exquisite this place really is."

In our rush to get to Mother's office, I'm thrown off track by Collette's sudden change of subject. I pass this part of The Club multiple times a day in my haste to get to and from tasks, but seeing it through the eyes of someone who doesn't come here very often forces me to take pause and appreciate it.

Taking in the sixty-five-foot-long turquoise masterpiece in front of us, I have to admit it is breathtaking. Set under a two-story double-height glass roof and surrounded by floor-to-ceiling windows, the top floor of The Club is an architectural masterpiece. Both sides of the pool are flanked by white-cushioned lounge chairs, meticulously spaced out evenly, running the length of the atrium. The back wall is the only surface not covered in glass. Instead, in place of a window is a wall garden, full of ferns, Japanese iris, begonias, orchids, and a wide range of hostas. With its own misting system built in, the garden is continually surrounded by a cloud of white haze. The finishing touch is the waterfall trickling down a white-and-turquoise mosaic of The Club logo, cutting the flora in half as it spills into the pool below in a sheet of pristine water.

Collette turns to me. "I can't believe you're going to inherit all this."

I look at her in astonishment. It wasn't so long ago she was begging me to take her place in this little legacy. I scoff at her and say, "It's not like Mother is ever going to hand this over. Do you know how long I've been stuck down in the dungeon of the accounting department? She has no immediate plans to change that, trust me."

Collette looks down at her hands and studies her nails, which I notice are chipped and bitten. "I guess we can chalk that promise up to another one of her deceptions." She looks back up at me, and I feel like she is trying to tell me more. But before I have a chance to ask her what's really on her mind, she grabs my hand and starts walking down the side hallway that leads to Mother's office. "Let's get this over with."

We stand facing the closed door. I glance over at Collette and can see the vein on the side of her neck pulsing to a silent rhythm. My eyes travel to her face, an unfaltering expression camouflaging her nerves.

"Should we knock?" I whisper, motioning to the door.

"Oh for Christ sake, just come in," Mother's voice calls through the door, making us both jump.

I reach for the handle and turn it. A waft of the air conditioning assaults my body as I walk through the door first.

"How did she know?" Collette whispers in my ear as she brushes past me.

"You two are so predictable. It was only a matter of time before this one here told you." Mother throws her thumb in my direction. "I knew you'd be coming here eventually," she says, sitting behind her desk, her chair rolling away, arms crossed over her chest. It's the same posture Collette and I have seen a thousand times, usually when we were young and paying our penance for wrongdoings.

Collette and I stand at attention, transported back to our youth, awaiting our punishment. It really is astounding how she possesses the ability to reduce us, even as adults, to children.

We are rooted to our spots as she stares us down. But when she hesitates a fraction of a second too long, I remember why we came here in the first place. We aren't the ones on trial this time, she is. I step forward and place a hand on her desk. "We need answers."

She doesn't respond right away and instead, points to the two chairs across from her. "Sit."

I begrudgingly take a step away from her desk, and we do as we're told.

She focuses her gaze on Collette, intentionally blocking me out.

"I'm going to go ahead and assume she already told you about your father, so I don't have to waste my breath repeating myself."

Collette narrows her eyes but nods mutely.

"Good, that saves me the trouble of recounting it. I'm also going to assume you two"—she lets her eyes glance over in my direction—"are here looking for information. Am I correct?"

Again, Collette nods.

"Well, let me be the first to disappoint you both. I have known that one day you two might find out about your father. Either by my telling you or by some act of God. I wasn't naive enough to believe this conversation would never happen. I've had a good, long time to think about what I would be telling you, and what the consequences would be with each piece of information I might give you. With that being said, I have decided that what I told Ireland last night is the extent to which I'm willing to share."

I open my mouth, ready to protest, but she shuts me down immediately by holding her palm open in my direction.

"This is not up for discussion. I made my decision a long time ago. The day I walked away from that place, I knew I was never going back. I had to move forward with my life, and now you do too. I know it's for the better, so don't go getting crazy ideas in your heads. You will not be looking him up or trying to find him. It won't do anyone any good at this point. What's done is done. There is no changing the past."

"You can't be serious." Suddenly Collette has found her voice again.

"Dead serious." Mother's steady gaze gives no indication she means otherwise.

"Do you even hear yourself?" I ask. "You come over in the middle of the night, drop a bomb on Collette and me. Tell us we have a father who might, or might not, still be alive. And to top it off he doesn't even know we exist. You give us less than forty-eight hours to process all this information, and then, when we come looking to you for answers, you shut the door in our faces and say, 'No'?"

I turn to Collette. "She's literally crazy!" I fling my hand in Mother's direction. And that's when I spot it, what I came here looking for in the first place. I squint my eyes trying to take a mental picture, then turn my attention back to Collette.

Speaking slowly, I say, "I don't think we're going to win this one. We should go. Maybe we can try again later."

"You can try, but nothing is going to change. I made my mind up a long time ago. No good will come from digging up the past."

I grab Collette's hand and pull her to a standing position. I look her in the eye and say, "I think we have everything we came for anyway."

"We do?"

"Yes, we do." I turn to Mother. "If you decide to change your mind, you know where to find us."

"I won't be changing my mind."

"Fine, then I guess that's it." I pull a confused Collette out into the hallway with me and shut the door behind us.

Chapter 10

"What was that all about?" Collette asks.

"Shh." I usher her into my office and close the glass door behind us so no one will hear.

"Just listen before you get all pissed off." Out of habit, I swipe my finger across the mouse pad, causing my computer to spring to life as I sit at the desk.

"I'm waiting," she says through clenched teeth.

"She wasn't going to tell us anything. You know Mother—once her mind is made up, that's the end of it. There is no reasoning with her."

"So you're just going to give in? I thought we were going to find out who he is, don't you still want to find him?"

"I do."

"Then why just give up and walk out?" She sits down in the chair opposite my desk.

"I saw her University of Berkeley diploma on the wall behind her," I explain.

"So?" Her lips purse, and her eyes narrow.

"So, last night, when she was explaining everything, she mentioned the class she was taking when she met him, her Behavioral Finance class. All we need to do is call the university and get the records of who was teaching the class that year. They must keep records of who the professors are for each class."

I stop tinkering with the computer and check to see

if she is keeping up with me.

"We get the name and then do a person search. There are a ton of them on the internet right now. I'm sure I can do a little research and come up with something."

"Do you really think that's going to work?" she says, looking doubtful. "Don't you need to have more than just a name? Most of those things go by birthdate or social security number. How do you propose we get those little nuggets of information?" she challenges, obviously not convinced by my argument. Bending over, she grabs her handbag. "Look, I have to get to work. We're going to have to pick this up later."

"Fine, but do me a favor? At least just try looking for information while you're at the office?"

She sighs. "I'll see what I can find, but I'm not getting my hopes up."

****

It turns out I don't have to wait very long. I'm trying to act busy, categorizing the expense account on QuickBooks, when my computer pings with an incoming message. I click on the mail icon and a message from Collette springs onto the page.

From: ColletteJ@gatesfoundation.org
To: IrelandJ@Belltrio.net
Subject: Operation: Find Dad
Listen to this! I called the university and got through to the admissions department. I told them I was looking for a professor who used to work in the business department. I told them I couldn't remember his name but knew what class he taught and what year. She didn't know anything, but she passed me on to the academic secretary, who pulled up the records from

that year. Not only was I able to find out his name but she told me he left the school twelve years ago and moved to Hawaii!

His name is Carl Martin!

My heart stops beating, I can't believe it. Collette did it. She found our father! I quickly reply to her message, my hands shaking, making it hard to type anything out.

To: ColletteJ@gatesfoundation.org
From: IrelandJ@Belltrio.net
Subject: Operation: Find Dad
OMG! I can't believe you found him! And you didn't think it would work! What do we do now?
Me

From: ColletteJ@gatesfoundation.org
To: IrelandJ@Belltrio.net
Subject: Operation: Find Dad
I'm going to put his information into Lifewire, like you suggested, and see what turns up. I'm not sure if it will work, seeing as we only have his name and state. But it's worth a shot.

Hold on a second, I'm entering it now.

I stare at the blank computer, waiting for Collette. The whiteness of the screen is hypnotizing. I try to count my heart beats to pass the time. I'm so mesmerized, I don't hear the door to my office open.

"You'd better be working."

I jump and look into Mother's steady gaze. I float my finger across the curser on the computer, make a small click to hide the e-mail, and QuickBooks springs back to life.

"Just inputting the expense account information," I lie, trying my best to look nonchalant.

"Did you need something?" I ask as I back away from the computer, looking at her.

"I'm working with Loraine. I need the accounts receivable and the W-3s for last year."

"I can have that to you in an hour."

I wait, knowing there's more. Mother rarely comes to my office, I'm usually summoned to hers, so I know she has something else on her mind. I watch as she looks up to my clock, then around my room, searching for something. Eventually, her gaze travels back to my face, and we lock eyes. Hers burn into mine, and I do my best to hold her blatant stare.

A challenge passes between us. I know why she's here. She has more to say about Carl Martin. I can tell she doesn't want to be the first one to break. It would seem having the last word is easy compared to being the one to start a conversation.

This time I'm not budging. If Mother has something to tell me, I most certainly am not going to help her find the words to do it.

She sighs. "Look, I know this all came as a shock, but I'm asking for you and your sister to let it go. I never intended to put this on you and Collette, but now that you know about it, it's best if we all just forget about it."

I give a snort of disgust and raise my eyebrows. "You were never going to tell us? That's supposed to make this better? No, saying you were never going to tell me *doesn't* make it better. It makes it worse. You had this…this secret for all these years. I just don't understand how you could look at Collette and me and know you were lying to us our whole lives. I can promise you one thing—it's not just going to go away.

Why don't you make it easier on yourself and give us the information I know you're hiding?" I try, knowing full well I am skating on thin ice.

"That's never going to happen," is her smooth, emotionless response.

"Why not?" I ask. It comes out sounding like I'm begging, even to my own ears.

"Because it's better this way. He was married. He was a professor at a college. If he had found out—if anyone had found out, for that matter—he could have lost his job, his family. I couldn't do that to him."

"But you could do it to us?"

She doesn't respond.

"You could have had more." My voice is low. "You still can."

She narrows her eyes at me, knowing where I'm going with this.

"No. I told you, don't go getting any ideas about trying to find your father. This is not some teenage rom-com movie where the long-lost parents find each other and fall back in love. He is no longer a part of my life, and he doesn't need to be a part of yours."

"How can you say that? Why wouldn't I want to have him be a part of my life? It's not like I'm exactly swimming in love and devotion over here." I scoff at her.

"You don't seem to be catching on to what I'm saying. Let me put it another way. If you try and make contact with him, you will no longer be my daughter. I will no longer support you in any way. Legacy or not, you will be dead to me."

I want to laugh in her face. The absurdity of it feels like a joke. She is continuing to play God with my life.

She has been making decisions for me since I was born and she is still doing it now.

But, at this particular moment, she has me. She knows I rely on her too much to go against her.

"Right, got it," I assure her.

Without another word, she turns on her heel and walks out the door, waving politely as an employee passes in front of her in the hallway.

For the first time ever, she let me have the last word.

As soon as I can no longer hear Mother's heels clicking down the marble hallway, I bring my computer screen back to life, ready to message Collette about what had just happened, but before I can compose one, I'm bombarded with a slew of messages from Collette.

From: ColletteJ@gatesfoundation.org
To: IrelandJ@Belltrio.net
Subject: I found him!
I think I found him! He lives in Honolulu Hawaii!
From: ColletteJ@gatesfoundation.org
To: IrelandJ@Belltrio.net
Subject: Did you hear me?
I'm envisioning palm trees in our near future!
From: ColletteJ@gatesfoundation.org
To: IrelandJ@Belltrio.net
Subject: Where did you go?
Did you hear me? What should we do?
What is going on? Where did you go? Call me soon as you get this!

I get up from my desk and walk around to the glass door. I peek left and right to make sure no one is coming and then sit back down at my computer. I pull out a protein bar from my desk drawer to silence my rumbling stomach and pick up my cell phone, speed dialing Collette.

"Where did you go?" she answers.

"Hello to you, too!"

"Sure, fine. Hello," Collette humors me, and then "Where did you go?"

"I didn't go anywhere. Mother paid another visit." I give her a quick rundown of the conversation before finishing with, "I don't think I can do it."

"You can't be serious? Ireland, I have the information. I have his freaking address! We could leave tomorrow and find him. We could meet our dad! This is our chance to make our own decisions. Don't let Mother get in the way of that."

"Collette," I start, "don't take this the wrong way, but when we drew straws all those years ago, you got the chance to continue with your life. You got to have dreams and accomplish them. And I couldn't have been more proud watching you do all of it. But while you were out there, living your life, I was stuck here. I've spent almost a decade learning this Club. Besides Lenny, The Club is the only thing I care about. It's true, I hate working for Mother, but I've spent so much time here, I really do care about it. I've already lost Lenny. Besides, I'm not qualified for anything else. What would I do? I'm just not ready to lose this too." I pause. "Please understand, I just don't know if I can handle much more right now. Maybe we can find him later, when it's not so new and controversial?" My head is spinning, and I can't think straight. Along with my head, my stomach starts to churn.

I rest my head in my free hand, so I'm staring straight down at the desk. "I don't know what to do," I say honestly.

"But don't you see it, Ireland? This is your chance. Your chance to get out, to start living your own life. You're young and free from obligations. Who cares if you don't get handed The Club? Is that really what you want anyway? You could start over, be free of Mother for once."

Everything Collette is saying is true. I'm so unattached right now that it's painful. There is no one I have to support, but also, there is no one there who will catch me if I fall. The more I think about it, the more I feel like I'm already falling.

The churning in my stomach reaches an all-time high. "Hold on, Collette, I'm not feeling well." I lay the phone down just in time to pull out the garbage can under the desk and empty the protein bar from my stomach into it.

I sit like this for a minute, with my head between my knees and one hand holding my own hair back.

Once composed, I tie off the plastic bag rimming the can and reach into the same drawer that housed my protein bar to grab a napkin and wipe my mouth. I pick out a packet of mints—I've started putting them everywhere since the memorial, when Mel gave me one—and pop it into my mouth. I suck on it for a minute, then pick up the phone again.

"Are you still there?" I manage into the phone.

"That was disgusting!" Collette complains. "I thought you were getting better at keeping it down?"

"I thought so too. I guess it's not getting better."

"Sorry. Maybe you should go home and take a break? We can talk more about this later. Why don't you come over tomorrow and have dinner with us? The girls can see their auntie, and we'll persuade Greg to take them out for ice cream while we talk."

"Yeah, okay. I'll see you tomorrow."

"Six o'clock?"

"All right, six."

"See you tomorrow. Go get some rest."

I hang up after I hear the click on her end of the line and rest my head on the desk. What was happening to me?

"Good God, woman, every time I come in here you're lying on your desk." The sweet sound of Jenna's voice puts a damper on my pity party.

I pick my head up and smile at her. "Just needed a rest."

"Mhmm, what is that stench?" She waves her hand in front of her nose as she stands in the doorway, making no effort to come in farther.

I point to the trash can.

"Regurgitated lunch."

"Oh honey," she softens and takes a step past the door. "What can I do?"

I look at the clock on the wall above the computer.

"Can you cover for me for a half hour? I think I just need to go home."

"Easiest thing I've done all day," she says.

"Thanks." I gather up some papers and my handbag so we can walk out together. We just have to wait the requisite two minutes for the computer back-up to be complete before I can shut it down and lock the door behind us.

"Are you teaching tonight?" I attempt to make small talk as we walk down the hallway that leads to the front lobby.

"I have twilight yoga at seven, and then I'm done. Want me to stop by on my way home?"

"No, I'll be fine. I just need to rest, re-set. I'll be better tomorrow."

Jenna faces me, stalling our progress down the hallway. "I'm worried about you. You've been under a lot of stress, and this thing with your Mother is obviously not helping." She leans against a side wall as two members walk past us. We both turn on our most megawatt smiles and say our most charming Hellos.

Soon as they move on, Jenna is staring me down again.

"Just promise me you'll tell me if you need anything."

"I promise. I just need to rest. You're right, it is a lot to process. If I can just have some time to myself, to figure it all out, I'll feel better tomorrow, I'm sure of it."

Jenna pinches her lips together and leans in to give me a hug.

I return her hug and bid her adieu, heading for the back entrance of The Club.

The crisp autumn air brings new life to my lungs, and I inhale deeply as I walk to my car.

I might have lied to Jenna about feeling better tomorrow, but I was truthful about one thing, I needed some time to myself. I needed to get away from this place for a while.

****

Determined to self-medicate with Netflix and about twenty macarons bought at Belle Pastry on my way home, I've managed to haul the TV from the living room into the bedroom and even fight with the cords long enough to figure out how to plug everything in right. Slightly satisfied with myself—this is something I would usually have asked Lenny do—I'm now snug under the covers trying to block out any semblance of reality with *Gossip Girl* reruns.

As I was going through the cupboard earlier, looking for a bottle of wine, I stumbled upon an old bottle of Vicodin left over from when Lenny had broken his pinkie finger while skiing at Stevens Pass. It wasn't even a heroic story of falling down the mountain doing some crazy moguls; instead, his glove had gotten stuck in the chairlift. When it was our turn to disembark from the chair, he jumped up to get off, only to be dragged around by his hand as the chair completed its U-turn to head back down the mountain. With me shrieking in terror, the chairlift operator had finally noticed our dire situation and stopped the lift, but not before Lenny's finger was a bent-up mess.

Remembering how I had taken him home and babied him for the whole weekend, I pick up the bottle from the bedside table and twist it between my palms, debating taking one of the little pills, deciding if this was a rabbit hole I was prepared to go down. Maybe if I just take one, I'll finally be able to relax. The idea of being in a sweet, medically-induced numbness is so appealing I can't help but twist off the cap and pop one in my mouth, chasing it down with a sip of wine.

I wait for the room to start spinning and am disappointed when it doesn't happen right away. I pop another macaron in my mouth and sit back on the pillows, the sweet bite of raspberry covering the sour taste of the pill. I close my eyes and listen to Blair Waldorf chatting to Chuck Bass about some party they are going to that night. Apparently, it's going to be "the party to end all parties." I'm struck by how they can lead such dramatic lives and yet be so composed all the time. But then I remember this is a TV drama and what I'm experiencing is real life. Soon the voices start mixing together, and I can't decipher if it's Chuck who is trying on a dress and Blair who's mixing a cocktail or if it's the other way around. As the Vicodin takes hold, I drift off into oblivion.

****

I wake up feeling totally disoriented. The sheets are tangled around my legs, and I'm covered in sweat.

I don't fully remember what I was dreaming about, but there is a lingering sensation of drowning. I am sure there was a boat and Lenny.

I lie utterly still, trying to evoke the dream back. Lenny was on the boat, and I was trying to swim to him. He was reaching out to me, to get me on the boat with him. Only I couldn't get there. I kept swimming, but he kept drifting away.

I pound the sheets in frustration, now fully awake. When was I going to stop waking up like this? Waking up in a panic, re-living the loss of Lenny. I thought for sure the Vicodin would take this away, but really the only thing it seems to have done is make me have to go pee.

The room is dark now, and I wonder how long I've been asleep as I pad into the bathroom and take a seat on the toilet. After finishing, I wash my hands and head back to bed, dreading round two of sleep.

I hadn't bothered to turn the lights on, on my way to the bathroom, so I have no idea what I trip over, banging my knee against the side table in the process, causing sudden pain to shoot up my leg. I flip on the light switch behind the side table, instantly illuminating the room.

My eyes take a few minutes to dilate, and when they do, I realize what it is I've tripped over—one of Lenny's Timberland hiking boots.

I feel like a statue, unable to move while I stare at it. Where did that come from?

I lean down and pick it up, examining it in my hand. The rage creeps over me slowly as I stand holding the boot. How dare he leave this out for me to trip over!

Somewhere in the deep recesses of my brain I know I'm being completely irrational. Lenny didn't "leave" the boot here.

But the anger that I feel at this stupid boot rips through me, consuming my thoughts to the point I don't want to fight it. I want to give in to it. I close my hand around the boot and chuck it at the wall. It makes a loud *thud* and falls back to the floor.

I walk over to the boot and pick it up. Again an intense urge to get rid of it rips through my body. Falling to my hands and knees, I crawl under the bed, where we store the suitcases. I pull one out, dragging the matching Timberland with it. I flip the suitcase open and throw the boots in.

They sit there, lying on their sides in the empty suitcase, and I feel a third surge tear through me.

I look around the bedroom, my eye settling on the dresser where I know Lenny's things are still stored, neatly folded in piles of clothes he's never going to wear again. I yank open the drawers and scoop up piles of Lenny's T-shirts and jeans. I deposit all of them into the suitcase.

I race around the room, in a frenzy of finding Lenny's belongings. A lone sock, his watch, some shirts and boxer briefs, chucking it all into the luggage as fast as I can get my hands on them.

I stop in front of his side of the bed, his nightstand in front of me. I yank the drawer open and rummage around in his belongings. I grab a handful of papers, ready to throw them in with the rest of the pile, but an e-mail receipt with Alaska Airlines along the top of the page catches my eye. Putting a momentary damper on my tirade, I pull the paper closer to my face.

Alaska Airlines
Flight 248
Departure SEA
Arrival HON
Lenny Evans, Ireland Jacobson

A week after our wedding, our honeymoon to Hawaii.

All the wind leaves my lungs. The fury that was just coursing through my body immediately drains out through my legs, leaving me unsteady on my feet. I sit down on the edge of the rumpled bed, my heart still thumping in my chest.

What am I doing? I can't just throw all of Lenny's worldly possessions away. His things being gone isn't going to stop me from thinking about him. I can't just zip up my sorrows into a neat little box and have it disappear. It doesn't work that way.

Besides, it's not just Lenny. It's Lenny, my mother, finding out I have a father, The Club. It's all of it. And all that won't fit into this useless suitcase.

I'm struck by an intense need to get away from

everything. To have a chance to start fresh, to figure out where my life is going.

Then it hits me—Hawaii. I stare down at the paper in my hand and wonder if I'm being childish, believing this is destiny.

I look up from the ticket, right into the eyes of Lenny, staring at me from the framed picture on the dresser like he's looking into my soul, telling me, "Go find yourself. I'm still here with you."

I turn the ticket over again in my hand and nod my head.

Before I lose my nerve, I dial the 1-800 number on the bottom of the paper.

I'm redirected twice before I'm connected to an operator, "Mary" she says her name is.

"So let me get this straight. You have a reservation under your name and one under your deceased fiancé's, to Hawaii. Departing on June 26th, and you would like to change the tickets for a departure tomorrow, one in your name and one in a Collette Johnson?"

"Yes, that's correct," I state like it's the most normal request.

"First, I would like to offer my sincerest condolences. We can certainly change the flight that is under your name to another date, as long as you have the correct ID. Just make sure you have your ID with you when boarding. I don't see any problems there. There is typically a fee associated with ticket changes, but due to the circumstances, I'll waive it for you."

"Thank you."

"However, due to TSA regulations, I'm not able to transfer the ticket of Lenny Evans into another person's name. What I can do is refund the card it was bought on, and you can purchase another ticket for the flight you will be taking under Collette Johnson's name."

I don't bother arguing with her that they would be refunding a dead man's credit card, but instead pull my wallet out and ask her to check for the next departing flight with first class availability, for Honolulu, Hawaii.

Ten minutes later I hang up with Mary at Alaska Airlines and speed-dial Collette. She needs to know she has a plane to catch.

Chapter 11

"I'm sorry, ladies, but the flight is all booked. There simply isn't anything I can do at this time. You're going to have to sit in the seats assigned to you." Brenda, as her name tag announces, is looking anything but sorry. I would actually call it more of a bored look, or maybe an "I've heard this argument before, and I'm so over it" kind of look. Either way, it was apparent she wasn't going to be doing us any favors today.

I roll my eyes at Collette and turn away from the counter. The cattle call of the boarding process has already started and the time Collette and I just wasted trying to move our seats together has now put us at the very end of the line.

We inch our way forward, following the crowd of people lugging their roller bags and carry-ons.

I'm resigning myself to sitting on my own for the next five and a half hours when Collette grabs my arm.

"I can't believe we're doing this."

"I know, I just wish we could sit together," I whine.

"Oh, come on. It'll be fine. A movie, some reading, a nap and we'll be there before we know it," Collette says, handing her ticket over to the gate attendant and gliding down the ramp leading to the plane. I step onboard behind her and follow as she finds her seat three rows behind mine. Once situated, she turns and gives a little finger wave before disappearing, leaving me to fend for myself.

I do my best to fight the urge to reach out for her as she leaves me in the aisle feeling deserted and forlorn. The last time I thought about airplanes or flights was when Lenny's plane went down. The rational part of my brain is telling me this is a commercial flight, whereas Lenny was on a private jet, but the irrational part is screaming for me to get off this potential fireball before it's too late.

With shaky hands, I pick up my carry-on and place it in the overhead bin, careful to make sure the wheels are pointing in. I shuffle into the middle seat, the only position left at such short notice, and drop my phone and a magazine into the mesh pocket in front of me, marveling at how they have managed to shove chairs so tightly together that only a child could possibly find themselves comfortable. I can count on my hand the number of times I've flown commercial, and of those times it was always on an international flight, and in first class. It was one of the few perks of being Mother's daughter. Flying commercial, and in coach, I was going to have to get used to.

"Excuse me." A soft voice interrupts my thoughts. I turn my head in the direction of the request.

A young woman, I'd estimate her to be close to my age, is looking down at me from the aisle. I take in the dark hair cascading in ringlets down the middle of her back. Her bronze eyes and tan complexion instantly invoke images of the girls I used to see on the Hawaiian Tropic sunscreen commercials on TV. I can almost smell the coconut, just looking at her. I'm so caught up in her beauty that it takes me a second to remember she has just addressed me.

"Excuse me," she repeats. Her voice is calming, a welcome diversion in the sea of chaos and commotion surrounding her as people push past in a rush to claim their own seats. "My son and I are seated in this row, and they weren't able to move our seats together."

I look behind her and notice a boy of about ten hovering close by, holding a backpack and shifting from foot to foot. He has her same hair but a slightly fairer complexion, and I'm struck by how alike they are.

"I was wondering if you would mind switching seats so we could sit together?" she continues.

Even though I've just gotten settled, I don't hesitate in my response. "Yes, of course! You should sit with your son." I start gathering my belongings, thinking how the service counter wasn't so great at actually providing service. Once I've collected everything, I step back into the aisle. "Do you want the window seat?" I ask, smiling at the boy.

"Yes, please, that'd be great." His polite manner catches me off guard. I've always been under the impression that all ten-year-old boys were supposed to be a combination of crazy and out of control, but this one was obviously well versed in proper manners.

I smile as they scoot past me and take their seats.

"Thank you," the mother says once we are all settled in our chairs with our seat belts fastened.

"No problem. My sister and I were trying to change seats earlier, but they weren't the most obliging."

"We must have talked to the same lady," she says

with a small smirk. "We didn't get much assistance either." She places her carry-on under the seat in front of her.

"You'd think they would have seen the logic in having a mother sit with her son. Honestly, I don't know what they could have been thinking." I stop myself before my ranting gets out of hand.

"I would have to agree, but, well, thank you all the same."

"Of course. You're welcome."

She gives me a warm smile and turns her attention back to her son.

The plane is starting to back away from the gate, and I watch as she naturally wraps her arm over her son's shoulder as they lean into the window.

I lean my head back on the headrest and close my eyes, mentally resolving to check on Collette when we are in the air and leveled off at our flying altitude. With my temporary distraction now engrossed by the plane's movements, I feel the anxiousness returning. Thoughts of Lenny, Carl, and Mother keep drifting in and out of my mind. No matter how hard I try, I can't persuade myself to relax. I open my eyes, searching for something to grab my attention, to help me focus on something other than the impending danger I keep fabricating in my head.

I glance to my right and see the woman leaning over her son, now busy getting him situated with a movie on an iPad she's pulled from his backpack.

I don't disturb them and instead turn in my seat to search for Collette. I spot her a few rows down, munching on snacks with headphones on. It strikes me as odd that she can be so relaxed, and it makes me burn with jealousy. She doesn't seem to mind the tight accommodations of her surroundings. She's obviously not comparing her current experience to our past luxury like I am. But then I remember that this is a luxury for her, to simply be traveling without the girls. It probably doesn't matter what or where she's sitting as long as there isn't someone on her lap, asking for a snack, iPad, game, or toy. I decide to not impinge on her quiet time for now and instead turn back and pull out the magazine I brought with me. *425 Magazine of the Eastside* is usually good for articles about up and coming restaurants, bars or events. I flip through, searching for ideas on new places to check out, momentarily forgetting I don't have anyone to check them out with anymore. My gut tightens when the realization hits me, and I turn the page, coming to rest on the advertisement for The Club.

Seeing The Club Logo in print takes me back to yesterday, making my stomach turn even more. I shut the magazine and lay it on my lap, tapping my fingers on it rhythmically, trying to drown out my own thoughts, until Miss Hawaiian Tropic turns to look at me, her eyebrows raised.

I realize my error and lay my hands flat on the magazine. "Sorry," I offer.

She gives me a reassuring smile. "It's okay."

"It's just I get a little nervous flying," I blurt out.

"That's perfectly understandable."

I nod my head and rack my brain for something to say that will keep our conversation alive, the distraction I'm desperate for. "So do you live in Seattle or Hawaii?"

"We live on the island, but my parents moved to

Seattle. They have an Asian fusion restaurant in the city, AOE Fusion."

"I've heard of that one," I say and flip open the magazine lying in my lap to reveal the advertisement of the exact restaurant she was talking about.

"Yup, that's the one." She chuckles and gingerly takes the magazine from my hands. "We come out so Kai can visit my parents. They used to live on the island, but now that they've moved and are busy with the restaurant, we don't get to see them that often," she says, tracing her fingers over the page.

"You must miss them."

"I do, but Kai misses them more." She nods at her son, who is still engrossed in his movie.

"Have you thought about moving to Seattle? To be closer to them?" I ask.

"I've thought about it, but Kai's father loves the Island too much to leave it. And I love Kai's father too much to make him leave." She gives me a wistful smile. "I'm his second marriage, and Kai and I are his life, but he's older than I am, and the island time agrees with his current lifestyle. He loves the weather and the freedom to be outdoors in the sunshine."

"Hawaii is certainly the place for that," I say, while mentally conjuring up the image of this youthful woman with an older retiree.

"I'm Kayla, by the way," she says as she passes the magazine back to me.

"Ireland," I respond, taking back the glossy pages.

"So, Ireland, how about you? Do you live on the Eastside?" she points to the magazine.

"I do."

"Headed on vacation, then?" She bends down and

reaches into her carry-on and pulls out a granola bar, passing it to Kai.

"Actually, I would say I'm more on a mission."

"Oh? How very James Bond of you." She turns back to me with a smile.

I laugh. "I did make that sound a bit more mysterious than I meant to, didn't I?" I shift in my seat to relieve some pressure on my backside. "What I was trying to say is, my sister and I just found out we have a long-lost father we never knew about...geez, that doesn't sound any better either."

She chuckles and raises her eyebrows. I notice how perfectly they shape her face. "I'll give you zero for two, but that is pretty intense."

"Yeah, that's a good way to put it."

"So I assume you're on your way to go find him?"

The stewardess is starting to approach with the drink cart. I reach down and push my bag further under the chair in front of me. "That's the plan."

"That's incredibly courageous of you. Have you talked to him already?"

I shift back into my seat, which is starting to feel more and more like steel under my bum by the minute. "We haven't exactly spoken yet," I admit.

Kayla turns fully in her seat to look at me with her mouth agape. "So you're going to just show up at his doorstep?" She shakes her head. "Wow, I don't know if I could do that. I'd be too afraid it would turn out in disaster."

I pinch my lips together. "Mmm, I guess we didn't get that far in our planning, it was more of a spur-of-the-moment decision."

Kayla looks at me for a moment without saying

anything, and I get the sensation she is trying to decide how she would feel if I showed up on her doorstep unannounced. "Well," she finally says. "I hope you find what you're looking for."

"Thanks, me too." The drink cart stops in our row, giving me the opportunity to think about Kayla's words. *I hope you find what you're looking for.* Did I even know what I was looking for? I watch as the stewardess doles out drinks to Kayla and Kai. When it's my turn, I order water and take the packet of pretzels offered to me, letting them sit on the tray table untouched. I watch the water start to wobble in my cup as the overhead ding, along with the voice announcing turbulence, reminds the cabin to fasten our seatbelts in preparation for a bumpy ride.

We hit a series of air pockets, and I feel the now-familiar sensation of bile starting to rise in my throat.

Kayla has turned away from me, re-addressing her attention to Kai and his seatbelt.

I take a sip of water and try to swallow down my rising panic. I can't decide if it's the turbulence, thoughts of Lenny, or thoughts of finding my father that have me suddenly sweating, but I'm now acutely aware of my desperate need for one of the white paper bags tucked into the seat in front of me.

With clammy hands I reach out and start rifling through the pamphlets and magazines in front of me. When I don't find what I'm after, I turn my attention to the next chair and start doing the same.

I can tell my sudden invasion of Kayla's personal space has caused her alarm, because when she turns to me, a look of surprise and concern are etched across her face.

By the grace of God, I find the little white bag but not before a small stream of vomit leaves my mouth, and in what seems like slow motion, sails through the air and lands on Kayla's pant leg. Horrified, but not able to do anything to offer her assistance, I rip open the bag and place it to my mouth in order to empty the rest of my tragedy into it.

"Oh my." I see Kayla recoil out of the corner of my eye as she takes in the scene before her. Recovering quickly, she reaches her hand up and pushes the button for assistance and then reaches down into her carry-on, pulling out a stack of tissue, taking half for herself and handing me the rest.

Holding the bag as far away from my seatmates as possible, I hover my arm in the aisle and twist the top of it. "I'm so sorry," I manage.

"Don't worry, really. Are you okay?" Kayla asks, wiping at her leg and looking at a loss for what to do next.

I see the steward coming our direction down the aisle, and I unbuckle my seatbelt. "I will be. I think I'll just go and clean up a bit. I'll bring you some napkins," I say into my hand as I cover my mouth with my free fist.

"That's probably a good idea." Kayla nods in agreement.

"I'll be back."

"Take your time," she calls after me as I ignore the seatbelt sign and hurry down the aisle to the back of the plane, avoiding the stewardess and passing a sleeping Collette on the way.

Once inside the matchbook of a bathroom, I rinse my mouth out and splash water on my face.

Clutching the sides of the sink with shaky hands, I face my ghostly reflection in the mirror. "You've got to get a grip," I chastise myself.

This is so beyond embarrassing. How could I have gotten to this point? I'm literally vomiting on perfect strangers. How am I going to go back out there and face Kayla?

Maybe I should tell her about Lenny, explain why I got sick in the first place. But on second thought, I'm sure she doesn't want to be unloaded on by a perfect stranger.

No, I decide, I'm just going to go back out there and apologize. It's really all I can do at this point.

I finish cleaning up and vacate the restroom, hoping the stench from my bag, now tossed in the trash, doesn't start to leak out.

Once I'm back in my seat and buckled, Kayla turns to me with a pack of gum. "This might help," she offers the package to me.

I take a piece and start to chew, noticing she has miraculously cleaned not only herself but the surrounding area. The chair and her pant leg are void of any signs of misgivings, and the air smells like disinfectant and lemon. "Thanks." I take a deep breath and sit back against the chair.

"I'm really sorry about all of that." I motion to her lap.

"It's okay, really. Are you feeling better now?"

"A little, maybe if I just rest a little…"

"That's probably a good idea." Kayla offers a small smile as I close my eyes and rest my head back, but even with my eyes closed, I can feel Kayla still taking me in.

I open one eye to check, and sure enough, she is full on staring at me. Sizing me up, taking stock of who and what is sitting next to her.

"Do you get motion sickness often?" she asks when she realizes I know she's staring at me.

"No, it's more of a recent thing I've been experiencing."

"Oh, I see."

I'm not entirely sure what it is she *sees*, so I don't respond.

"So you said you're here with your sister. Do you have any other family, back in Seattle?" she asks, switching topics.

"Just my Mother and my sister's family. She's married, and they have two little girls."

"So no children of your own?"

Her question brings me back to Lenny.

"No, I didn't get the chance to," I say absentmindedly.

"How so?" she asks, and I realize, too late, my mistake.

"I recently lost my fiancé. He died a month ago," I whisper, breaking my promise to myself to not go into this with her.

Kayla, obviously not expecting this answer, knits those perfect eyebrows of hers into a frown. "I'm so sorry."

"I know, everyone is."

"Is there anything I can do to help?"

I smile at the kindness of this stranger, knowing full well there is nothing she can do for me, but I appreciate her sentiment nonetheless.

"You know, I think I just need to try to rest for

right now," I say, bringing us back to my earlier suggestion.

"Yes, of course. You rest, and let me know if you need anything, okay?"

"Thanks, I will," I say as I put some earplugs in my ears. I search for the right music to fit my mood. There doesn't seem to be a wide variety of tortured/ horrified music on my phone, so I finally settle on Ed Sheeran. Kayla has returned to her own in-flight entertainment, graciously letting me once again become invisible.

For the rest of the flight, I concentrate on clearing my mind and keeping out of Kayla's way. I can feel her look at me from time to time, but I keep my earplugs firmly in place. Eventually, I drift into a restless sleep, only waking to Collette nudging my shoulder.

"Get up, sleepyhead. We're here!"

Chapter 12

It's still dark out when my phone buzzes. Blurry-eyed, I reach over to the nightstand and search the top with one hand. Grabbing the nuisance, I bring it to my ear.

"Hello?" I croak, not bothering to look at the caller ID.

"Ireland?" Mother's voice screeches through the other end of the line. "Just what the hell do you think you're doing?"

I immediately regret not checking the caller ID. "Good morning to you too, Mother."

"No, Ireland. There is nothing good about this morning. Finding out from Human Resources that my accountant, my own daughter, is taking a few *unplanned* sick days is not how I wanted to start my day. Did you think I would be pleased with this little stunt you're pulling?"

"You can't blame me for not feeling well. I'll be back in when I'm better. It should only be a few days." I pry open one eye and glance around the hotel room. The shades are closed, and I can't tell what time it is.

"Cut the crap. I know you're not at the condo. I also happen to know that wherever you are, Collette is with you. You don't think I'm so stupid as to think you're not out doing the exact thing I told you not to do."

"No, Mother, I don't think you're stupid." Unfortunately, that had never been her downfall.

"If you want me to believe you, that you are indeed sick, and still in Bellevue, you will be walking through the front doors of The Club in one hour."

I think about the waves gently lapping against the sand just outside our suite. "I'm sorry. That won't be possible."

"And why, exactly, is that?"

I sigh and confess, "Because it's going to take changing plane tickets and about six hours of flight before I can walk through the doors of The Club."

I wait but hear only silence from her end of the line.

When she does finally talk, it's with a calmness that makes my skin crawl. "You know, I believed in you. I believed that you would take my feelings into consideration when making decisions, but I see clearly now where your loyalties lie."

"You know as well as I do that this isn't about loyalties. This is about finding out who we are. There are answers available to us now. Can't you understand that?"

"No, Ireland, I don't understand that, but I'll tell you what I do understand. I understand all the hard work I've spent my whole life doing, to provide for you and your sister. If you weren't such spoiled little brats, you would see it too. I've put blood, sweat, and tears into this Club. Can't you see? It was all for you and Collette. To put food on the table and clothes on your backs. I did it all on my own. I didn't have anyone to hold my hand, to show me the way. And this is the thanks I get?"

Mother's high-pitched tirade has caused a rhythmic pounding to start in my head. I'm half listening to her as I rest my phone on the pillow next to me.

"Ireland! Are you listening to me?" Her screeching makes me flinch, and I pick up the phone again and place it next to my ear.

"Yes, Mother, I'm here."

"Good. Now, you and Collette show me the respect I deserve, pack your things immediately, and get back here! Your little vacation is officially over."

"I'll see what I can do about the tickets," I mumble into the phone, knowing full well I won't be calling the airlines to change tickets again.

"No, you will not *see what you can do about them*, you will get them changed. Today! I expect both of you to walk through my office door tomorrow at noon. Do you understand me?"

"Yes, Mother. Goodbye, Mother." I wait for her reply, but there's just a click on the other end of the line as she hangs up on me.

"Argh!" I toss the phone to the other side of the bed, careful not to throw it off the edge, for fear of cracking the screen. I push the covers off and amble into the bathroom.

On the way back, I peek into Collette's room and find her still sleeping, blissfully unaware of Mother's diatribe. I turn back to the shared living room and walk over to my suitcase, which I had haphazardly rolled into the room last night. I grab the handle and make a beeline for my bedroom. Picking through the contents, I select a pair of pink speed shorts and an old tank top. I pull them on and throw my hair into a ponytail.

Heading back through the living room, I grab a

piece of scrap paper and scribble a quick note to Collette—*Going to the beach to take a walk, be back soon*—and leave it on the counter.

I close the door quietly, careful to make sure it locks behind me, and walk barefoot the few feet to the water's edge.

The sun is just starting to make its way over the horizon, the air still cool from the night before. It's silent except for the sound of the water lapping against the sand.

I close my eyes and breathe in the sea air. When I open them, I glance right and left trying to decide which way to head. I turn right, in the direction of rows of bungalows lining the shore, and start a leisurely walk. The sand is cool and refreshing under my feet, yet to be warmed from the sun.

Coming out here, to the Kahala Resort and Spa on Oahu, seemed like the perfect solution to our problem when I was back in my room in Bellevue, but now I'm not so sure.

How could I have thought that coming on my honeymoon, without my fiancé, was going to be a good idea? Sure, the view is breathtaking, the food undeniably decadent, and the accommodations plush and luxurious, but not a single bone in my body is willing to let any of that sink in. Ever since the moment I stepped off the plane I've been tense and on alert, like what I'm doing is somehow scandalous.

I switch from my leisurely canter into a slow jog, letting my legs get used to propelling my body forward. I concentrate on my breathing as I increase my speed. But the harder I try to ignore them, the quicker the thoughts of Lenny, my father, and Mother and the conversation we just had invade my head.

I can't help but wonder how old I was when I really let Mother take over my life. Was it when Collette and I were children, so young and impressionable? Or was it later, when I had caved and started working for her? I look back at all the opportunities she had to control me, and I'm appalled at myself for letting her become the sole determinant of my every move.

Over the years we've created such a web of our lives, it's become impossible for me to untangle myself from it. I started out working for Mother because I lost the bet with Collette, but over the years The Club has become a piece of me too. Working from the ground up, I've become a fixture there, just like Mother, pouring my own heart and soul into it.

If I go back now, change the tickets and get back in time, maybe Mother won't be so mad. I could stay at The Club and work into the management position she's been promising all along. But that would mean Collette and I would never know our father. Never have the chance to find out what he's like. "*What are you hoping to find?*" That was what Kayla had asked me on the plane. Did I really think that finding my father was going to save me? What could a complete stranger do for me right now? He couldn't take the pain away, but maybe he could be a distraction. And don't we owe it to him to tell him about Collette and me? It would be like keeping this awful secret from someone. To never tell him, now that I know, would be just as bad as Mother never telling him.

I wish I knew what to do.

Lenny would have known what to do. How to deal

with all of this. I stretch my legs further and try to conjure up Lenny's voice in my head. What would he tell me? He would say, *"Ireland, when are you going to stand up to her? You can't let your Mother run your life forever. You can't let her affect you like this."* He would tell me that I don't know my own strength and that it was about time I found it. Lenny was always making little speeches at me, about going out and living a life I deserved.

As his words rattle around in my head, I pump my arms in rhythm with my legs. I can feel my quadriceps burn as I kick my feet out in front of me, landing on the heel, rounding over my foot and pushing off my toes as I flex my hamstrings, digging up the sand behind me. My lungs gasp for each breath as I fly down the beach. My heart aches as it pounds to keep up with my legs. It is an ache that is drastically different from the heartache I've been suffering lately. I welcome every beat, daring my heart to pound harder, to hurt more. I'm sprinting until I can't take it any longer. Finally, not able to keep up with my own pace I bend over and grasp my knees, sucking in the air as if there isn't enough of it on the beach.

Sweat drips down my nose and lands on the sand under my feet. This feeling—of not being able to catch my breath—is a feeling I've been yearning for. A physical pain, not a heartache or a betrayal, but a manageable, self-inflicted pain. One that possesses my whole body, providing a distraction. And one that ultimately will help me become stronger.

I know I need to hold on to this pain, to remember it and come back to it. I have a feeling this isn't the only time I'm going to need it.

****

I pretend to be asleep when Collette checks on me lying on the chaise lounge.

"Ireland?" she nudges my shoulder and waits. When I don't respond, I hear her gather her towel and head back inside our beachfront lanai to take a shower.

Only when I hear the shower running through the open doors do I open my eyes again. Safely hidden behind mirrored sunglasses, I continue watching a family playing on the beach in front of me.

The father has scooped up sand in a bright blue plastic pail and is now instructing his son on how to use the plastic shovel he's holding to pack the sand down, making it stable for when they turn it over to create their sandcastle masterpiece. The boy's mother comes over and kisses his toddler forehead, opening her hand before him to show the white shells she has collected for decorating their masterpiece. She's wearing a bikini, and it is obvious to me that she is carrying the little boy's sibling in her belly. The dad stands up, dusting the sand off his knees, and leans down to kiss his wife. They are a picture of happiness, contentedness. It makes my stomach hurt, watching them, and yet I can't tear my eyes away from them. I continue to spy on them, careful to look like I'm dozing off rather than taking in every detail, categorizing it under memories I'll never experience.

After my run, I had walked back to the hotel with a new determination that I would take control of my life, but as the endorphins of the run wore off, my resolve followed. I realized that I can't just simply decide to overcome a lifetime of emotional neglect and accompanying parental control. I couldn't just wash away my grief in the shower as I scrubbed at the sand and sweat. Too many parts are still missing from my puzzle. I don't know how to create a new life picture when it contains so many holes.

As I watch the families, enjoying themselves, making memories they will take back and place in an album for future reference, I'm reminded of another hole. Lenny and I will never have that time of being so happy together, so relaxed together. I can just picture the family in front of me poring over their photos next year, marveling how their family used to be only three, and now it's four. Looking at their boy and remarking on how much he's grown over the year.

I burn inside, not from the heat of the sun or from the humidity in the air, but from the knowledge that Lenny and I will never have the opportunity to take these pictures.

"Are you feeling okay?" Collette asks, sticking her head out the sliding glass door.

I was so lost in thought, I didn't hear the shower shutting off or her getting dressed in the room.

"Yeah, I just have a headache." I remove my sunglasses and move to the edge of the lounge chair.

The family I was watching is now starting to pack up their beach supplies. I hear the mom say something about bathing the boy before nap time as they walk past me. The boy runs ahead of them, in that way toddlers do, excited to see what is around the next corner, without any fear of what lies ahead. The father dashes after the boy as the mom waddles behind them carrying towels and buckets.

They are out of sight when Collette sits beside me on the lounge chair.

"I miss the girls," she says, holding her hand up to shade her eyes, watching the family I had just been spying on. "They would have loved it here."

"They would have," I agree. "Why don't we give them a call? I'm sure they would love to hear from you."

"Good idea. Come on." Collette heads into the suite, and I follow behind. She grabs her phone off the counter and pushes the FaceTime button, holding it up so both she and I are in the screen, the ocean behind us through the glass doors.

It takes a few seconds for the connection to come through, and when it does, we are bombarded from the other end with squeals of "Mommy!" and pudgy little legs and arms tangled all over the screen. One chocolate-covered hand reaches toward the camera, and I wince in reaction, right before Greg snatches it out of Molly's reach.

"Hey there." Collette chuckles into the screen. "How are my loves doing?"

"We had chocolate pancakes for breakfast, Mommy!" Maggie announces.

"Auntie Ireland!" Molly graces me with acknowledgment.

"Hi, girls. Hi, Greg," I offer.

"Hi, Ireland. Hey, Honey." Greg emerges from the pile of toddlers.

I sit back and let Collette chat with the girls for a bit, but eventually they lose interest and drift off to do art or play with their dolls, leaving Collette to chat quietly with Greg.

I'm only half listening to their conversation, I've settled back into the couch, content to wait for Collette.

"So have you made any contact yet?" I hear Greg ask.

"We just got here last night." Collette turns from me slightly. "Ireland took a run this morning. We'll get ready to head out soon."

"Right, might as well get some R and R while you're over there."

"It's not like we're at the spa all day or something. Geesh, you make it sound like we're vacationing and goofing around. I told you we just got here last night."

"Relax, Coco. I didn't mean anything by it."

"Look I know you want me to hurry back. I'll be home as soon as I can. You're just going to have to hold it together until I get back."

"Collette, I know you've been too busy to notice, but I've been holding things together. Have been for some time now."

I don't look at the screen, but the tension in Greg's voice is evident.

"Well, then you'll be able to handle it for a little longer." Collette sighs. "Look, I'll call you later, okay?"

"Sure, fine. Later."

Collette signs off and leans back on the chair that is covered in palm tree fabric that somehow manages to match and clash simultaneously with all the other tropical prints in the room.

I rub my lips together, debating if I should voice what's on my mind. I bite my lower lip and say, "You should give him more of a break."

"What do you mean by that?" she snaps back.

I wince at her immediate response. "He's doing a good job. He's changing roles, you know. Just give him

144

a little slack."

"He's not the only one changing roles here, you know. Where's my slack? I'm expected to work full time and still carry the housewife role. And why? Because I'm a woman? Forget that." Collette sniffs to herself. "If Greg and I are going to make this work, he needs to step it up. I didn't go to school all those years to be a stay-at-home. You're not married, and you didn't go to school for a master's degree. You wouldn't understand."

"Right, you're right, Collette. I didn't get the chance to get married and have that kind of relationship, but that is because my fiancé died. And if I did have a chance to have him here, you're damn well certain I would treat him with love and respect. And you're also right, I didn't get a chance to get a master's or to further my education, but that was because I literally chose the short straw. I took the brunt of our fate so you could go out and live yours. So you're right, I don't have the experiences that you got to have, but you know what, it's not that I didn't want them. You better believe I would have treated them better than what you are." I'm leaning forward in my chair, all worked up.

"Well, if that's really what you believe, then I guess there's not much more to say. Other than that you can think whatever you want to, but until you're in the middle of it, you really just don't know. You can't live with Lenny on a pedestal forever. If you had been with him for as long as Greg and I have been together, I'm sure you would have different feelings. So don't go around judging others just because you have a vision of what your perfect life would have been."

"I'm not judging you. I'm only suggesting you give him a little more credit."

"Fine." Collette huffs, and stays silent for a second before changing the subject. "But in the meantime, let's go do what we came here for in the first place. Let's go find our dad."

Chapter 13

"There are so many fences here," I say absentmindedly, as I stare out the window at the homes along North Kalaheo Drive.

"Earth to Ireland, a little help here?" Collette cuts into my momentary serenity while taking in the sights, frantically waving at the GPS sitting on my lap. "Why don't you save the sightseeing for later and start giving me directions."

"Geesh, I was just admiring the lawns," I shoot back. It's not like she's piloting an F15 and I'm her copilot or anything.

Collette scans the surroundings of Kailua while still keeping an eye on the road in front of her.

"Okay, you're right, there are a lot of fences. Now, can you do your job and be my copilot?"

I glance at her out of the corner of my eye. It really is eerie how she does that, read my thoughts and all. I decide to let it go and look down at the slim phone in my hand. "Turn right, here."

"Here, like now?"

"Now!" We almost miss the turn as Collette swings the topless Jeep around the corner, the tires screeching.

"Nice one, Ireland. That's exactly why I wanted you to pay attention." Collette chastises me like she would her girls.

"Sorry," I say and duck my head, still stinging

from our earlier argument.

I check the address on the phone again and start counting down the house numbers on the left side of the street. "It should be just up ahead." I point two houses down.

Collette slowly rolls the Jeep to a stop in front of a charming, custom-crafted gray house with white shutters flanking the windows. A wraparound porch is scattered with all kinds of different sports equipment, most of it the water sports variety. Surfboards, boogie boards, and a low-seated bicycle with a brown basket hold places of honor next to the front door.

Collette cuts the engine on the Jeep, but the two of us have become glued to our seats, and neither of us makes a single move to get out of the Jeep. I look at her and wonder if her heartbeat is as irregular as mine.

She swallows, and I catch sight of the blue vein on the side of her neck, and I know my answer.

"It's cute," she says.

"It is."

"We should probably go knock on the door," she says, still making no effort to unbuckle her seatbelt.

Silence descends on us as we sit motionless in the vehicle.

I can't take it any longer, so I say, "Are we sure we want to do this? Once we go in, there's no going back."

"I think we have to. We've come this far. It would be silly to turn back now."

"I agree, but then why is it so hard to walk up there?" I point to the stairs leading to the front door.

She twists in her seat so that we face each other. I try to see her as a stranger would. As someone who would have to decide if she was acceptable to bring into their lives. Her open smile and her athletic figure, coupled with her proper etiquette and her charisma, instantly stir a feeling of pride deep within, and I know the answer. A slow smile spreads across my lips. It's so obvious to me that anyone would be an idiot to turn Collette away.

"What are you smiling at?" She huffs and reaches down for her mirrored sunglasses, blocking my eye contact with her and reflecting a mirror image of what I had just been looking at, a perfect replica of Collette, if only a little worse for the wear. I pull my shoulders back to try to emulate Collette's posture. I can't do anything about the dark circles under my eyes, but the sunglasses buried deep in my own purse will do well to hide them.

"I was just thinking anyone who turned you away would be classified as an idiot, in my opinion."

She reaches out and takes my hand in hers. "No matter what happens in there"—she cocks her head in the direction of the house—"we will always have each other. You're my family, Ireland. I couldn't have gone through this life without you by my side," she says, her voice heavy with emotion.

"I know, you're my everything too. Now, more than ever. With Lenny gone, well, you're all I have." I concentrate on a spot embedded into the foot-mat, determined to keep my composure.

Collette gives my hand one last squeeze before releasing it. She reaches down, unbuckles her seatbelt, and grabs the door handle. "Let's do this."

I copy her motions and place my hand on the opposite door handle. "Let's do this." We swing our doors open simultaneously and walk up the wooden walkway, shoulder to shoulder.

We pause a beat when we reach the front door. I can hear Collette's breathing beside me. Her breath has taken on the cadence of being in a cycling class. I take a deep breath in and out, hoping she will mimic me.

She nudges me with her elbow and gestures to the doorbell on my side of the door.

I feel like I'm moving through mud as I reach my hand out and press the tiny button. We hear a soft chiming throughout the entire house like someone just passed their hand across a wind chime.

The sides of my lips turn up at the sound.

We wait.

Collette turns to me. "We should have called first. He's not even home."

"No, remember, we agreed to do this in person? No phone calls with 'Hi, I'm your long-lost daughter' and click." I stick my thumb and pinkie finger out. As I make the motion with my hand slamming down a pretend phone, I catch sight of an old Ford truck over Collette's shoulder, parked in the garage. "Look, there's a car here. Maybe he's out back."

Collette turns in the direction of the garage and turns back around, her eyebrows raised. "So there is."

Without discussing it, we walk down the steps and follow a gravel path that leads into the back yard.

The yard is lush with a profusion of tropical plants running along the borders—bird of paradise, mini palm trees, a few avocado and mango trees, their branches bending from the weight of the abundant fruits, create a secret tropical garden. In the middle, there's a pergola, with what looks like a bed hanging from thick steel chains, piled high with pillows. Orchids drip down from the wooden beams. I'm stunned by the beauty of it all.

"Wow, this is incredible," I breathe.

"Yeah, and empty."

I had momentarily forgotten our goal of coming back here, I was so caught up in my surroundings. Reluctantly, I tear my eyes away from the outdoor, rock-wall shower attached to the side of the house and start to look around.

Collette was right. It was empty.

"Look over there," she says, pointing to a path separating the hedges, leading farther behind the house.

"Let's go." Boosted by our real earthen surrounding, I start walking toward the path, the discarded palm branches cracking under my sandals.

Collette hurries to catch up with me as we make our way another hundred yards down the path, spitting us out onto a perfect white sand beach. The sun assaults my eyes as we pass from the shade of the trees into the direct light. Instinctively I bring my hand up to cover my brow, providing some shade. As my eyes adjust, I take in the glittering sand and the clear Pacific Ocean. Even though it's already midday, there are only a scattering of people on the beach, most of them clad in wetsuits with a surfboard under their arm. A few beachcombers and even fewer sun worshipers litter the shore.

"Now what?" I turn to Collette as she bursts through the tree-lined walkway behind me. She immediately imitates me and brings her hand above her eyes, shielding them from the sun's rays.

Once she adjusts, she shifts left and right, looking up and down the beach. "It's like a needle in a haystack. We don't even know what the needle looks like!" She huffs a sigh of disappointment and dramatically flops down on the sand.

I'm not sure what she expects me to do, so I sit down next to her, gazing out into the surf.

"Maybe we should just go back," Collette says, the wind taking her words and whipping them away quickly. I lean in to hear her better.

"What if he's some drinking, smoking, jerky guy that we wouldn't want to be around anyway? Then we'd just be wasting our time, really." She keeps staring out at the ocean, watching the surfers bobbing on the waves in front of us.

I cock an eyebrow at her. "You really think he lives out here with surfboards, a bicycle, and snorkel gear and that he's a heavy drinker and smoker?" I let out a laugh. I could be wrong, but the probability of that was sure to be on the low side.

"I'm just saying, what if he's not someone we want to invite into our lives?" She turns and looks at me.

I heave a heavy sigh, still staring out at the water. "You know, I wake up in the middle of the night with nightmares. From that night when they told me Lenny was gone. I wake up shaking." I glance at her out of the side of my eye.

"You've never told me that."

"I know," I say and look back out at the water. "I didn't want to worry you. There's really nothing you could do about it anyway, but I've had this feeling like things need to change in my life. I was waiting for Lenny to whisk me away on some white horse and ride off into the sunset. Maybe I should be the one to change my future, instead of waiting for someone else to do it for me. Maybe this is my chance to do just that. Change my own destiny. I don't know why yet, but I just have this feeling like we need to find Carl. We need to know who our father is."

Collette leans into the side of my shoulder, her way of showing affection. "Okay, I'm still in." She gets up off the sand with renewed determination in her eyes, dusts off the back of her shorts, and reaches down to pull me up. "I guess it's time we figure out our next move, then. What do you think about leaving a note on the door? You know, 'Long-lost daughters, just stopped by to say 'Hi.' Here's our phone number, call us when you get back in?"

"Um, not so much. What else do you have?"

I'm momentarily blinded as the sun reflects off a surfboard one of the surfers is dragging up the beach, having just finished a run.

Once I regain my eyesight, I find myself staring at a man wearing a wetsuit that hugs his body in all the right places. I can't tear my eyes off him as he reaches behind him and pulls on the string that's attached to the wetsuit zipper.

Collette notices my staring and turns to see what I'm so fixated on.

"Oh," is all that escapes her lips as she becomes as transfixed as I am.

We watch as the man peels the wetsuit the rest of the way down, revealing perfectly cut deltoids and biceps. The show continues as he brings the wetsuit to his waist, showing off his muscular chest and chiseled stomach.

He makes his way to the water's edge and picks up the board, slings it under his arm, and continues up the beach, shaking his head as he goes. Little droplets of water fly off his short beard like water flies off a wet dog after a bath.

As the surfer gets closer, I'm shocked to discover that what I thought was blond hair slicked back in a ponytail is actually silver hair slicked back in a ponytail. Our eye candy has at least a generation on us.

Colette and I stand transfixed as he continues up the beach and heads for the path we just came from.

It can't be. That would be too easy, yet there is something about him. Something that makes me feel like I already know him.

Collette, sensing the same familiarity as me, somehow regains her composure first and calls out, "Carl? Carl Martin?" Taking a step in the direction he's heading.

Surfer guy stops to turn and look at us. The wind leaves my lungs as I behold a third copy of my own eyes. The first two copies belong to the set of twins staring back at him.

"That's me. How can I help you?" His good manners prevail over the surprise of being called on by two strangers in the middle of the beach.

I still can't seem to make my mouth work as I stand, transfixed by him. He is a male version of Collette and me, only a few decades older.

"Sorry? Do I know you?" His eyes light up as he takes in Collette and me.

"No, not yet, at least," I eke out, realizing how horrible that must sound at the exact same moment the words leave my mouth.

"Am I going to get to know you? Boy, this is my lucky day," is his rude comment.

I can't blame him. He has no idea who we are, but

my blood turns cold at the sexual innuendo of his comment.

Collette holds her hands up in protest, having the same visceral reaction I'm experiencing. "Hold on there, buddy. Nobody's getting lucky today. We're just wondering if you might have a few minutes, for a chat?"

Carl's eyes narrow. "Is this a religious thing?" He turns and picks up his surfboard as he continues to talk. "Because I told them last time that while I appreciate your beliefs, they aren't what I'm interested in right now." He walks along the beach, heading down the path leading back to his house.

Collette and I watch as his footprints in the sand grow in the distance between us, neither one of us moving to follow him.

As he walks away, I can see the muscles in his back tighten as he adjusts his grip on the surfboard. His is the back of someone who spends his time outdoors.

I feel Collette's elbow in my ribs. "Aww!"

"We can't let him get away," she whispers.

I look to where Carl's footprints have faded from the sand onto the dirt path and take off at a slow jog, quickly catching up to him. I can hear the leaves and twigs crunching under Collette's sandals as she hurries after me.

"Um, excuse me, Carl?" I try.

He looks over his shoulder at us. "This is private property." There is a warning in his tone.

"I realize that, it's just...I was hoping we could have just a minute of your time. We're not affiliated with a religious group I promise."

I gesture to Collette, who is nodding her head in

agreement with me. I look back at Carl.

"So what's this about, then? Are you students at the college? I don't teach there anymore. If you have a problem with the program, you need to see the Dean of the department. I can't help you."

Again I glance at Collette, waiting for her to help me out.

"No, we don't attend the university. This is more of a private matter. One we could discuss in a more relaxed setting maybe?" she says.

"What do you mean by private?" He still wasn't budging.

I try a different method. "I think we got off on the wrong foot. What my sister, Collette, is trying to tell you is we have some information regarding family. We were wondering if we could have a moment of your time to give you some information that we recently came across in that regard." I give my best used-car-salesman voice and mentally cross my fingers that this is the right angle to approach Carl.

He eyes me suspiciously, but I can tell I've piqued his interest. "Ten minutes," is his gracious response. "C'mon, this way." He leads us the rest of the way through the brush, depositing his surfboard on the side of the house, leaning it against the white trim. Collette and I follow him into the garden and take a seat on two wire chairs, separated by a bamboo table.

I place my hands in my lap as Carl walks over to the outdoor shower, turns the knob, and steps into the steady shower stream. He washes the sand off his body. I watch as the muddy stream of water follows the lines of his muscles before being deposited into the grate below.

I avert my eyes as he peels the rest of his wetsuit down the length of his body, revealing swimming briefs underneath. He snaps a towel off the nearby rack and quickly wraps it around his torso.

I look up as his feet come into my viewpoint, the spot on the grass I was concentrating on now blocked by his thick calves. He doesn't approach Collette and me, but rather takes a seat on the hanging bed under the pergola, a few yards away but still facing us.

"So what's this information you have about my family?" he asks, cutting to the chase.

I turn to Collette who just stares back at me. I rack my brain on how to begin. "Um, hi, I'm Ireland, and this is my sister Collette."

Carl tilts his head in acknowledgment. "Nice to meet you both," are the words that come out of his mouth, but his voice sounds more like *Get to the point*.

I take this as my cue to dive straight in.

"Do you, by any chance, remember a student you had back at Berkley, one by the name of Cynthia Jacobson?"

Carl looks down to the left, studying the grass seeming to try and remember.

"She was in your Economics for Business Decision Making class, the year of 1989." I try again, hoping to jog his memory.

His eyes narrow as he looks back up to Collette and me. His next word is slow and drawn out.

"Yeesss?"

"Would you mind telling me what you remember about her?" I ask.

He averts his eyes to the same spot on the grass, speaking slowly. "She was a bright young girl with a certain spark about her. I knew she was going to go far. Why? Why do you want to know about her, and what has this got to do with my family?"

"Did you have a relationship with her?" Collette asks, not so casually jumping into the conversation. I shoot her a look. I would have eased into it a little slower. But now that it's out there, I look at Carl for the answer.

"You said you weren't from the university. Look, I haven't worked there in ages. I don't know what you're trying to dig up, but there isn't really anything you can do to me at this point." He presses his hand down on the bed, pushing himself off the edge.

"No! No, we're not from the university." I try to reassure him. "We know her."

He pauses mid-stand and looks at me. I hold my hands up, signaling that we are here in peace. Sighing, he sits back down on the swing.

"Okay, so how do *you* know her?" he counters.

I look to Collette again, who just shrugs her shoulders at me and tilts her head to Carl in a silent "You tell him."

"She's our mother."

There's silence as Carl looks between Collette and me, finally saying, "I should have known. I thought you looked familiar. I see it now."

I snicker to myself. He doesn't realize just how familiar we look to him. Like looking in a mirror, more like it.

Carl either chooses to ignore my outburst, or he didn't hear it because he continues talking as he takes us in. "You're like a replica of her all those years ago. Just looking at you both brings back fond memories of her."

"So you have *fond* memories of her?" Collette asks.

He pauses just a beat before confessing, "Yes, I suppose the memories I have of her are fond ones. I suppose your mother told you about our time together. Is that why you're here?"

"Yes," Collette says.

"And no," I follow.

"I was married at the time your mother and I met," he says slowly. "She, on the other hand, was not in a relationship," he clarifies.

"We know," Collette confirms.

We were both keeping our answers short and concise. It seemed the less we spoke, the more Carl did.

"My marriage had hit a rough patch. Judy and I had been married for four years. We were so young when we got married. I was working on my Ph.D., and the stress was getting the best of both of us. We decided to take a break. That's when I had your mother in my class."

I nod encouragingly, but Carl hesitates, seeming to have caught on to the fact he was the only one doing the talking.

"What did you say you came here to find out exactly? I didn't disgrace your family or anything. I'm sorry if you think I did, but I'm pretty sure our relationship ended before your time or the time of your father." He incorrectly tries to put an explanation together.

"We know. We know she was single when you two met. That's not why we're here."

"Okay, why are you here?" he asks, still trying to

connect the dots.

"Did you ever wonder where she went? Did you ever try to get back in touch with her?" Collette questions.

Carl looks at the spot on the ground again, seeming to think about her question. "No, I didn't try to get back in touch with her again. After I broke it off with Cynthia, Judy and I decided to make things work. I figured Cynthia found out about it and was pretty mad. I was thankful to her for making a clean exit. No drama. Not many girls would do that, you know. I could have gotten fired for having relations with a student. I could have lost my job, my education, and my wife. Honestly, I lived in fear for a long time that she would come back and turn me in to the university. But she never did."

"And you never wondered where she went or why she never came back?" I ask. It seemed cruel to me that he could just leave her so easily.

"I did wonder about her, of course. But you have to realize, I had a marriage to save and an education I needed to get through. She was just a blip on my radar in the scheme of things. I had so many other matters on my mind. I couldn't have spent the time and energy tracking her down. From what I heard, she finished her degree and moved up the coast somewhere."

"Seattle. She moved to Seattle," I offer.

"So that must have been where she met your father? Honestly, I only ever wished the best for her."

Collette gives me a quick look, eyebrows raised. This is our chance to tell him. I give her a tip of my chin so small Carl can't notice. She was older by two minutes. She should do this.

Collette, knowing precisely what I'm trying to do,

narrows her eyes at me, takes a deep breath and turns to Carl.

"Our mother never dated anyone after you," she states, nothing added, just the facts. She waits to see if it's enough for him to catch on.

"Why not?" Carl asks, apparently not putting all the puzzle pieces together yet.

Collette's shoulders visibly drop, and she looks at me again, her eyes large and pleading.

"Um, because she was busy raising us and building her business," I try, not doing much better at explaining than Collette had.

"Well, she must have dated someone to get you two, or did she just adopt you?" He chuckles to himself and looks away. "Women nowadays don't need men for anything, think they can do it all on their own." He looks back at us. "I knew Cynthia was independent, but I have to admit I'm surprised. She struck me as the more traditional type."

"She is—traditional, I mean, at least in that sense," I say.

"I'm sorry, I'm just not following you. Your mother never dated or married anyone after me, but yet you two are sitting here in front of me claiming to be her twin daughters?"

"That's correct." I feel almost cruel at this point, like I'm talking in circles. I'm going to have to spell it out for him, I take a big breath.

"You were the last person she had a sexual relationship with before we were born." I raise one eyebrow and look him in the eye, waiting for the words to sink in.

There's a long silence, only the birds and the

waves crashing on the beach making any sound.

I watch Carl as his eyes leave mine and search the sky for answers.

Collette and I wait.

"But that can't be. She never contacted me, she never told me, she..." His voice trails off, and his eyes come back down on Collette and me, seeming to see us for the first time. Taking in every detail, every feature of our faces. I look at Collette and try to see what he is seeing. The low hairline, the oval face with a strong jaw. The straight nose and the high cheekbones. They all matched mine, and now they all matched Carl's as well.

"But why wouldn't she tell me?" The hurt in his voice is evident.

"She never told us about you either," Collette says.

"What do you mean?"

"Ever since we were little our mother told us that our father died before we were born. She never elaborated, claimed it was 'too hard to talk about.'" Collette makes quotation marks with her fingers. "Said that it was just the three of us. That's the most explanation we ever got, that's all we ever knew."

"Then how did you find out about me?"

Collette looks at me.

I study the grass in front of my feet as memories of Lenny flood my mind. I hadn't thought of him in almost a day, having been so consumed by other things. The wind is knocked out of my lungs as the guilt of not thinking about him slams into my chest, and I make a silent gasp for breath.

"My own fiancé died in a plane crash." I manage to get out before the tears start to fall. I look desperately at

Collette, silently begging for her to finish for me.

This was one of the perks of being a twin. She just knew, and without my having to say anything she finishes for me.

"Ireland was having a hard time around the time of the funeral."

"As well she should be," Carl interjects with sympathy, the kind that I had so desperately wanted from my own mother.

"Yes, I agree," Collette concurs. "But our mother had a different view. When she was approached by a local reporter about your fictitious death, she got spooked. She was afraid her story would be released. She was more worried about her appearance than how it might affect us."

I've regained my composure, so I jump in to take over. "She cut a deal with a reporter to keep it quiet, but she was worried that the news would still get to us. So she came over to my condo one night and laid it all out for me. She told me about you and about the relationship you had with her."

Carl nods, taking it all in.

"She told me how she found out about you being married, and how you were trying to make things work with your wife, about the same time she discovered she was pregnant. She didn't know what to do. She didn't want you to lose your job or your marriage, so she didn't tell anyone. She finished her degree and left town. She didn't have anyone to help support her, so she moved to Seattle, where she had a friend who could help her find a job." I spread my hands out in front of me, finishing the story.

Carl keeps nodding his head, even though I'm done

talking. Like it's on a spring. Up, down, up, down, in time to a silent metronome in his head.

I look at Collette, who gives a minuscule shrug to her shoulders.

We both wait again.

The sound we hear next isn't what we're expecting. It starts as a low rumble in his chest and then begins to bubble up his throat until it explodes out of his mouth. Laughing for what seems like forever. Tears forming in the corner of his eyes.

He regains control of himself and wipes the tears away with the back of his hand, looking at Collette and me, he says, "I don't believe it."

Chapter 14

Collette and I stare at each other across the table. He didn't believe it?

"Sorry, but what exactly don't you believe?" Collette asks. "It's all true, we swear."

"Oh, no, sorry." Carl pauses to collect himself. "I believe you and what you're telling me. Well, at least, I have good faith in what you're telling me." He waves his hand dismissively, like this isn't what's bothering him. "No, what I can't believe is, all this time, I allegedly had two daughters." He suddenly becomes contemplative. "You see, Judy and I, we could never have children of our own. We tried for years. Judy made herself crazy with it all. Planning her cycle, taking her temperature, tracking her hormone cycle. There wasn't all this IVF stuff back then, like you have now. Soon Judy lost hope. Every time another disappointment came, it would just crush her. Seeing her so dejected would shatter me. You can't imagine what it's like to be a man, to want to give your wife the one thing you should be able to, and just not." He spreads his hands out wide like there should be something there besides empty space. "Eventually we learned to accept our lives without children in it. We kept ourselves busy by traveling the world and picking up every activity under the sun." He motions with his arm to the wide variety of equipment scattered around the property. "We came to accept that we had each other, and that was enough." He looks solemn for a moment. "And then she got sick."

I can literally feel his pain. It creeps up over me and surrounds me like a hooded sweater, covering me from top to bottom. Here I am, meeting what in reality is a complete stranger, and nevertheless I feel like we're connected. Connected by our mutual tribulations. It's funny how people can become attached to each other merely by sharing an experience. Going into this, it never occurred to me how we would rattle his existence. Yet here we are, facing the fact that Carl has his own story, his own pain, and his own hardships he's been through. I had been so caught up in my own that I never stopped to think how all of this might affect his world.

He pushes back on the bed swing, the muscles in his thigh tightening and releasing as the swing moves forward, lifting his feet off the ground by an inch or two.

"About twelve years ago, Judy was having her routine mammogram when they found the lump." He swallows. "She gave a good fight. She was a fighter." He directs his words to the flowers that are dripping down toward him, hanging from the wooden beams over his head.

"I quit my job toward the end, and we moved out here so she could be near the water. I built this for her"—he motions to the pergola—"so she could still be outside, even when she was at her worst. She loved being outdoors." It was evident to me that Carl was a man of dignity, staying with Judy to the very end.

"If she had known about you"—he gestures with

his chin to Collette and me—"she would have opened her arms to you in a second, no questions asked. She would have loved you like you were her own."

Tears prick the corners of my eyes at the notion of a perfect stranger having enough tenderness in her heart to offer the kind of motherly love that was so lacking in our own lives. Life was cruel, teasing us, letting us look at the type of experience we could have had, full of adventure and kindness.

"She sounds lovely," Collette whispers.

"She was," Carl says. "I was a shattered man after her death. I didn't want to go anywhere or do anything. I didn't know my own purpose in life anymore." Carl looks at me like he's looking into my soul. I feel like he's speaking for me. Somehow he knows what is inside me better than anyone else I've run across in the last few weeks.

"You know, there is no time limit on grief, it never truly leaves, but it does dull. When mine dulled enough for me to re-enter the world, I decided to continue on with life as Judy would have wanted me to. That's when I met my wife."

I'm about to ask Carl about her but am cut off by a blur of something passing through my vision.

"Hey, Dad! Think fast!" A water balloon sails through the air, colliding with Carl's knee and ricocheting off, but not before causing a liquid explosion just a couple of feet from Collette and me. Droplets of water fill the air and force me to raise my hand in protection against further assault.

"What the—!" I hear Collette utter beside me, clearly as shocked as I am.

"Hey, sport!" Carl calls out as a flash of dark hair

and tan skin races past us and heads straight into the house, letting the screen door slam behind him on his way in.

I lower my arms and glance toward the back door. What just happened? What, or I guess I should say, who was that?

I turn to Carl, looking for answers to my unasked questions, but he is already rising off the daybed and jumping to his feet—again his litheness impresses me—and heading toward the side of the house.

Only when I let my eyes follow Carl do I realize we have been joined by another person. A woman is striding down the walkway, carrying grocery bags in each hand. Her tall, slim figure is caught off balance by the heavy bags, and I watch as she sways a little on her descent into the yard. A baseball cap with the Hawaii Five-O logo across the front is pulled down low, covering her face from view. A ponytail extends from the back of the baseball cap and winds down past her mid-back, almost touching the top of her cut-off jean shorts.

I watch as Carl reaches her and easily lifts the bags out of her hands while simultaneously giving her a quick kiss on the mouth, tilting his head to the side to avoid the brim of the hat.

"Hey, baby, how was shopping?" Carl asks, and I instantly catch on that this is his wife while simultaneously following his game of downplaying the presence of Collette and me loitering in their back yard.

"It was fine. I couldn't find the roasted chestnuts you like, but I'll try to get them the next time I go to Don Quixote," she says as she follows him down the path, still unaware of our presence.

I feel like a voyeur as I study her walking toward us behind Carl. There is something familiar about her when she speaks, and I find myself trying to figure out who she reminds me of.

It's not until she's reached the yard's edge and finally notices us that she lifts her head and I can see past the brim of her baseball cap. In the instant I see her face I understand why she seems so familiar.

"Kayla?"

She stops to look in my direction, apparently caught off guard by my outburst.

"Ireland?"

I know I shouldn't be impressed that she remembers me, but something in me feels a slight sense of satisfaction that she does.

Kayla regains her composure and continues walking toward us. I rise out of my chair, but before I can take a step, Collette grabs my wrist. "Wait, you know her?" she asks at the exact same moment Carl says, "You know each other?"

Kayla looks from Carl to me and back to Carl. "We sat next to each other on the plane." She looks back to me. "What are you doing here?"

I take a step closer and open my mouth to speak. "I, I mean, we…" But the words get stuck in my head as I make the mental connection. Carl and Kayla, Kayla and Carl. Carl is Kayla's retired husband. Kayla is Carl's second marriage.

It all hits me so fast that I'm at a loss for words. I've forgotten what it was Kayla just asked me. All I can do is manage to stand there like a mute halfwit as the heat spreads across my face.

I watch in horror as she takes in what I'm now sure

is the blush rising from my neck to my face, her eyes growing in size by the second. There is a sharp intake of breath before she turns to Carl and, without uttering a single word, speaks a million things to him, her face saying it all.

"We sat next to each other on the plane," she repeats. "I told you about her," she continues in a hushed voice.

Carl shifts the groceries into one hand and reaches for her elbow with the free one. Holding on to her, I hear him whisper, "She's the one who got sick?"

Kayla nods and looks back to me.

"Kayla, I had no idea," I offer, floundering for an explanation, "that Carl—"

Kayla's head snaps back to Carl. "You mean, you think Carl is him? I mean that he's your... Oh, damn it."

Collette has walked across the yard during this interaction and is now standing at my side. "I'm sorry, but I'm obviously missing something here." She turns to me. "Mind filling me in?"

I speak to Collette while keeping my eyes on Kayla to judge her reaction. "I sat next to Kayla on the plane." I pinch my lips together, measuring my next words carefully. "I believe I shared our reason for this trip with her."

"Oh," Collette says, catching on quickly.

"Yeah. Oh!" Kayla repeats.

"And you're Carl's wife?" Collette needlessly confirms.

"Yes."

"And that flash of lightning, that was your son?"

"Yes."

Collette takes a deep breath through her nose and lets it out slowly. "Okay," she says, drawing the word out.

"Actually, no. Not okay. Absolutely not okay." Kayla suddenly turns to Carl. "We need to talk." She tilts her head toward the house and, without waiting for him, turns and starts walking away from us.

Carl, looking from Kayla to us and then back to Kayla, says, "Sure, let's take these inside and get them put away."

"I'll be right back," he offers politely as he follows Kayla up the stairs and into the house, leaving Collette and me alone in the back yard.

Not sure what to do, I look at Collette, who just shrugs her shoulders and walks back to the lawn chairs we were sitting in.

She pats the one next to her, and I walk over and sit down, staring at the door Kayla and Carl had disappeared through.

"She wasn't so happy to see me again," I say.

"Well, you did say you threw up on her, didn't you?"

"I don't think that's the reason she's upset."

"Right," Collette deadpans.

"What do we do now?"

"We wait."

"What if they don't come back?" I contemplate out loud.

"Oh, they'll come back. Besides, we came all this way, so I'm not going to leave here until I know for sure it's over."

There is a clatter as the screen door opens and closes. Collette gives me a knowing look and then shifts her gaze to Carl as he makes his way back down to the yard. Disappointment fills me when I notice he's alone.

"I'm so sorry," I start to say, but stop when Collette places her hand over mine.

Carl clears his throat. "Um, yeah, right." He shakes his head, clearly at a loss for words, and finally comes out with, "This is not what I was expecting this day to be like."

"I know. We're so sorry—" again Collette squeezes my arm for me to stop.

I glare at her and narrow my eyes.

She stares back and gives me a minuscule shake of her head.

"It's a lot to take in all at once," Carl continues, oblivious of the exchange between Collette and me. "I think Kayla and I could use a little time to process all of this."

I look to the back porch and think I see the blinds moving in the window. Is she really watching us right now? Why wouldn't she just come out here and ask us all the questions I know she must have?

"I know it's a lot." This time it's Collette doing the talking. "But I hope you can understand we want to know more about you. This is new to us too. Don't you feel like it would be mutually beneficial to explore a bit more of what this could all be, before we shut it down?"

Carl scratches his head at his temple. "I do think there is more to discuss." Pausing, he glances toward the back porch. "But I'm sure you understand that it's not just about me anymore. I have a family to consider."

I nod my head but notice Collette is sitting stoically, not moving a muscle. "We would like to see you again," she says pointedly.

Carl sighs and says, "Why don't you leave your information. I'll get in touch with you after I've had a chance to speak with my wife. This is quite a shock to her. I'm sure you can understand that some things need to be explained and discussed between us before I can go any further here."

It's clear to me that we are not going to be making any more progress today, so I remove my arm from under Collette's grasp and dig into my purse for a paper and pen. I scribble our phone numbers and the hotel we're staying at on the paper and stand to give him the note.

"We only have a couple of days. I know you have some things to work out, but we'd really like to hear from you again." I turn to Collette. "We should go now."

Collette turns from me to Carl and back again, throws her hands in the air and brings them back down again to push out of the chair. "Fine!"

She brushes past me and makes her way back up the yard, heading for the side walkway.

I turn to Carl. "Please call us."

Carl just nods his head and holds up the piece of paper.

I follow Collette wordlessly to the car. Once inside, she starts the engine and backs out of the driveway. We are two blocks away before she slaps the steering wheel, causing me to jump in my seat.

"Damn it, that's not how it was supposed to go."

"And how was it supposed to go, exactly?" I challenge. "We went in there with no expectations."

She scoffs at me. "Oh, come on, Ireland. You

seriously didn't have any expectations coming into this? We flew all the way out here, and you didn't have any hopes or images in your mind of a happy reunion between father and daughters?"

"I mean, yeah, I guess I had hope. But that doesn't equate to me knowing how this was all going to turn out. You can never be sure."

"You might not be sure, but you can encourage it to go a certain way. What was it with all that 'I'm sorry' shit? For God's sake, don't apologize. We haven't done anything wrong. When you apologize, it makes it sound like we have."

"That's not what I was trying to do. Besides, it didn't have anything to do with what I said. That was all Kayla. She probably went all momma bear on him as soon as they got in the house. It didn't have anything to do with us."

Collette snorts and tightens her grip on the wheel. "God, Ireland, you really are dense sometimes. It had everything to do with us. You had to go and blab to a complete stranger on a plane about your life, and now look where it's gotten us."

"I didn't blab to a stranger. I was just having a conversation. Besides, how was I supposed to know she was the wife of our long-lost father?"

"Do you even know how ridiculous you sound? That's the kind of personal information you keep to yourself. You don't just tell every person walking down the street."

"Fine! From now on I'll just be quiet. I won't talk to anyone." I hear myself and instantly think my behavior is the equivalent of Molly or Maggie or another five-year-old, but the exhaustion of the day was starting to settle in, and I couldn't come up with a better comeback.

"Fine."

"Fine." I sit back in a huff as we speed through the streets of Honolulu, destined for our hotel and a long silent wait for a phone call we don't even know will come.

Chapter 15

Sitting down to our second breakfast buffet at the Plumeria Beach House Cafe, I'm beginning to suspect the probability of Carl getting in touch with Collette and me is becoming slimmer by the minute.

Picking up my fork, I stab a lone piece of golden pineapple from my plate and take a savage bite out of it, letting the juices roll around my mouth as I chew and swallow.

Directly across the table from me, hidden behind dark sunglasses, Collette is sitting, staring out into the Pacific Ocean, just a few feet in front of us. Letting out what seems to be a contended sigh, she says, "This is paradise."

I study Collette for a moment, noticing her relaxed posture and how slowly she is sipping her coffee. I let my gaze drift across the restaurant, following hers to the breathtaking view.

The sun is glistening in the sky, causing long shadows from the palm trees to dance across the immaculate lawn as they sway in the gentle breeze. Immediately in front of the grass, the beach stretches into the soft waves lapping against the shore. The brown-sugar sand, smooth from the night's tide, is bare except for the few footprints left from swimmers trickling in and out of the water for a morning swim.

"I suppose it could be paradise," I say, feeling

generous in my answer.

It's probably my lack of an enthusiastic response that makes her turn to me. "Oh, Ireland, I wish you could see past your own fog, if only for a minute, and just receive this for what it is. There is so much beauty around us. Most people would give their right arm to be where we are right now."

I'm silent as I try to conjure up the gratitude Collette is requesting of me, but the more effort I exert for the task, the more her words permeate my consciousness in an incompatible way, and I begin to feel the sting of her desire to categorically brush my feelings to the side.

"It's not that easy," I say quietly, being mindful of the couple seated at the table directly behind us.

Collette seems to digest this as we turn back to the lawn and watch as a set of young girls, similar in age to Molly and Maggie, prance around gathering plumeria flowers that have fallen from the trees, making a pile of white and pink flowers on the grass.

Collette moves her head in my direction, almost imperceptibly, and I know she is trying to study me through her darkened glasses.

"I think you should consider going on an anti-depressant. You know, to help with how you've been feeling and all."

I stare at Collette like she's the one on drugs. "You can't be serious."

"Look, being on meds to help you through a tough time is nothing to be ashamed of. And you, you've been through the toughest time of them all. I know lots of people who've used them to help. I even used them after Maggie was born."

My ears perk up, as this is new information to me. "You did? Why?"

"Having Molly first was a big adjustment for Greg and me, but somehow we always seemed to be able to make it work. We would tag team so that one of us was on duty at a time." She smiles, seeming to be caught up in the memory of them as first-time parents.

"He was able to have his personal time, and I was still able to have mine. We worked in tandem, but when I had Maggie, there were two children for two adults." Collette's smile falters. "I wasn't able to have any time to myself, and I don't know, that coupled with a mixture of hormones going wacko in my body caused me to feel nothing. I was numb to being a new mother again. I couldn't conjure up the joy I had experienced with Molly's birth. And the worst part was I didn't even care. Instead, I just felt sad and lonely all the time, even though there were plenty of people around." She pauses and looks out at the water before continuing. "When it got to the point where I didn't want to get out of bed anymore or take a shower or leave the house, Greg stepped in and made an appointment for me to see my ob-gyn. And I'm so glad he did, because as soon as I started taking medicine, I was a new person. It didn't change me completely or work immediately, but it took the edge off, enough that I could start to concentrate on being a mom again. As time wore on and I felt myself readjusting to our new life, it got easier, and eventually, I felt like I didn't need to take the meds anymore. With the help of the doctor, I slowly came off them and haven't had to use them since. But like I said, I'm so glad they were there when I needed them. I'm not ashamed of what I went through, and I don't think you should feel ashamed if that's what you need to help you get through Lenny's death now."

As the sun casts a glow across Collette's face, I feel like I'm seeing her in a new light, and I wonder how I had never been privy to this secret part of her life. She managed to keep it hidden away so that even I didn't have a clue about it.

"I had no idea you were going through that," I say. "How did I not know?" I ponder, more to myself than actually expecting an answer from Collette.

"Anyway, it's also part of the reason Greg and I agreed I would go back to work. I needed to feel a purpose besides being a milk cart and a taxi. We've been talking about it for a while, and when the opportunity came up, I jumped on it. Greg has always been so supportive of me, you know that. He's always just wanted me to be happy, but I'm not sure he was expecting my actual return to work to come to fruition. I think to him it had become one of those things we talked about to help me feel better, not that I would actually go out and do it."

"But you did, and I'm so proud of you for going after the thing that you knew was going to make you happy."

"Thanks, but that's what I mean. Ireland, I just want you to be happy again."

"Of course," I say, knowing she means well. "And I appreciate the thought, and I'll let you know if I change my mind, but I think I'm going to try and weather this particular storm on my own for now."

Collette pinches her lips together with the universal look that says she wants to say more, but she merely nods and turns back to the view, leaving the conversation on the table.

Trying to find a distraction from the silence that has suddenly descended over us, I pick up my phone and, for the hundredth time in the last two days, check for any messages. Much to my disappointment, the screen is steadfastly blank. No text, no calls, not even messages from Mother, harassing me about my whereabouts. Just eerie silence.

"Do you think he'll call?" Collette asks, breaking back into my thoughts.

"It's not looking like it," I answer, trying not to sound like the perpetual pessimist.

Collette pours herself some more coffee from the stainless-steel pot that comes with the breakfast and takes a tentative sip before putting the mug back down on the table and leaning back in her chair.

"Well, I guess all we have on our hands is time. What are we going to do with it?"

"Keep waiting."

****

My sides hurt, and I have to wipe a tear away. Trying to catch my breath from laughing so hard, I dab my eyes with my napkin. Collette is just recalling a story about how, when Molly and Maggie were little, they used to stuff toilet paper down the toilet and then flush it until it overflowed. Collette had found them floating paper sailboats in the water, singing, "Hi-ho, hi-ho, it's off to sailing we go." I'm in stitches by the time she's done recounting the events, and I've heard this story before.

Collette and I are packed into one of the small, turquoise-painted tables of Kono's, a fun, surf-inspired, casual diner. A picture of a pig riding a surfboard takes up residence on the wall opposite our table. The diagram of each part of the pig reminds me precisely of what we're eating, or rather devouring at this exact moment, the best pulled-pork tacos I've ever tasted.

It was pushing forty-eight hours since our last encounter with Carl, and Collette and I had grown weary of hanging around Kahala Resort and Spa waiting for our phones to ring. We had walked the beach multiple times, visited the Dolphins at the Dolphin Quest, checked in on the turtles, and lain by the pool or beach for so long our legs were turning the color of honey. With only one day left before we're scheduled to fly back to Seattle we decided it was time to get out and explore a bit, so this afternoon we looked up the best "local" place for eats and headed out for some comfort food.

Considering the amount of time that has passed since I handed over our phone numbers, I am starting to think the possibility that Carl might call is gone.

As I listen to Collette recount the story about Molly and Maggie, I'm struck with the idea that Carl doesn't even know he's a grandfather. The thought that the girls could possibly grow up with another grandfather to love on them is temporarily heartwarming.

Something flashes in my mind about the night Mother was making cookies in my condo. She said her own parents had abandoned her when she was pregnant with Collette and me. All for the simple reason it was against their beliefs. Would Carl have opinions of his own that would prevent him from wanting anything to do with us, with them?

I can't imagine a person who could be so closed off in their heart as to not want to be a part of Molly and

Maggie's lives.

I'm about to bring this up to Collette when her phone starts vibrating on the table. We both look down at the caller ID.

Unknown.

Collette looks up at me.

"Well, answer it!" I practically yell, wondering why she's hesitating.

My words shock her into action, and she grabs the phone.

"Hello? This is Collette."

There is a silence while she waits for the person on the other side.

"Mm-hm, okay, yes, she's here with me."

I lean over the table, trying to hear both sides of the conversation.

Collette holds up a finger. "Sure, one minute. We just need to get to the car. Hold on."

Collette is already grabbing her handbag and scooting out of the booth. I grab my things and follow her out of the restaurant and across the street. Without speaking, we both hop into the Jeep. The sun coming through the window has made the inside unbearably hot, causing us to immediately roll down the windows, letting the scent of plumeria waft in on the humid breeze, filling the car with its sweet perfume.

Once we are both settled, Collette touches the speakerphone button.

"Okay, we're both here," she announces.

"Hi, girls," comes Carl's voice through the line, and I almost swoon in relief.

"Hi," we answer in unison.

Even though I'm dying to ask a million questions, I

hold my tongue and wait for him to speak first.

"Sorry I didn't call sooner. Kayla and I had a lot to go over." His voice sounds forlorn, and I wonder how much tension we've caused in their marriage. A hypothetical image of Lenny and me, married and a few years down the road, with a child, fills my mind. I place a strange woman claiming to be his daughter into the scene in my head. How would I react? Would I have been pissed? Taken it in stride? I honestly don't know. How could Kayla have known what to do? Sympathy grips my heart before Carl continues.

"I don't want to burden you with the details, but I'm sure you can understand that this has all been a shock to her, and to myself."

"Of course," I say as I watch Collette from across the front seat of the car.

"So after a lot of discussions, Kayla feels that it's best we get a blood test before moving forward with any sort of relationship."

I look at Collette and wonder if she is thinking the same thing as I am. That a blood test wasn't necessary, because any person could simply look at the three of us and see we were related. It was like looking at an older, male reflection of myself every time I looked at Carl.

"Well, I suppose if that's what she wants, we'd be okay with that?" Collette lifts the end of her sentence, so it comes out as a question directed to me.

"It's just that with Kai and everything, well, we don't want to complicate his life if there is no reason to."

"No, we understand," Collette says and nods to the phone, indicating I should go along with this.

"Yeah, okay. But we leave tomorrow. How can we

get the information before that?"

"Kayla has contacted a friend of mine who's a physician here on the Island He can see us tomorrow morning for a blood draw. They would be able to do a DNA test from the blood sample and tell us if I am, in fact, your biological father," Carl says. "Would you be willing to do that?"

Collette looks to me for confirmation, I nod, and she answers for both of us. "Yes."

"We won't get the results right away. It'll take a few days."

My eyebrows knit together. "So we won't know the results before we leave?"

"That's correct. I guess there's no way around it. They have to send the samples to a lab and do the work up there. We have to wait, no matter what."

"So how will we get the results?" Collette asks.

"I think they'll send us each a copy in the mail," Carl clarifies. "I'll call you as soon as I get mine. After we know more, we can decide what to do from there."

I twist my lips as I contemplate what to do. I want answers, and this seems like the only way to get a definite one, but I want them sooner. The idea of leaving here without clarity makes my stomach hurt.

"Okay," I finally concede.

"I'm in too," Collette answers.

"Then it's settled. I'll see you both tomorrow."

"Tomorrow."

Chapter 16

The taxi deposits Collette and me onto Punchbowl Street—which sounds more like a party staple than the location of the Queen's Medical Center—where we are to meet up with Carl. Despite the fact the Medical Center is only a few blocks from the hustle and bustle of the beaches of Waikiki, there isn't a single tourist in sight. Instead, the sidewalks are filled with locals, either clad in professional clothing, hurrying to their jobs, or in jeans and tank tops. Carrying grocery bags and attending to the day's errands, vacation is not even a speck on their radar.

After dodging a few sidewalk patrons, Collette and I turn to enter the building through the automatic sliding doors. A whoosh of air-conditioning assaults our bodies the second we step into the lobby, causing goosebumps to rise on our arms and legs.

Carl texted over the physician's suite number earlier in the day, along with the time of our appointment. I had to resist the urge to text back, asking him to grab coffee after, and instead just sent a simple

—*thank you, we'll be there*—

I refer to the text message again, and we quickly find the correct door, entering the office right on time.

Aside from the brown-and-tan decor that could lend to visions of shag carpet and lava lamps—both of which are appropriately missing from this space—it is a neat and tidy office. Patient chairs are scattered about the waiting room, separated by tables with the latest gossip magazines fanned out on the top.

My eyes scan the room, eventually landing on Carl. I watch as he absentmindedly flips through one of the magazines. Shifting my weight from one foot to the other, I mentally wrestle with my own insecurities. I can't decide if it's hope or fear making it difficult for me to walk the rest of the way into the room. This man, in all his island charm, with his blue Hawaiian shirt, white shorts, and leather flip-flops, is quite possibly my father. And after today we will know for sure. But if he is, then what? Does he scoop us up in his arms and declare his parental love for us? How does a person you've never known before quietly slide into your life? Is it similar to dating, taking days, weeks, and months to feel comfortable around this person, to trust them and let them know the real you? And what about Kayla and Kai? Would they want to share Carl with Collette and me? Standing there watching him, it was getting harder and harder to devise a plan, to make sense of the future. The more I tried to come up with the answers, the less sure I was about everything.

I watch as Carl checks his watch and then looks up, scanning the room until our eyes meet and he smiles. His is the kind of smile that reaches his eyes before his lips even have a chance to move. The kindness behind those eyes kicks Collette and me into action, and I follow behind as Collette makes her way across the room. He stands as we approach and gives each of us an unexpected hug. The warmth of his body, coupled with the affection being shown, is such a foreign feeling that I freeze the second he touches me. I do my best to avoid my awkwardness and lean in for a side hug and pat on the back.

"You found it okay?" Carl asks.

"No problem at all," Collette responds readily and takes the seat next to his, leaving me the one on the opposite side of the L-shaped waiting room. A fact which does not go unnoticed by me.

"Thanks for meeting me here." Carl addresses Collette and me once we are settled.

"Well, it's a place to start, I guess," Collette says, while I mutely bob my head up and down next to her.

I rack my brain but can't come up with a single thing to say that will take the awkwardness out of this situation. It appears Carl and Collette can't think of anything either, because we all dissolve into silence, feigning an interest in the cheap artwork gracing the walls.

"I'm sorry it took me so long to call you," Carl says, breaking our silence.

"It's okay," I say, not entirely meaning it. Collette and I were on pins and needles waiting to hear from him for the last few days.

Carl leans forward, placing his elbows on his knees, and grasps his hands. "I wish this could be about just the three of us, but it's not. I have a family, and my sole purpose on this earth is to protect them." Carl pauses and takes a breath. "You both seem so lovely, and I'm excited to get to know you better, but I have to proceed with caution. I hope you understand. I need to think about Kai and how this might affect him. Kayla is right. He is simply too young to make sense of this situation. If you are indeed my daughters, then we need to be absolutely positive before I introduce you to him as his half-sisters."

A wave of heat passes through my body with the words *half-sister*. I have longed my entire life for someone to protect me the way Carl is protecting his son, but where does that leave Collette and me? On the sidelines waiting for answers.

"I have two little girls as well, Molly and Maggie. I know how you feel. I would never want to put them in harm's way. It's perfectly understandable to want to protect your son," Collette says.

Carl sits up and shifts to the side so that his upper body is facing Collette. "Wait a minute, you have two girls? That would mean I could possibly be a grandpa?" Carl lets out a laugh and slaps his knee. "Get out of town!"

Collette looks at me with amusement on her face. I smile back and shrug my shoulders. But before we can say anything further, the door separating the waiting room from the back office opens. An island-sized dark-haired girl, dressed in scrubs and holding a clipboard, stands in the doorway. "Carl, Collette, and Ireland?" She addresses the entire waiting room even though we're sitting right in front of her.

Carl recovers quickly and gives her a small wave as we all rise in unison.

She smiles at each of us as we walk through the door she holds open. After we have all passed through, she hurries in front of us and starts down a narrow hallway. We follow behind automatically and only stop when she pauses to deposit us into a small consult room. After a brief moment of awkwardness, while the nurse realizes there are only two patient chairs in the room and scurries out into the hallway, then returns dragging a chair behind her, we find our seats and wait for the doctor.

Sitting in a line, all of us with our hands in our laps, we settle into silence until we hear the handle turn, and our heads swivel simultaneously as the doctor enters into the room.

Carl stands and gives the doctor a firm handshake and a manly clap on the back.

"Good to see you, Carl," the doctor says. "How have you been?"

I take pause at the familiarity between the two men and then remember Kayla was the one to set up this appointment. Of course it would be with someone they knew.

"I've been good! You know, trying to keep busy. Only, recently I've been bestowed with a little surprise, one that has my heart rate slightly elevated." I inwardly roll my eyes at his little attempt at a joke. So this is what it would feel like to have a father that embarrasses you.

"I did notice you weren't alone today." The doctor pauses and flips through the file he's holding. "I also noticed what's on the appointment for today." He keeps a professional tone but raises his eyebrow at Carl. Coming around to his side of the desk, he sits down and turns to acknowledge us. "I'm Doctor Collins," he says, extending his hand to each of us.

"Collette." Collette shakes his hand

"Ireland," I say, repeating her motions.

"It's a pleasure to meet you both. Now, why don't you tell me, in your own words, the reason for this visit." He steeples his hands together under his chin.

"I had the pleasure of meeting these two ladies a

few days ago. Turns out, they're looking for their biological father, and they think it might be me," Carl says, diving right in.

Doctor Collins raises his eyebrow again. "I see, and you'd like me to perform the test to see if this is a fact?"

"Yes, that's correct," Carl answers.

"There certainly is a way that can be done," Doctor Collins says. "We can use a DNA paternity test called Restriction Fragment Length Polymorphism. It will use blood samples to compare the DNA between that of yourself"—he indicates Carl—"and that of the girls. We'll be looking for a match of the DNA patterns on two or more probes. With an accuracy of ninety to ninety-nine-point nine percent, we're looking at a test that will give us the information you're seeking. Once we get the results, we will know, without a shadow of a doubt, whether you are their biological father." Doctor Collins lays his hands out on the table, palms facing up. "It's a fairly simple test. We just need to do a quick blood draw in our lab here, and then we send it out to a nearby lab for the processing. The results will be back to our office in two days, at which time I'd be happy to go over the findings with you."

Carl looks at both of us. "I'm not sure what all that means, but I do like the idea that it's so accurate. What do you think?"

"Yes, I'm okay with it," I say looking to Collette, who's nodding her head in agreement.

"I'll just need each of you to sign a treatment acceptance form for the blood draw." Doctor Collins slides a piece of paper from his file folder across the desk to each of us.

I sign mine without reading it and push it back across the table to Doctor Collins. Once he has gathered all three papers, he stands and walks around his desk.

"Okay then, why don't you three stay put for just a minute, and I'll let the nurse know to set up for a blood draw." Doctor Collins heads toward the door. "I'll be right back." He excuses himself and slips out, leaving the door slightly ajar behind him. We can hear him talking to the nurse in the hallway, and then he's back before we've even missed him.

"Right this way, please." He ushers us out the door and down the hallway, into another small room on the left, the in-office lab.

"Hello!" comes the overly cheery voice of the nurse. "Looks like I'm going to be taking a sample on all of you today. So who wants to go first?" She is setting up the vials for our blood samples, and there is a long printout of what looks like name-tag stickers in front of her.

"Why don't I start us out," Carl says, taking the seat with only one armrest.

"Okey-dokey, I just need you to state your full name and date of birth for me, please." The nurse leans over the name tags on the counter.

"Carl Martin, born nineteen sixty." Carl confirms for her.

Satisfied, she picks up one of the empty vials and plasters his name tags onto it. Next, she places a suction cup onto the top of the vial. It has what looks like a long thin line attached to a needle at the other end of it. She ties a tourniquet around Carl's upper arm and tells him to make a fist. Quickly and efficiently she pokes the needle into the vein that is bulging out of Carl's inner elbow.

The sound of the tourniquet being snapped free from Carl's arm briefly breaks the silence in the room.

Just as quickly as she stuck the needle in, she's pulling it back out, placing gauze over the spot the needle was in, collecting the blood that was going to determine our fate.

The nurse repeats the process with both Collette and me, leaving all three of us with matching Snoopy Band-Aids covering our inner arm.

"It should have already stopped bleeding, but you can keep the Band-Aid on for another ten minutes or so. Call us if you have any adverse reaction later in the day, but I really don't think you'll be having any problems," she says. "You're all finished and free to go. I believe Doctor Collins said he will be calling you when he has the results."

We each thank the nurse for her time and make our way back into the office waiting room.

"That was fairly painless." Carl sticks his hands in his pockets, leaving his thumbs sticking out on either side.

"And quick," Collette says.

Had it really been that easy? Just a few pricks of a needle and a few vials of blood and we would know for sure if we were genetically matched.

It happened so fast, and now, without planning for what to do after, we are left standing in the waiting room awkwardly looking at one another. This could possibly be the last time we see Carl. If the DNA results come back negative, there will be no reason to pursue a relationship. But, I'm not ready to just let him walk out the door. I don't want our time together to end just yet.

The fact that Carl doesn't want to move forward until he gets the results is not wasted on me, but surely a cup of coffee and some light conversation wouldn't be out of the question.

"Know any good coffee places? Collette and I were just talking, saying we wanted to get some coffee after we were done here. Feel like joining us?"

Collette eyeballs me, probably because there was no conversation earlier about coffee, but I nod my head toward Carl, and she seems to understand what I'm trying to accomplish.

"Right, you must know the best places! We'd love for you to join us."

It's evident to me that Carl is wrestling with something inside himself as he pauses before he answers us. Finally, he checks his watch and replies, "I was supposed to meet up with Kayla and Kai, for Kai's soccer game, but that doesn't start for another forty minutes. I guess a quick coffee would be all right."

Carl holds the door to the office open, and I wink at Collette as we pass through into the hallway. Carl follows us as we head to the elevator. "I know just the place. The Honolulu Coffee Company makes a great cup of joe. They have teas and acai bowls if you want, too." Carl stops as we approach the entrance to the hospital.

"Sounds perfect," I say.

"Why don't we follow you in a taxi, since you have to head straight to the soccer game after?"

Carl digs into his shorts pocket and pulls out his car keys. "Okay, I'll swing around and pull up beside you so the taxi can follow me."

Collette digs into her purse and pulls out her cell

phone to call the taxi, but before she has a chance, her phone rings.

She glances at the caller ID and quickly shoots me a look before answering.

"Hello, Mother," Collette monotones.

Carl's eyebrows raise on his forehead. This is the first time Mother's name has been mentioned—other than the initial explanation of our visit—while we've been with Carl.

I hold my breath, remembering that I had yet to tell Collette about my earlier conversation with Mother. I listen to Collette's side of the discussion, trying to garner information about what Mother is saying.

"Slow down, Mother. I'm not understanding you."

There's a pause as she listens again.

"Hold on a second. I still don't understand. I was never planning on being in your office yesterday. What made you think I was going to be there?"

Collette's eyes slide over to mine, her eyebrows knitting together as she listens.

"You did? When? I see. No, she didn't tell me about that." I can hear Mother's voice growing louder through the phone now.

"I'm not sure why she's not answering her phone." She looks at me again, and I dig in my purse to pull mine out. There are at least a dozen missed messages on it, all from Mother. I check the ringer. It's switched off. I show Collette as she continues talking.

"I guess the ringer was turned off. Sure, she's right here."

She starts to hand me the phone, but I put my hands up in protest, mouthing a silent "No" as she pushes it at me again, apparently running out of patience.

Reluctantly, I take the phone and put it to my ear. "Hello, Mother."

There is silence on the other end of the line.

"Hello?" I try again.

"Do you remember what I told you earlier? Did you think I was joking, Ireland?" she hisses into my ear.

I try to block out the heat rising in my body. "No, I didn't think you were, Mother."

"Then I want you to tell me right now. Where are you?"

I take a deep breath. "Hawaii, Mother. Collette and I are in Hawaii."

There is a long pause on the other end of the line. So long that I actually remove the phone from my ear to check that we haven't been disconnected.

"Mother?"

There is a distinct sigh on the other end of the line but still no words.

I wait.

"So that's where he lives? In Hawaii?"

"Yes."

"And you found him?"

"Can we talk about it when we get back? It's probably better if we do this in person."

It only takes a split second to know I've made a mistake, as a peal of laughter from the other side of the phone ricochets off my eardrum, and I pull the phone back.

"When you get back? Oh, I see. You still think you get to just waltz back in here and have a little chat with me. Like I've just been waiting around for you to come and have tea. You expect me to sit there while you tell me some grand story about your gallivanting around some tropical island, all in your quest to find your father?" The sarcasm is literally dripping from her voice. "What on God's great Earth gave you the impression I would be welcoming you home, let alone talking to the two of you again?"

My throat tightens, making it hard to respond to her question. I swallow. "Because we're your daughters."

"Ireland, seriously, I don't know why you still don't get it. I was explicit with my requests. And yet you and Collette thoughtlessly disregard them and go behind my back, doing whatever it is you darn well fancy. I'm not sure why you don't take me seriously." She pauses. "It looks like I'm going to have to spell it out for you. You and Collette are no longer welcome anywhere near me."

"Mother, you can't be serious!" I hear my voice, and I sound like a defiant teenager, even to my own ears.

"Try me."

"But we're your daughters. We didn't do this maliciously! We needed answers, answers about who our dad is. Can't you see that?"

There's another long pause on her end of the phone. I can hear a knock on the door through the phone line, and she is forced to speak to me again.

"Hold on, Ireland. I need to speak with someone for a minute." Her tone has instantly changed back to the constant professional.

There is a muffled conversation on the other end of the line, but I can't make out what is being said. I press the phone closer to my ear, trying to decipher who she's talking to.

"Ireland, Loraine is here with me," she says, her voice loud—because I had pressed the phone so close to my ear—and businesslike—because there was now another person to witness this conversation. "Since you are not easily accessible, I'm going to need the password to your computer. Loraine is looking for additional information for the taxes. Please hang up and text it to me immediately. I will pass it on to her. We will finish the rest of our conversation later," she says curtly and hangs up the phone.

I stare at the black screen in front of me. The speed at which she was able to turn the conversation has left me disoriented. It takes me a few minutes before I remember my own surroundings and the company I'm in. I quickly send off a text with the password and then hand the phone back to Collette. She takes the phone from my hand with a little too much force.

I look up and see she is staring at me, hard. "Why didn't you tell me she called?"

"Would it have made a difference? We were already here. We both knew she wasn't going be happy about it."

"That's not the point. You didn't even give me a chance to make my own decisions."

A fake laugh escapes my lips before I can think about it. "Like you let me make my own?"

"What's that supposed to mean?" Collette questions.

"Oh, come off it. You know you've been dictating my life as much as Mother has. That short straw that we never talk about. That wasn't my decision. You made that for me."

"That wasn't a decision I made for you, that was fate. You choose that straw fair and square. Besides, I didn't force you to stay there all these years. That's all on you."

Carl's head is now ping-ponging back and forth between the two of us, a worried expression on his face.

I pause to acknowledge him.

"Sorry, it's complicated," I offer.

"It sounds that way." It's more of a question than a statement. "Your mother, she didn't want you to come to find me? Why?"

"I think she's embarrassed by her decision. You know, time takes over, and then it feels like it's too late. It's one of the few mistakes she'll admit to," Collette answers, clearly enjoying diverting the conversation back to Mother and away from herself.

Carl averts his eyes and looks at the ground, searching for answers in the pavement. He crosses his arms over his chest and cocks his head to the side. "I should have been more honest with her. Then maybe all of this wouldn't have happened."

"You were honest with her." Collette reassures him.

"No, actually, I wasn't," he counters. "I didn't tell your mother I was married when we first got together. She didn't find out until after I broke up with her. I'm sure I hurt her. She must have been mad." He trails his toe against the pavement. "But I still don't agree with her never telling me about you. That is, if I am your father."

"So you're saying you led our mother on? In essence, you cheated on Judy with Mother and then dumped her to go back to Judy?" I can feel the fire from my earlier conversation being carried over onto this one.

"When you put it that way, it does sound shady. You have to remember what I said earlier—Judy and I were going through a rough patch. We were separated."

"Right, but that doesn't change the fact you led on another woman. One you just happened to get pregnant."

"I obviously never knew about the pregnancy, remember?"

"Right, sorry," I concede.

"Forgive me for saying this, but that conversation you just had with your mother, it didn't sound enjoyable."

"Conversations with Mother are rarely pleasant," I scoff.

Carl gives me a questioning look and continues, "If she was so against you coming here, why did you?"

"You don't understand," I start, knowing he has painted a version of her in his own mind, one of her that is entirely wrong.

Carl holds up his hands, stopping my protest.

"You're right, I probably don't understand. You have a lifetime of history that I don't know anything about. But if I'm honest here, I'm starting to think Kayla was right, this has all become very complicated very quickly. I'm not sure this is the right time for us."

A wave of electricity passes through my body as I stare at him with my mouth agape.

"You can't be serious," I say, feeling the blood draining from my head. "We just took the test." I point to the Band-Aid still on my arm. "You're really not willing to find out the truth before you toss us aside?

That would be like the equivalent to Mother not telling you in the first place."

"That's a little harsh, don't you think? The difference here is Cynthia took fate into her own hands. She didn't take anyone else's thoughts or feelings into consideration. She made all the decisions for us herself. It's the complete opposite for me. I have to take a whole load of people's feelings into consideration. How do you think I'm supposed to explain to my son that he now has two half-sisters virtually the same age as his mother and that now he's an uncle to two little girls who are only a few years younger than him? What I do from this point forward will affect those closest to me. I can't be selfish like your mother was." Carl's demeanor has switched to the defensive, and I'm keenly aware that I've had a lot to do with it.

"No." I surprise myself at the venom in my words. "You're wrong, you're just like her, thinking you can determine our fates." I point to Collette and me. "You might be considering your family but when has anyone considered us? Collette and me, we've been the casualties of our parents. Neither of you have acted with our interests at heart. It's just about you. How this all affects you. Well, when is anyone going to care about how it affects us?" The blood is returning to my head, but now it's boiling hot, casting a red hue across my vision. Carl is willing to turn his back on us, just like Mother always has.

"Ireland, we just met him a few days ago. Give him a break. This is all a lot to process," Collette says, trying to cool me down.

But her words only add fuel to my inferno.

"Oh, knock it off, Collette. If he really wanted to

be our father, he would be fighting for us. But instead, he's just standing there, moving to the side, afraid of rocking the boat of his perfect life." My tirade continues, as the steam starts to come off me in waves.

I turn to Carl. "If you want to know the truth, our mother has never been there for us. She never actually cared about us. I can count the number of people who were there for us on one hand, and she isn't one of them. Collette and Lenny, those are the people I've relied on in tough times, and then Lenny had to go and die, and I was left with one less person I could call family. I really thought you might be someone I could have added to my diminishing corner. Someone who would stand up for me, care about me. But it's clear now I couldn't have been more wrong about you."

There are tears in my eyes as I hurl the insults at Carl. People are staring as they try to walk around us on the sidewalk, but I don't care. I'm tired of being let down.

"That's enough, Ireland," Collette seethes at me. "You need to stop it with this 'poor me' crap. Or did you forget that there are more people than just you in this situation? It's not always about you."

I want to lunge at her, to grab her and make her take the words back. How could she imply it was always about me? Have I not just said the words *us* in every sentence? I was fighting for her too. I've spent my life catering to our mother, doing the exact opposite of thinking about myself, all so Collette could have the life she dreamt of. Taking the brunt of Mother's abuse so Collette could go off, enjoying her white picket fence.

I walk into the street and hail the first cab passing

by. Carl and Collette stand watching as I open the door to the cab.

"Wait, Ireland. We can't leave it like this," Carl pleads with me.

"It's too late. I'm going home now. It's obvious this"—I gesture to the two of them standing across the street from me—"is over. Maybe I can at least salvage my job."

"You can't be serious. You're going to go groveling back to Mother? You really think going back to being her little puppet is going to make you feel better?" Collette spits out, too worked up to stop now.

I lift one leg into the cab. "No. Nothing's going to make me feel better. Now it's about knowing where I belong, and you've made it quite clear. I don't belong here." I close the door behind me, leaving Collette and Carl staring after me.

I will myself not to look behind me as the cab pulls into traffic. I wipe the tears away that are running down my checks in steady streams. The cab driver asks where to, and I have to take several deep breaths before I can give him the name of the hotel.

When I first walked into the lobby of the Kahala I was so full of anticipation and hope. But now, looking out the window as we speed through downtown, all I see is disappointment. It is time to go home.

Chapter 17

I flip the switch, instantly illuminating the office with fluorescent lights. Tossing my handbag on the chair next to my desk, I take the seat in front of my computer. The familiarity of my surroundings is comforting. I can't even begin to calculate the number of hours I've spent behind this desk, and I can't help but wonder if I'll get the chance to clock any more hours here or if today will be my last day at The Club. Taking a deep breath, I switch on the computer and sit back, waiting for it to boot up.

I can't believe it's only been five days since I last sat in this office. The circumstances of the last few days have played tricks with my internal calendar. I let my eyes drift around the room, taking in the assortment of objects I decorated my office with. Even though it's comforting, my space seems foreign to me. Like all the trinkets from trips, my diploma, framed pictures of Collette and me, Lenny and me, one goofy picture of Molly and Maggie and me with our tongues sticking out at the camera, and the picture box of the straw were all put there by a stranger. Amongst all of these sentimental objects, there isn't a single picture of Mother and me. An absence I'd never noticed until just this moment. Searching my memories, I desperately try to grasp one of Mother and me appropriate for framing. Even the briefest of moments of us being silly or loving. The longer I sit trying to recover one, the more clear it is that I can't come up with anything, not a single interaction I would have deemed worthy of capturing in a photograph.

All my memories of Mother and me are contaminated, either by a threat, a put down, or a standard that was expected but never met.

The computer screen suddenly comes to life, lighting up the room and illuminating the sticky notes cluttered all over my keyboard, left there by various people needing attention in my absence. I pile all the notes together, with the intention of completing them later today. I place them on top of the utterly full inbox and turn my attention back to the computer, bringing up my e-mails.

I click on the mail icon and am reminded of the e-mail from Mel Evans I received before leaving for Hawaii, the subject line "Nice seeing you" still at the top of the page.

I haven't thought about Mel or Sheila since I left, which seems like a lifetime ago. So much has changed in me, yet I'm still in the same position I was the first time I came across this e-mail, only this time I don't hesitate as I click on it.

From: MelE@Evansenterprises.com
To: IrelandJ@Belletrio.com
Subject: Nice seeing you
Hello Dear,

I just wanted to take a minute and tell you how nice it was to have your presence with us during the memorial. I know it is a difficult time for all of us. It's important to Sheila and myself that we make sure you have the support you need.

We brushed on the topic lightly at the service, but I wanted to reiterate what I said earlier. If you need anything at all, we are here for you. Sheila and I want to give you support in any way you might need. On that note, I have gone over Lenny's estate and would like to have an opportunity to meet with you in person to go over his beneficiaries.

Please write back and let me know when a good time for you to meet up would be.

As always, I think of you as my family.

Much Love,

Mel Evans

Lenny's estate? I'm not exactly sure what Mel is talking about. I'm simultaneously curious and cautious. I don't want the Evans to feel an obligation toward me. I'm still mortified about the circumstances at the memorial, and I don't want what Mother said to be the sole reason for our continued contact. I'm still debating as to how to respond to Mel's e-mail when I hear, "Boy am I happy to see you."

"Hey!" I say, relieved Jenna's hospitable face is the first one to grace my office today.

"Girl, you better not let your mom see you here. She was on a tirade the whole time you were gone. If she sees you, she might just rip your head off." She continues into my office and leans against the door.

I groan. "Unfortunately, I've already had the pleasure of talking with her yesterday, when she made certain I was fully aware of the trouble I was in."

"You have no idea, Ireland." Jenna hesitates only for a beat. "I tried to cover for you for as long as I could, but when she found out you left, she completely lost her shit. I've seen her mad at you before, but this time, I don't know…" She trails off.

"Don't worry, this isn't the first time I've had to deal with her. Remember I grew up with this. I know how to handle her." I don't even believe my own words. I don't know why Jenna would.

"If you say so." Jenna looks hesitant, but then decides to change the subject. Pointing to the computer screen, she says, "What were you looking at?"

Before I can answer, the intercom on my phone buzzes. It's the caller ID I've been dreading all morning. I try to steady my nerves and push the button for speakerphone. "Hello?" I say, careful to keep my voice even.

"Don't you dare 'Hello' me. Since you've managed to get your ass into the office today, you better carry it all the way up here to my office. Now." She is seething, leaving nothing to the imagination as to how furious she is.

Jenna sticks her fingers in her ears and makes a "la-la-la" motion silently with her mouth.

I pinch my lips together, so no inadvertent giggles can escape, and turn to look at the wall, shutting Jenna out of my eye line. "I'll be right there."

Without another word the line is disconnected.

I turn back to Jenna, whose eyebrows are virtually touching her hairline, they're so high on her forehead.

"Relax, I'll be fine." I assure her.

"If you say so." She shrugs and heads out the door. "Let me know if you need anything. You know where to find me."

"Thanks, but really, there's nothing to worry about." I follow her around the desk and out into the hallway, where we separate, her to the right in the direction of the exercise studio and me to the left, through the winding maze of corridors and stairs leading to the lion's den.

****

Facing the closed door, I shut my eyes and say a silent prayer. *Please let this be over and done with quickly.* I'm hoping for a quick execution.

Taking a deep breath, I open my eyes and knock once.

"Come in," Mother barks.

I open the door and walk to the center of her office as she stares me down with her steady gaze.

I stand awkwardly, not wanting to sit down until she invites me to, which she does not. She remains silent, watching me squirm under her gaze.

It seems like hours go by before she finally speaks. "Truly, Ireland. The audacity of your actions is shocking, even to me. And I'm used to being disappointed by you. But this, well, everything else pales in comparison to this." She brings her hands up in front of her and starts counting her fingers. "Let's get it all straight. You abandoned your job, leaving everyone here scrambling to cover for you." She ticks off one finger. "You leave without getting permission and without leaving any way to get hold of you." She ticks another finger. "And finally, and most importantly, you went behind my back, fully disregarding my request regarding not searching out your father." She places her hands on her desk in front of her. "Am I missing anything?"

I don't know how to respond, so I do what comes naturally and remain silent. Anything I try to articulate now will just work against me.

"So you have nothing to say?" she presses.

"No, I do have something to say," I answer, doing my best to think quickly.

"And what would that be?"

"I'm sorry."

She laughs cruelly. "Sorry? You think 'sorry' is going to cut it?" She pauses. "It's going to take a lot more than sorry."

I take a deep breath, gathering my courage.

"I understand I made a mistake."

Her eyes narrow at me.

"I wasn't thinking straight. After the memorial, I lost my way." I continue, "I needed the chance to re-evaluate things. I was wrong to go away. I know that now. But I had to figure it out on my own. I had to have time to think about where I belong and who I belong with. And I now understand that's here, with you. If you let me, I've decided to re-dedicate myself to you and to this job. I know I can perform my duties at a higher level, now that I've had time to process everything. Please give me a chance. My loyalties are here." I indicate The Club by spreading my arms wide. "And with you." The words taste bad in my mouth, but I force myself to say them.

"Why should I believe you? You've already proven I can't trust you. Why should I change my mind now?"

"Because I've changed. I've seen with my own eyes. This is where I belong."

She stays silent but maintains eye contact with me. I can tell she's mulling over what I just said.

Still standing in the middle of the room, I do my best to not fidget while I wait for her decision.

"Now tell me, why would I keep an employee who

clearly has no regard for the way things are done around here? I am not particularly inclined to keep you on my staff." She pauses for effect. "But, and honestly I don't know why, I've decided to give you another chance. But Ireland?"

"Yes?"

"Don't think this means I've forgotten what you did. As far as I'm concerned, you are here on probation. If your loyalties truly do lie here, as you say they do, I'll expect you to prove it."

"Yes, of course. I can do that, I promise," I say, inching toward the door, ready for this embarrassment to be over.

"There's one more thing."

"Yes?"

"While you were gone, we had a request for an audit."

"An audit?" I ask, confused by the transition in subjects. "By who?"

"By the Internal Revenue Service, who else?" She flicks her hair off her shoulder. "They've been poking around for a while," she says, clearly irritated. "I couldn't delay them any longer. They needed to start while you were away. I was able to get them some information they needed from your computer with the password you gave me yesterday. However, I'm going to need you to meet with them to explain all your entries. You can do that, can't you?" she says.

The hair on the back of my neck is standing up. Mother gave them access to my computer. Without asking me first? Was she waiting for me to give my little speech before she dropped this little nugget of information in my lap? It dawns on me. She was.

"Yes, of course I can. When?" I ask, my brain already going full speed, categorizing all the work this is going to require. I need to itemize the expense account, get all the receipts in order, double-check the dates of deposits and make sure the accounts receivable and the bank accounts match up. My heart rate increasing by the minute.

"The auditor will meet you in your office in an hour," she says, the sides of her mouth turning up.

She thinks this is funny? No, she doesn't think this is funny. She's smiling because she's getting her revenge. I disobeyed her orders, and now she is paying me back, handing me over to the executioner.

"I won't be ready for them," I say.

"Well, that's a problem you're going to have to figure out. There really isn't anything I can do. We already had to reschedule once because you were off gallivanting around the country." She pauses to look at the clock. "They'll be here in an hour. I suggest you go get ready what you can."

"Did they tell you what information they'll be reviewing?" I'm grasping at straws, trying to get my thoughts in order. If I can prioritize the information, they need I just might have a chance of getting it prepared in time.

"Didn't say," she says, her eyes boring into mine. Daring me to back down from her challenge.

Baffled, I turn on my heel and head out the door.

"Ireland?"

I stop in the doorway and look over my shoulder.

"I'll be gone the rest of the day. I'll be forwarding my calls to Julia. Just thought you should know." She gives a rare smile as she twists the knife, the one sticking out of my back.

****

Back in my office and behind my computer, I shoot off a quick Hail Mary message to Jenna and then click out of e-mail, knowing I won't be getting around to sending any other messages until the end of the day, at best. I quickly bring up the books and scan the last few months. I'm busy looking over the reports when there's a knock on my door.

"Excuse me, I'm looking for Ireland Jacobson?"

I look up into fresh blue eyes, partially hidden behind thick, black-rimmed glasses. Standing at close to six foot, he takes up most of my doorway.

I stand up and extend my hand to him.

"Yes, I'm Ireland Jacobson. Please come in."

He takes two steps into my office and takes my hand in his. I'm surprised by how soft and cushy his hand is in mine. "I'm Brandon Shelton, with the Internal Revenue Service." He reaches his hand into his coat pocket and produces a card: Brandon Shelton: Internal Revenue Service. "I was told you'd be expecting me."

"Yes, please come in," I say, stepping around my desk and ushering him into what now feels like a tight space. I close the door behind him as he takes a seat in one of the guest chairs.

"As you know, I'm here to conduct an audit. The IRS sometimes gets anonymous tips, and we have an obligation to look into all situations. With your support, I'll be conducting an audit of your previous three tax years. I'll be looking for any inconsistencies in the information we have on record with what you have in your bookkeeping." He is strictly professional. There is

211

no warmth in any of his words.

I nod to let him know I'm willing to provide whatever information he might need.

"I'll keep you informed as to what I procure moving forward. I'll need access to your books, either through you or through other means."

"I'm happy to provide you with any information you need," I assure him.

"Great, let's get started, then." He pulls out a notepad, pencils, and his own laptop computer, which he boots up and places on the desk next to my own.

He picks up his chair and brings it around to the same side of the desk I'm on, scooting it closer to my own. Sitting back down, he turns to me. "Let's start with the accounts receivable for the previous three years and go from there."

I nod and pull up the information on the computer, settling in for the long haul.

****

My back is cramping from sitting for so long. We've been working on matching receipts to expenses for over five hours now. I reach my hands over my head and stretch.

Brandon glances over and gives a little nod, pushes his glasses back up his nose, and focuses back on the papers in his lap.

"So you're Cynthia Jacobson's daughter, huh?" he asks as he compares figures from his computer to what he has in his hands.

"Yes," I answer, failing to elaborate further.

"Do you have a share in this company?" he asks.

"Not a share, no. But I do have a trust fund set up. It's funded by this company," I offer, not sure if this line of questioning pertains to the audit or if it's just friendly chit-chat.

"So you have a vested interest in the success of the company, is that safe to say?"

I'm trying to figure out where this conversation is leading. Of course I have a vested interest in this company. I've worked here for seven years, and the owner is my mother.

"You could say I'm invested in the success of this company, yes. My mother is the owner, after all."

"And you say you're the only one who does the accounting for The Club?" Brandon asks.

"That's correct," I confirm.

"That's a big job. Lots to keep track of for such a prestigious company."

Is he trying to flatter me or is he fishing for something else? I'm not entirely sure.

"I've worked here for a long time. It's second nature to me now."

"Hmm, I see."

"I'm sorry, is there a problem?" I ask, running out of patience.

"Let's just say there seem to be some pretty consistent inconsistencies between the amount of income that is being recorded at the end of the year and the income you are showing on your computer."

"I'm sorry, what?" It's not that I don't understand, it's that I don't agree with what he's implying. I know my numbers, and I know I've kept track of The Club's income to the penny.

"Your past AR reports are showing that the net income for Cynthia Jacobson and in turn The Club should be in the three-point-five area. However, the past W-2s are showing an income of only two-point-four. That's close to a one-million-dollar discrepancy."

He pulls his glasses off his nose and rubs the bridge. He turns to look at me.

"That's not possible," I state because it's true. It isn't possible that there is over a million dollars not accounted for.

"It seems it is." He gestures to the screen that's up on the computer, filled with numbers and dates. Glancing at it quickly, it looks like a jumble of numbers, impossible to read or decipher, but I knew every transaction and where it belonged. There was no possible way I could have sifted one million dollars away.

He pinches his nose and squeezes his eyes shut, mumbling to himself. "This is the part of the job I hate," he says to no one in particular.

When he looks up, any kindness or familiarity that had been building between the two of us has now vanished. He replaces his glasses on the bridge of his nose and starts to gather all the materials he laid out just a few hours earlier—stacks of multi-colored sticky notes, colored pencils arranged by color in a rainbow, and two notebooks with dividing folders.

"Let's call it a day. I need to take some time, look at the figures, and get back to you." He took a copy of my data at the beginning of our work together, and now he ejects the memory stick with all the information on it. Pinching it between his two fingers, he slips it into the side pocket of his briefcase.

After sitting side by side for so many hours, it's jarring when Brandon suddenly rises from his chair and walks around to the other side of the desk.

"When will you be returning?" I ask.

"I'll touch base with you tomorrow."

"Okay, is there anything you need me to do in the meantime?" I ask, hoping for a better clue as to what he's looking at.

"Let me just go over everything, and I'll get back to you," he assures me.

"Okay, have a good night," I call as he heads out the door. He gives a small wave, closing the door behind him, leaving me alone in the office.

I realize I've been standing watching Brandon leave. I sit back down with a whoosh of air as my body sinks into the leather cushioning.

I glance at the computer screen blinking at me and notice the numbers staring back at me do look higher than I recall seeing them last. How is that even possible? I haven't looked at this data for over six months. I'm sure I didn't change anything since the beginning of the year.

A headache that was a dull presence earlier is now starting to make a grand performance in the back of my eyes. Probably from all the screen time Brandon and I just clocked.

Deciding to pick up tomorrow where I left off today, I do a backup before closing down the computer and heading out the door, down the same hallway Brandon traveled a few minutes earlier.

Chapter 18

Tossing my keys on the hall table, I shrug off the jacket I've been wearing since the drive home. Shivering from the cold that engulfs the condo, I have second thoughts about taking my coat off. Hurriedly, I push one of my Hunter boots against the heel of the other, freeing my feet from the rubber columns I long ago abandoned my sneakers for, leaving them on the floor next to the front door.

The plush rug running the length of the entranceway keeps my bare feet from freezing on the hardwood floors.

It's been ages since I considered this condo my oasis. My safe place to come home to. Now it just feels like an empty box carton. Four walls holding up a roof over my head. The solace I used to find here, coming home to Lenny after a long day, curling up on the couch with him and a glass of wine as we hashed out the day's events, that's what made the condo feel like home. I sigh and pick up the framed picture of us on the side table.

I've yet to move any of Lenny's belongings out of the condo. Except for the night when I tripped over his hiking boots, I haven't touched a single one of his things. I'm pretty sure his toothbrush is still in the bathroom, along with a razor and his aftershave. The drawer full of clothes is still untouched. His papers still lie in the bedside table, ready to be attended to, but never will be.

"I sure missed you today," I say to the picture in my hand, and I actually feel disappointed when his smiling face doesn't respond. What am I expecting? A full-on conversation with an image of a dead person?

Shaking my head at myself, I take the frame with me into the kitchen and place in on the counter. I pull out a wine glass and a bottle of Riesling and pour myself a glass. With the first sip, sweetness dances on the back of my tongue, granting me the tiniest moments of pleasure. The buzzing of my phone cuts into my contentment all too quickly.

I place the wine glass by the frame and rush to get my phone before voicemail picks up.

"Hey," I say into the mouthpiece.

"Hey," comes Jenna's voice. "Are you home?"

"Yeah, just got here. Having a glass of wine and then going to go slit my wrist in the bathroom. How was your day?"

Jenna sighs. "Do I need to come over there?"

"No, I'm fine. Still just getting used to my new normal. It's quiet. I don't know what I hate more, the stress at The Club or the quiet here."

"I know. I'm sorry. It'll get easier. The quiet, I mean. The Club is always going to be stressful, as long as you keep working for that bitch boss of yours."

"Um, you mean my mother?"

"Yup, that's the one. Come on, you know she's a bitch. You even said it yourself. You hate working for her. It's not the stress of the job that gets to you, it's the stress of her."

I close my eyes. "I suppose you're right."

"I know I'm right," she confirms. "But tell me what happened today anyway."

"You got the e-mail about the auditor, right?" I ask.

"Yup, that was the last I heard from you until now. Did everything go okay?" I can hear her tinkering with pots and pans, probably getting some kind of healthy dinner involving kale and quinoa ready.

"I think so. Well, actually, I'm not quite sure. He left rather abruptly. He said he needed to look at some of the entries on his own. I don't understand what he was referring to, but he said he'll get back to me tomorrow. It's probably nothing." I skim over it.

"Really? Hmm." She says, sounding distracted. "Well, I know you take impeccable records. Remember that time when you were reconciling and you had a difference of two cents?"

I laugh at the memory.

"Right? Most people would have let it go; I mean two cents! But not little Miss OCD here. You stayed there and missed dinner with me, just so you could have the perfect close. Two hours later and two cents different, you found the problem and had your perfect books."

"I remember. It was totally worth it!" I say.

"Or not!" Jenna retorts. "But that's my point. I'm sure whatever he's looking at will come back as nothing."

"You're probably right. I can't think of a single thing that would be out of place with my records."

"I'm sure I'm right. Now, you never told me about your trip. I'm assuming it wasn't exactly the homecoming you were hoping for, since you're back at The Club, kissing some major ass."

I'm quiet for a moment, reflecting on all that happened in Hawaii. I still haven't heard from Collette or Carl. Not that I was expecting to hear from Carl anytime soon. I made sure to screw that relationship up before I left town. But I should probably check on Collette, or at least text Greg to make sure she made it home safe.

"Oh, Jenna, I might have messed up big this time," I say, before explaining the whole horrid mess to her.

"Well, I'm not going to lie to you," Jenna says after I'm done talking. "that probably did not increase your chances of getting a birthday or Christmas present from him. But, seriously, Ireland, you need to give yourself a break. You've been through more in these last few months than most people go through in a lifetime. I'm personally surprised you haven't cracked before now."

"I don't know, Jenna, I'm just so tired. I feel like no matter what I do or what path I take it doesn't take me in a direction where I feel like I'm in control of my own life. I just really need a break from it all."

I look at my glass of wine and the bottle next to it. "In fact, I think I'll take one tonight," I say pouring myself another drink.

"That a' girl. Take a bath, get some rest. You'll feel better in the morning. Or at least hopefully you will."

"Right now, I don't want to feel anything."

"I know, but trust me, it's going to get better. I promise."

I don't know how she can make a promise like that without a crystal ball, but it's still comforting to hear at least one of us think things might turn around.

"Thanks, Jenna. I'll talk to you later."

"Okay, try and have a good night. I'll check on you tomorrow."

Soon as I click the phone off, the profound realization that Jenna is the only person I'm probably going to talk to tonight falls over me.

Picking up the bottle of wine and the picture of Lenny, I wander into the bathroom. Pulling directly from the bottle like it's a Colt .45, I manage to down half of it in one long gulp.

Feeling the lightness start in my head, I reach over and turn on the tap for the bathtub, then watch the tub fill with steaming water from my viewpoint on top of the toilet. I twist my engagement ring off and place it on the counter next to the sink. I finally start to feel some relief as the alcohol starts to take effect..

I strip off my clothes and plunge my body into the hot water, not hesitating when the scalding liquid touches my bare skin. It's only a matter of seconds before I'm as red as a lobster being cooked in a boiling pot of water.

I barely notice the scorching water as I lie listless in the tub, staring at the ceiling. I reach over and take another swig from the bottle as my internal temperature adjusts to the inferno surrounding me.

The ceiling starts to swirl, the paint twisting in with Lenny's face. I hear Mother's words echoing in my ears, *You must show me your loyalties now*, and Brandon's warning, *There's something I need to check on*. I'm having trouble focusing on one thing at a time. Every time I attempt to chase a thought down, it slips out of my grasp.

I close my eyes and feel the swaying of my body, I

can't tell if it's from the water or the alcohol that I'm swimming in, but it feels nice. Like a cradle being rocked, lulling me to sleep.

****

The cold surrounding me has permeated deep into my bones. I'm numb across the entirety of my body. I wiggle my fingers, afraid to open my eyes, and am relieved to feel the hard ceramic of the tub.

Good God, I must have passed out taking a bath! What was I doing? Trying to kill myself by drowning or, better yet, hypothermia?

What a sight that would be when…

Wait, who would find me? The realization that no one is looking for me is colder than the ice bath I'm currently sitting in.

With a jolt, I sit up, sloshing water onto the tile floor. Goosebumps cover my entire body as I frantically try to wrap a towel around myself. Once the shivering has subsided enough that I can walk, I grab my phone and make a beeline for my bed.

Still feeling woozy from the bottle of wine I single-handedly downed earlier, I don't bother getting dressed and instead crawl under the covers, wrapping them tightly around me.

I wait for my body's thermostat to return to normal and am relieved when I start to feel the sensation of the comforter against my skin.

I long for Lenny's body to snuggle up against. I used to use him as my own personal space heater, sticking my feet between his legs to get them warm on cold nights. It strikes me that what I've really missed is the intimacy of our lives, over the act of actually being intimate. Not that being intimate was ever that bad. My mind flashes back to a few nights before the crash.

I had been making dinner in the kitchen when Lenny came in from the study. Our song was playing on the radio—"Home" by Michael Bublé. He had come into the kitchen and wrapped his arms around my waist from behind, nuzzling my neck and whispering, "I love this song." He started moving side to side, swaying to the music, listening to Michael crooning about how he just wanted to come back home. "You're my home now," Lenny had said as I felt his affection for me literally growing on my backside. A slow smile crept over my lips as I turned to him. He was my home now too. He leaned down and kissed me, the kind of kiss that left me breathless. Moving his hands from around my waist, he lifted me up and placed me on the kitchen counter, where I wrapped my legs around his torso.

It was the kind of lovemaking meant for the movies. Dishes clattered to the floor. Food was forgotten on the stove. That night we explored what it would mean to be each other's forever and what our home really meant.

When he left a few days later, I never expected our forever would be gone in the blink of an eye.

I snuggle deeper into the covers, reliving that night in my head. If I try hard enough, I can pretend the warmth now surrounding me is coming from Lenny. I close my eyes again and drift back to sleep.

****

Who in the world has decided to jackhammer on a Saturday morning? And at what time? It has to be too early for construction to start. I reach my hand out of the covers and realize that it's not a jackhammer at all but, rather, my phone ringing, causing vibration in every nerve ending of my brain to fire simultaneously.

I glance at the clock on the nightstand: 8:30 a.m. Okay, so it's not that early. Still, I'm not expected anywhere on a Saturday, and being woken up a second time within a matter of hours is not encouraging.

"Hello?" I croak into the receiver, already abandoning the idea of getting any more sleep.

"Ms. Jacobson?"

"Yes, this is Ireland."

"Oh, yes. Ireland, this is Brandon, from yesterday?"

"Yes, Brandon. Good morning. How can I help you?"

"I'm sorry to bother you so early."

"Not a bother at all," I lie.

"It's just that I was reviewing the accounts this morning—"

"You work on a Saturday?"

"I work all the time."

"I see."

"Like I was saying, I was reviewing the accounts, and I can now confirm what my suspicions were when we were in your office yesterday. Ms. Jacobson, I'm calling to inform you I have detected your attempts at covering up the obvious tax evasion being conducted at The Club. I have spoken with my supervisor, and—"

"Already? All this before nine a.m.?" I interrupt.

"Yes, contrary to popular belief, the IRS is quite efficient when conducting an audit."

"So it appears."

"Like I was saying, I have reviewed the data from your computer, and it shows that you switched the dates on the income entries so that it wasn't reflected on the accounts receivable until after the taxes were completed, and then you went back in and added it after. This is blatant tax evasion for two years of income reporting. I've spoken with my supervisor," he continues, "and we are requesting a meeting to go over the charges that will be brought against you by the United States Government. You may have your lawyer present at the time of the meeting."

All of a sudden, I'm wide awake. "The what? What kind of charges?"

"As you may or may not be aware, any person who willfully attempts to evade or defeat any taxes shall, in addition to any other penalties by law, be guilty of a felony, be fined no more than $100,000 or face imprisonment for no more than five years, or both." He rattles off, as if he's reading off a script.

"You can't be serious!"

"I'm afraid I'm completely serious. We will expect you in our offices on Monday at ten a.m. Can I confirm this with you now?"

"Yes, yes. I'll be there." I say, barely understanding the words coming out of my own mouth.

"Good day, then, Ms. Jacobson."

"No, this is definitely not a good day," I say, but the line has already gone dead.

I'm still curled up in the blankets from the bed, but my whole body is starting to tremble as words bounce around in my head.

Imprisonment.

Felony.

Fines of $100,000!

This can't be happening. There is no way my records show any sort of tax cover-up.

All of a sudden, I know what I have to do. I throw the covers off and hastily get dressed, grabbing my phone and keys as I rush out the door, not bothering to turn off the lights in the condo as I leave.

****

I pull up to The Club with a renewed calm. All I have to do is access my computer and the accounts, and I can prove that there is no cover-up. Easy. And it will be easy to show because there isn't one.

I walk into The Club and past the receptionist, catching a glimpse of myself in the mirror. Maybe I should have taken a few extra minutes getting ready. My hair is pulled back in a sloppy ponytail, and the part of my eyes that is normally white has morphed into a road map of red lines.

The receptionist gives me a tiny nod to acknowledge my existence and then moves on to check in the next guest.

The Club is quiet at this hour, so I don't have to hide my face from too many members as I make my way through the hallway to my office.

As I approach my office door, I dig into my coat pocket to produce my keys, but when I try to put my key into the lock on my door, there is obviously something wrong. I check the keychain to make sure I'm using the right key. Sure enough, it's the same key I've been using for over seven years now.

I try again, this time making sure to line up the key slowly. I try giving it a little jiggle, but still no luck.

"A guy was changing the locks this morning." Comes the voice of one of the other employees from human resources. I can't remember her name, so I just smile back.

"Oh, that's right," I lie quickly. "I was supposed to stop by and get the keys later." As I put the puzzle pieces together in my head, I try to work out a plan on the spot. "You don't have the new ones, do you? I could just get them from you now, if you do?"

"I'm sorry, but no. The keys were given directly to Ms. Jacobson."

I nod my head, now in clear understanding. Mother changed the locks on my office door. She was keeping me from my records. This is what she meant when she said I was to prove my loyalty to her and The Club. She set me up, and now I am supposed to take the fall. To go down willingly.

The heat building in my cheeks as I stand riveted to my spot rivals the temperature of last night's bath. "That's right. I'll just go pop in on Mother and collect them myself." I turn in the direction of the elevators.

"She's not in today. I believe she's working from home," the Human Resources girl says.

"Oh, yes! I just don't know where my head is today. I knew that. Thanks. Okay, see you later." I make a hasty exit, retracing my way back out of The Club. With only one destination in mind.

The heat that has started in my checks is now making its way through my entire body. A rage I didn't think I could possess is beginning to grow within me.

If Mother really thinks I am going to take the blame for her financial crisis, she has another thing coming.

Chapter 19

Knowing there would be at least one lock Mother wouldn't have thought to change, I don't bother knocking as I barge into the house I've known since my childhood. Memories of Collette and me flood my head as my rain boots sink into the modern abstract design silk rug lining the entrance hall. I shake my head and do my best to push back all thoughts of my sister. This is no time for distractions. If I let myself go down memory lane, I'll lose all track of my original purpose. I kick my boots off, my previous etiquette training prevailing, preventing me from dragging mud through the entire house, even though that is precisely what I feel like doing. Dropping my bag on the round marble entry table, currently housing a magnificent display of white orchids and greenery in a Baccarat vase, I head left, down the hallway, to the one place I know I'll find Mother, her office.

She calmly looks up from her computer as I enter the room, and I know without a doubt she's been expecting me. She smiles at me as I hover in the entrance, and with a blank stare, takes a sip from her floral ceramic teacup, two Earl Grey tags dangling off the side. Without so much as a word, she swivels her high-backed, white captain's chair to the side, leaving me to stare at her back as she takes in the view of Lake Washington from the bank of west-facing windows.

Left with nothing to spew my negative energy at, I look around the expansive office, done in all white, of course. Unable to find anything to focus on, I silently begin to count the ticks of the Tiffany clock, the one hanging prestigiously on her wall. The silent treatment is a discipline tactic of Mother's I am very familiar with. It is always done with the same purpose, for me to know she is the one who holds the power.

Not willing or able to hold my own in this particular silent match, I voluntarily lose the battle. "How could you? I don't understand." My head has been swirling with contempt and unanswered questions since I left The Club, so much so that I am no longer able to idly stand by.

"Ireland." Mother takes her time rotating her chair back around so she's facing me. "You seem to be missing the big picture here." She sighs like it's so obvious. "The question isn't 'How could I?' Rather, you should be asking, 'How couldn't I?' You see, I own a multi-million-dollar company. I employ hundreds of staff, who have to go home with their meager salaries and provide for their own middle-class families. I am the brand of the company. I run the company. I am the company." She flicks her hand in the air like she's directing an orchestra. "Without me, there wouldn't be anyone to keep this ship running. Hundreds of people would lose their jobs. Employees would lose their income. Families would have a hard time putting food on the table. If The Club is in danger of financial ruin or collapse, other people will be affected. I can't let that happen, and neither can you."

My natural instinct is to reply with, *Of course I can't let that happen.* I've known most of these employees my whole life. Like Josie, the head chef in the dining room. Collette and I would sneak into the kitchen when we were kids, and she would slip us PB&J sandwiches, sending us back out with a wink.

Or Lindsey, the locker room attendant, who for the last eleven years has kept me up to date on her grandchild, Mia, sharing photos of her from her birth to her latest birthday.

Mother was right to assume I wouldn't let harm come to The Club's employees, but there is one part she has miscalculated. And that is my inability to take the blame for something I didn't do. Gathering my courage, I push down the natural reply and instead respond with, "I didn't cause this. You did."

She leans back in her chair, staring at the lofted ceiling, rocking her head back and forth like she was replaying a tennis match in her head. "You still don't seem to understand. You see, The Club is my business. I worked my entire adult life to build it to what it is now. Every marble tile, the exact temperature of the exercise studios, the number of wait staff on hand in the dining room depending on the time of day, the scent of the oil in the massage rooms. All of it is me, my decisions, my expertise. If I need to take a trip on the company plane, that's mine. If I need to write off expenses for trips, that is my choice. If I need to have some of my personal accounts go through the office, that is my prerogative." She clicks her crimson-colored nails together, making a ticking sound matching the clock on the wall.

"Actually, that's not what the IRS says," I challenge. "and you know that is not all that I'm talking about. You broke into my computer. You changed my data." I pause.

"First off, I can't break into something that I own. Second off, I really have no idea what you're talking about." Mother narrows her eyes at me.

The sound of her voice starts a cold shiver in my spine that quickly spreads through my entire body, reaching the top of my head in seconds. "You did this on purpose."

"Like I said, I really have no idea what you're talking about." She steeples her fingers under her chin, resting her elbows on her desk as she stares at me. "You are the only one who does the accounting in the office. When Brandon told me there was a need to investigate The Club for suspicion of purposeful wrongdoing, you can only imagine how shocked I was." She mimes sincerity.

"How long have you known about this?" I seethe through clenched teeth.

"Well, darling, if you had been paying any attention whatsoever, you would have noticed I've been speaking of an audit for days now and that I was in need of your accounting information. It's not my fault that you chose to not listen to what I was saying and go gallivanting all over the Pacific Ocean when you should have been here doing your job."

"You did not mention any audit. I was paying attention. If you had told me what was going on, I might have made a different decision."

She presses her lips together. "Hmm, well, when you don't give me any notice about leaving, I don't feel it's my obligation to provide you with any more consideration than what you've shown me."

"I'm not going to go down for this."

"I'm sure you'll figure it out," she says, seemingly unconcerned. She is dismissing me like she would any other employee she had just explained a job to. "Go and carry out your duties now" is what she meant.

"I will figure it out."

I'm met with a sneer. "Yes, we'll see how that goes."

Not able to look at her another second longer, I turn and leave without another word. She doesn't stop me as I go, and I can hear the chair swivel back to the window as I trace my own steps back to the entrance.

In the foyer I pull my boots back on, and just for good measure, walk up and down the silk rug, digging in my heels and leaving muddy footprints tracking after me. Once outside the front door, I grit my teeth and let out a low, "Grrrrr," a sound slightly akin to a wild animal, which truth be told is how I feel right now. I trudge up the steep forty-five-degree-angle driveway and stop to catch my breath at the top.

I open the door to the Rover and jump inside. Turning on the heater full blast, I mentally will the air to get warmer faster. The chill that was running through my body earlier intensifies as I watch a lone snowflake drift onto the windshield of the car.

This is usually the exact moment when I would pick up the phone and dial Collette, the desire to contact her so deeply ingrained in me that I don't even hesitate as I reach for the phone. But as I hold it in my hand, looking at it, I stop and make myself put it back down. I haven't heard from her since the day I left her on the sidewalk with Carl. Not once has she contacted me to check and see if I am okay, or if there is some way we can resolve things. Just like in the past, she has brushed me aside and gone about her own life.

I put the SUV into drive and merge onto Mercer Way, forcing my thoughts back to what just happened at Mother's. How was I going to get out of this? If only I could get into my office at The Club, I could access my computer and figure out what she changed.

I reach again for my discarded phone, careful to keep my eyes on the road, and hit the speed dial for Jenna.

"Hello, you've reached Jenna. Leave a message and I'll get back to you. Namaste."

"Jenna, call me when you get this. I need a favor. I'll explain when you call back."

I throw my phone onto the passenger seat and grip my steering wheel. The streets are starting to get slippery with the buildup of new snow. On automatic pilot, I pull onto Main Street, headed for home, but at the last minute, the image of my empty condo passes through my mind, forcing me to take a right and head in the direction of the Bellevue Square mall. It's the best alternative I can come up with at the spur of the moment, and the idea of being lost in a sea of people oblivious to my troubles feels like the perfect solution for where I want to be right now.

****

The glass wall separating Woods Coffee from the rest of the shopping plaza provides an ideal sense of privacy. Like being back on the beaches of Oahu, watching people though reflective glasses, it gives me the sense of being camouflaged while being completely out in the open.

I watch as a mother calls out to her two children to slow down in their haste to get to the arcade, and I sympathize with her battle of trying to control something which, in reality, she actually has no control over. My eyes leave the mother and follow in the opposite direction as a couple stride by in front of the window, hand in hand, oblivious to myself or any of the chaos surrounding them. I envy their ability to block out the rest of the world, to merely concentrate on each other and the pure pleasure of being together. I remember when Lenny and I used to walk around like that, so totally engrossed with each other that we assumed time was built for our enjoyment only.

My envy slowly manifests into jealousy as I mentally count backward, trying to place how long ago it was that I was able to actually enjoy time like that.

More and more, it feels like time is speeding up, not willing to slow down, taunting and challenging me to catch my breath or find my bearings.

I am due in a meeting with the IRS in less than forty-eight hours, and I am still clueless as to what my plan is going to be. Mother obviously had time to concoct this little plot of hers, and now I am at a loss as to how to make my way out of this maze, with such little time left.

I sigh out loud and let my eyes slide over to my phone, face up on the table between my hands, the black screen silently mocking me for the last hour. As soon as I ordered my coffee and sat down, I placed it on the table, thinking there has to be someone out there I could call, someone who will know what to do. But the longer I sit sipping my coffee, the more my attention is drawn to the fact I have yet to receive a single phone call or text from anyone. How did I manage to find myself in this position? Wasn't it just a few short months ago I was surrounded by all the people who were closest to me? Lenny, Collette, Jenna, all the other people I could count on. And now? Just a blank phone screen.

The notion that I should have simply stayed in the bathtub last night keeps floating into my head. Would it really make such a difference if I wasn't here? Who would notice? Who would care? Maybe I should just take the blame for the tax evasion. Being locked away for a few years couldn't possibly be any lonelier than how I am feeling right now. I'm sure they would put me in a minimum-security prison. I've heard the accommodations aren't even that bad. I mean, if Martha Stewart and that one Housewife of somewhere could handle it, why can't I?

Because I didn't do what they say I did, is my immediate thought. I didn't do it, damn it, so why should I have to take the blame for it? I slam my fist down on the table, surprising myself and a few patrons at the table next to mine. "Sorry," I offer quickly, which thankfully seems to appease them.

A new resolve starts low in my chest, building like the slow simmer of a campfire ready to turn into a blazing wildfire. This is not my fault. I should not have to take the blame.

I feel like I'm suffering from a severe case of bipolar disorder as the reality of my situation descends on me once more. I don't have anyone to help me. Who can I call to get out of this situation? I don't have the first clue how to defend myself in a meeting with the IRS.

I rub my temples, begging my mind to find the solution. I do my best to recollect the last twenty-four hours, recalling the conversation with Brandon this morning. There is something in what he said, but I'm having a hard time grasping what it is my memory is trying to tell me.

"You can have your lawyer present at the time of the meeting" were his words. And then it hits me. I know exactly who it is I have to call.

Chapter 20

I press the phone to my ear, silently counting along with the rings. By the third one I'm contemplating hanging up, but before I get the chance to, I'm met with, "Ireland? Oh, my God, how are you? I haven't heard from you since the memorial. Mom and Dad were starting to get worried. I was too, to tell the truth. I've missed you. I'm so glad you called." She must have read the caller ID before answering, because she doesn't stop for a single breath between sentences.

I let out a sigh of relief that she isn't angry with me. I've thought about contacting her so many times, but every time I've gone to pick up the phone, it was only to put it down again, unable to actually dial the numbers. "Oh, Violet, I've missed you too. I'm so sorry I didn't call earlier. I just…" I let my voice trail off, unable to explain myself.

"Hey," she says, saving me from having to elaborate, "me too." Her solemn tone matches my own. "But I'm so happy that you did call. It's been hard, you know, after Lenny was gone, and so suddenly, well, it's just been so lonely. I've missed having someone to talk to." Her frankness is refreshing, and I wonder why it's so hard for me to reciprocate.

That old saying, "Misery loves company," flashes through my head. I should have known Violet was just as miserable as I was. But I have been so trapped in my own sorrow, it was impossible for me to see through the fog around me. If I'd been able to, I would have noticed how similar Violet and I are, lonely and feeling lost. I'm saddened at the thought of so much wasted time. We could have helped one another get through this tragedy together. But certainly, it isn't too late, is it? Could now be our chance? I just need to learn how to rely on someone, to trust them and let them help me as much as I can help them.

"I know, I'm so sorry, Violet. I guess I didn't think about how everyone else was feeling. I was trapped in my own darkness, and to be truthful, I still find myself in that space. I'm not sure when that's going to change."

"Believe me, I'm there too. I don't know about you, but for me the nights are the worst."

"Oh, God, yes, the nights. I hate them," I confirm, again slightly shocked by how her way of dealing is so similar to mine.

I stare out the window of the coffee shop, wondering how I could have missed the undeniable fact that we are trapped in the same never-ending agony, that we could have relied on each other or, at the very least, softened the loneliness. I feel like such an idiot. I should have been better to Violet, to Lenny's whole family. Collette was right. I've been stuck, only thinking about myself.

"How are your parents? I feel so bad about not calling or reaching out," I say, suddenly remembering the e-mail Mel sent me earlier.

"Honestly, Mom's having a rough time of it. She hasn't eaten much, and I feel like she's starting to lose too much weight. I go over every night and bring them take-out or a casserole, but the next day I come back, and it's barely touched. I don't think Dad is eating much either, but you know Dad, always putting on the brave face. He has this absurd notion that he needs to be this pillar of strength for our family. I don't think I've seen him cry once. Honestly, I find it more unnerving. It's not natural."

"I can't imagine what it must be like for them," I say, searching and failing to come up with a better response.

"They would love to see you. It might help them to have you stop by sometime. You know, if you think it wouldn't be too hard on you."

"No, it wouldn't be too hard, I can do that," I say, knowing full well there are many demons I will have to fight in order to walk into that house again, the one filled with so many memories of Lenny. But also understanding it would be a step forward, one that would benefit not just me but the Evans as well.

"You know, Mom and Dad love you like a daughter. They were so excited to have you joining our family. I think they would do anything for you, even still."

"I appreciate that. I love them too. I guess I just assumed with Lenny gone... I don't know—"

"That you wouldn't have a place in the family anymore?" she finishes for me.

"Something like that," I allow.

"Ireland, whether you choose to realize it or not, you will be bonded to our family forever. You're the closest thing to Lenny that we still have. If you need anything, we will be there for you."

I take a deep breath, realizing this is the cue I need.

"Well, that's actually part of the reason I'm calling."

"Oh?" She sounds surprised, and I hope I'm not tainting our moment with what I'm about to ask of her.

"I have a problem you might be able to help me with. It's a legal problem." I press forward.

"What kind of legal problem?"

"I think my mother might be framing me for tax evasion."

I'm met with silence on the other line. There is no screeching *What?* or *I don't believe it!* like I might get from Jenna or Collette. Afraid we've been disconnected, I ask, "Hello?"

"Where are you? I can come to meet you now." I hear shuffling of papers in the background, and I realize she must be at her office.

"I'm at Woods Coffee in Bellevue Square."

"I'm just down the street. Don't move. I'll be there in five minutes."

****

Getting to the cafe in record time, Violet strides through the door with an air of determination, the kind that is akin to all lawyers. Her hair is pulled back into a tidy bun, and her pantsuit doesn't have a single crease in it—which I find fascinating, given that it's midday and she's been wearing it for at least four hours now. Arriving with only a handbag thrown over her elbow, and no briefcase, I wonder at how hastily she must have left her office.

When I know she's spotted me, I wave at her from across the cafe.

"Ireland!" she exclaims once she's in front of me.

I stand, and she immediately envelops me in a hug,

her head only reaching to my shoulder, but her arms are tight around my waist. We probably stay this way for just a few seconds, but her embrace is so inviting that I get lost in the timing of it. Afraid I've committed some kind of social error by holding on too long, I let my arms become limp until Violet pulls away, cocking her thumb in the direction of the barista, and says, "There's a raspberry scone with my name on it. I'll be right back."

Feeling slightly awkward from our sudden separation, I reposition myself in my seat and wait as Violet strides to the counter to order herself a scone and a Cedar Americano.

Returning with her pastry and coffee, she places them on the table next to mine and claims the seat opposite me.

I observe our drinks, placed next to each other, while she takes a minute to stow away her wallet and settle her belongings. Staring at her Americano, I decide that if I were one of her clients, looking for representation, my faith in her courtroom skills would be significantly increased simply by her drink order. Like Violet herself, the coffee she has ordered has authority. Compared to mine, in which even though halfway gone I can still make out the leaf design running through the foam, it shows she obviously has no time or need for nonessential designs or dressings.

Once settled, she takes a big swig of the steaming liquid and sets the cup back on the table.

I watch as her throat bobs up and down with her swallow of coffee before she starts talking. "So what's going on with your mother?"

"Oh, Violet. It's all so confusing, and now it's such

Violet is quiet for a minute, seeming to digest the information I just unloaded onto her. Finally, she says, "I'm going to need the contact information for Special Agent Shelton, and I want you to stop talking to him. And to your mother, for that matter, at least about this case. From now on, all questions are filtered through me, got that?" she directs with authority.

I nod.

"I assume you back up your work?"

I nod again.

"I'm going to need all those backups, starting from three years ago. I can go through them and try to see when the changes were made."

"That's the problem. Mother changed the locks to my office. It seems I am officially no longer welcome."

"This just keeps getting better, doesn't it?" She pauses and takes a deep breath. "Is there any way you can get access to your computer? Without it, we don't have much to go on."

"I'm working on it." I don't bother telling her Jenna is my only chance of gaining access to my office. Nor do I tell her that Jenna hasn't bothered to call me back yet.

"Work hard. We need physical evidence."

I nod my head in understanding.

"Look, I need you to prepare yourself. The IRS likes to use high profile cases like this one as an example of what can happen if you cheat on your taxes. I'm guessing they are planning on using The Club as one of those cases. If they decide to go to trial, we are looking at it being tried as a criminal tax crime. If what you're telling me is correct, you are going to have to defend yourself as well as explain the setup. That's not just tax evasion, that's obstruction of justice."

I look at Violet. "You're saying I would have to defend myself and…" I can't bring myself to finish the sentence.

"That's right, you'd have to defend yourself and turn in your mother."

"Can't I just defend myself, show my innocence?"

Violet closes her eyes for a second, takes a deep breath and then opens them again. "Look, I get that it's hard for you to stand up to your mom. But Ireland, she is framing you for her wrongdoings. She is willing to send her own daughter to jail! Besides, this is her company. She is ultimately responsible for the accounts and any negligence associated with it. However, if they see you as an accomplice to her, she could still pull you down with her. We need to clear your name completely, and we need to do it quickly."

I blow out a long breath through the side of my mouth. "All right, what do we do now?"

"You go home, focus on finding me any hard evidence that proves it wasn't you who changed that data. I'll call Brandon and see if I can set up a mediation with the prosecutor. That's where we sit down and explain our case to him before he takes it all the way to the courts. Honestly, the odds of being convicted once prosecuted are high, and the odds of going to jail are high too. The Department of Justice, Tax Division, requires their attorneys to request jail time in all tax cases. Seventy-five percent of those cases get jail time."

I can feel the blood drain from my face. I know she is trying to drive her point home, but all she is managing to do is scare me into submission. I remain motionless as I once again picture my life in jail.

"Ireland. Now. I want you to go now!"

Violet's words pull me out of my brooding, and I uncurl my hand from around my coffee cup and smack it down on the cold, flat surface of the table. "Yes, I have to go now." I grab my handbag off the back of my chair and dig through the side pocket until I find my cell. Swiping my finger to the right, I bring the screen to life. A few quick touches and I hear Violet's phone ping.

"I just sent you the contact info for Brandon Shelton. Let me know what he says."

Violet picks up her phone and touches the screen. "I'm calling him now," she says and puts the receiver to her ear. "Meet me back at my office tomorrow at nine. I'll let you know what I find out."

I push out of the booth with a renewed sense of determination. I have work to do. It is time to go do it.

****

"Is there any way you can get the data? Is it backed up somewhere else?" Violet picks up a ceramic mug boasting Seattle University School of Law on the front, and takes a small sip. The aroma of her freshly brewed coffee takes up the entirety of the small room. "Are you sure I can't get you some?" Violet asks, indicating her cup.

I'm sitting at one of the mahogany wood conference tables in Violet's law office. Having arrived promptly at nine, Violet is wasting no time getting to work. I sit, as Violet recounts our plan, in a tall black leather chair, nervously crossing my left leg over my right and then switching to right over left, the sticky leather peeling off the backs of my legs each time I cross and uncross my legs.

"No, thank you, I'm fine." The thought of coffee on an empty stomach has me nauseous just thinking about it. "No, we have two backups. One is on the hard drive in my office, and the other is at an off-site location somewhere in Missouri. We do an online backup once a month. Those can only be accessed by Mother with a password. I wouldn't even know where to start to get access to those."

It is less than twenty-four hours since I left Violet at Wood's Coffee and went home determined to work on getting a defense ready. But when I got to my condo, all I was able to do was sit at the counter with a notepad and a pen. I had drawn a line down the middle of the page, but when I couldn't decide what to write at the top of the page, I scribbled out the line. I am due at the meeting with Brandon and his supervisors in less than twenty-four hours, and I am no closer to having something figured out than I was yesterday.

I know of only one way I can get access to the hard drive, but Jenna has yet to call me back from yesterday. It's unlike her to not respond to me right away, and I am starting to wonder if something is wrong. Is Jenna another person in the long procession of people with whom I haven't been able to see beyond my own problems? The possibility that I have been a sub-standard friend to her is crushing. Desperate to make amends for my insensitivities, I had left her one more message before walking into Violet's office.

"I spoke with Brandon before you got here. He refused to change the time of the meeting tomorrow. He said that if you don't show up, it will be seen as an admittance of guilt. So we really need to get our story straight. We have to figure out how to prove you were not involved in this. If we can clear your name and give him proof that you weren't part of the tax evasion, they will clear your name from the case and focus on Cynthia. Which is what we want them to do."

"I understand, but how are we going to prove that it was Mother who changed the entries, without the backup?"

"Brandon sent over the accountants' copy they've been working off of. Maybe we can comb the entries date by date to look for any discrepancies."

"That's going to be like looking for a needle in a haystack. I don't even know which entries were changed." I take a deep breath. This is going to be a long haul.

"I know, but right now this is all we have. Unless you have any other ideas."

"No." I hang my head in defeat. Undoubtedly, Violet is doing her best to come up with something, but there isn't much we can do.

Violet stands from the table and pops her head out the door. Within seconds a paralegal materializes out of nowhere.

"I'm going to need two laptops," Violet states.

The girl nods silently, turns on her heel, and walks purposefully in the direction of Violet's office.

A minute later she's back with two laptops.

Violet places a computer in front of me and then takes one for herself. "Okay, let's get started."

Chapter 21

I want to bang my head against the wooden table, we have been scouring computer entries for the last four hours and have yet to come up with a single clue as to what was changed. The problem is, I don't know what numbers have been changed without having the original to compare it to. As it stands, they're just a bunch of numbers and dates.

"This isn't working." I rub my sore back, which is getting sorer by the minute from sitting so long at Violet's conference table.

Violet leans back from her own screen, slumping into the chair, and rubs her face. "I know, but we have to find something," she says through her hands. "If this case boils down to your word against your mother's, I'm afraid you're not going to have a leg to stand on."

I let out a long breath. This is ridiculous. We could stay here all day and all night, and I still wouldn't know what to look for. Unless Mother marked the changes with a yellow highlighter, this is going to continue going nowhere.

"Maybe we need to find another way to defend me?" I offer hesitantly, not wanting to offend Violet, but it is becoming abundantly clear her defense strategy is shot through with holes.

"It's looking more and more like you're right. Let's think this through for a minute." Violet falls silent and stares up into the left corner of the conference room. Her immediate silence alters the mood in the room, but I don't interrupt her. I'm intrigued by her unusual brainstorming process.

I watch as she slowly starts to mumble out loud to herself. She has managed to completely shut me out of her consciousness, ignoring the fact that I'm even in the room, let alone sitting right next to her. It's clear she is fully engrossed in what's happening inside her head, I just hope whatever that is happens to be a stroke of brilliance because that is precisely what we need right now.

My phone vibrates, breaking Violet's trance.

Apologizing, I reach into my bag and pull my phone out, checking the caller ID.

Jenna!

Yes! She is finally calling me back.

"Jenna." I offer to Violet, holding up the screen to her, like a kid offering their friend a new toy.

"Well, answer it!" she says impatiently.

I swipe my finger across the phone. "Jenna, I'm so happy you called me back, you have no idea!"

"Wow, you certainly know how to make a girl feel loved. I'm happy to be talking to you too. What's up?"

And then I remember Collette's words and the fact that Jenna hasn't called me back for over a day. "Are you okay? I mean, not just okay, but is there anything wrong? You usually call me back right away, and this time, well, you didn't." I hope I'm coming off as concerned rather than a needy friend who wants to know what and where she was every minute of the day.

"Oh, no, I'm fine. I didn't mean to worry you. I've just been busy these last few days—classes, family in town, and all that. But the message you left sounded like you weren't so fine. What's going on?"

Relieved there is nothing serious happening in Jenna's life, I feel free to reveal the details. "I need your help."

Violet walks to the other side of the room, and I assume she is trying to give me some privacy while I'm on the phone with Jenna.

"Sure, anything for you. What do you need?"

"I need you to help me break into my office at The Club," I say, now that Violet is out of earshot.

"Break in? What are you talking about? Did you lose your key or something?"

"I wish. No, Mother changed the locks on the door to my office. It seems I've been evicted."

Jenna inadvertently laughs on the other end of the line. "Wait, what? Why?"

I give her a quick rundown of what's been happening in the last twenty-four hours. "So that's why I need your help to get into my office. Do you think you can score a pair of keys from Human Resources? Maybe tell them you left something in my office, something that can't wait until later to get?"

"Ireland, I can't believe your mother could do something like this! I knew she was devoted to The Club, but this totally blows my mind!"

"You have no idea. My mind has been blown twice over."

"I can only imagine," Jenna sympathizes with me. "I'm at The Club now. Give me a few minutes, and I'll call you back."

I hang up the phone, and it's not even five minutes of silence in the conference room before her name is lighting up the caller ID again.

"Ireland, I got them!" she enthuses into the phone.

"Really? How?"

"I talked Brandy into giving them to me. Told her I forgot my yoga mat in your office and needed to get it back. She totally fell for it."

"Oh, my God, Jenna, you're a superstar. Really, I don't know how to repay you."

"Don't worry about it, but if I were you, I'd get down here. I'm going to have to get these keys back to her in an hour. I think she might start poking around if I'm gone with them for too long."

"Right. I'm on my way now." I'm gathering my coat and bag, waving goodbye to Violet as I speak. "I'll meet you in ten minutes."

Violet mouths, "Go," as I scuffle out the door.

"Wait—" I turn in the hallway to see Violet running toward me. "You'll need this." She presses a memory stick into my palm. "Download the backups onto this. We can review them back here at my office."

I take the memory stick from her and hurry out the door to the Range Rover parked across the street, now covered with a dusting of new snow.

****

I nod at the receptionist as I walk unhurriedly through the main entrance of The Club, deliberately not entering through the back Cast Member entrance, where the security cameras are on twenty-four hours a day with a direct feed to Mother's assistant's desk.

Instead of heading directly down the back hall to my office, I swerve and enter the women's changing salon. Compared to the stark whiteness of The Club's reception sanctuary, the women's salon is bathed in varying shades and textures of mauve and lavender, leather and velvet. Chrome and crystal fixtures are present at every turn, and if this isn't enough to deliver The Club members into instant nirvana, the lavender scent pumped in from the central air system is sure to send them there.

I walk through the central salon, where on my right, behind a curtain of glass, is a carousel of mannequins modeling the season's most current fit wear by Sweaty Betty, Lululemon, and Ola, all available for immediate purchase from Emma, The Club's fashion concierge. I throw a quick wave to Emma, who is busy changing one of the mannequins behind the glass, plaster what I hope is a believable smile on my face, and continue walking past the blow-dry bar, a bank of seven mirrors flanked by vanity lights and lavender partition curtains, each station complete with the newest Dyson blow dryer, curling irons, and every possible hair accessory a woman could want.

"Ireland!" I jump and turn at the sound of Jenna's voice calling my name.

"I'm here," I say as I approach where she stands by the lockers, passing a shelf lined with water lilies floating in crystal bowls.

Once we are within arm's reach of each other, she immediately envelops me in a hug. "Oh, my God, Ireland, are you okay?"

"Um, I'm not entirely sure yet," I answer, hoping the outcome of this meeting will make me surer.

"Here." She presses her hand to mine, palm to palm, like we're exchanging something more illicit than just a set of keys. "Let's go."

I take the keys from her, and we both silently leave the women's salon from the back, smiling at the clientele as we go.

Once we are in the hallway of my office, I pause in front of the door.

Jenna nods to it, silent but encouraging.

A sense of relief floods through me when the door actually opens. Until this very second, my mind was whirling with irrational fears, like Mother might have known what I was up to and changed the locks again or given Brandy the wrong keys.

Once in my office, Jenna keeps post at the door, acting as a lookout, as I get to work quickly, starting up the computer and bringing up the accounts. As the accounts download onto the memory stick Violet gave me, I look around. The office seems to be in the exact same condition as when I left it just hours before, the only change being the locks on the door.

I say a silent prayer that Violet and I will be able to find the discrepancies later in her office. I glance at the clock on the side wall and take a mental tally of the hours remaining before I'm due in the meeting. Only fourteen hours until my fate is determined. Calling it close might be a cliché, but it's also an understatement.

As soon as the backup finishes, I close down the computer, careful to leave everything as it was before Jenna and I walked in just a few minutes earlier.

I turn off the lights and hurriedly lock the door behind me. I press the keys into Jenna's hand. "Thank you so much. I don't know how I can repay you."

"Are you kidding me? Ireland, you don't have to repay me. I just want to see you happy again. You deserve a happy ending. You can't go to jail for something you didn't do. I'll do anything to make sure that doesn't happen."

"I don't know what I would do without you."

"You will never have to find out. I'm always here for you."

"I don't mean to interrupt your little love-fest, ladies, but Ireland, I do believe you have something that belongs to me."

My head whips around in the direction of Mother's voice. The sound of it actually causes my ears to ache.

She's holding out her hand, while looking at the memory stick in mine. I grip it tighter.

"These are records I've taken. This is my work. I should be allowed access to it. You know I need them."

"I have no idea what you're referring to," Mother monotones, "but those records are the property of The Club. You will hand them over now, or I'll call the authorities."

I stare at her in disbelief. Was she serious? She was going to call the cops on me?

"Don't test me," she says, reading my mind.

I hold out my hand and release my death grip on the memory stick, watching it drop into her outstretched hand.

"Good decision," she says. "Now, I think it's time for you to go, isn't it?"

Jenna takes my arm and starts to lead me out of The Club.

"Oh, and Ireland?" Mother calls after me in a raised voice, "I think you should take that leave of absence you've been needing."

I stop in my tracks and look around us at the scattering of employees now turning our way. "I just returned, remember?"

"Yes, but I don't think you've taken enough time. I'll contact you when it's time to come back. Until then, I'll expect you to stay away. We just want you to truly get the rest you need."

She is doing this on purpose. She is making a show in front of the other staff. Making sure others know she is giving me time off under the pretense that it is for my own benefit. So no one will wonder why I'm not at The Club anymore. She is saving her face at the expense of mine yet again.

I narrow my eyes at her. "Of course, Mother. You won't see me here again."

She turns slightly, addressing Jenna, who has been remaining silent during the whole exchange. "And Jenna, I'll expect you to alert me to any changes in the arrangement."

Jenna shoots me a look. "Of course, Ms. Jacobson."

"Run along now, Jenna. I believe you must have a class to get ready for. I'll just walk Ireland out myself and see that she gets to her car and all."

Jenna hesitates.

"Go on, or did you have something you'd like to add?" Mother raises her eyebrows expectantly at Jenna, daring her to cross her.

"No, nothing to add," Jenna says. "Bye, Ireland," she whispers before heading down the hall in the direction of the yoga studio.

Mother turns back to me. "I believe it's time for you to leave now." She is turning the tables, kicking me out of her house, like I did earlier to her.

"Yes, I believe it is."

****

I slam the door to the condo and literally throw my keys across the room, only feeling the slightest satisfaction when they make a thud upon hitting the wall and dropping to the floor.

I stand in the doorway, momentarily petrified. I'm due to meet with Agent Brandon Shelton in less than twelve hours, and I have nothing, not a single thread to defend myself with. I left a message for Violet on the way home from The Club, but she didn't answer and has yet to call me back. She's probably given up hope and is reluctant to call me back with the sad news that she simply can't defend me because there is nothing to defend.

I reach up and pinch the bridge of my nose with my thumb and finger, willing myself to move forward. I finally make it from the hallway into the bedroom, where I sit on the edge of the bed, numb and unfeeling.

I reach up to scratch an itch and am surprised to find tears running down my checks. Not just a drop or two but what seems to be rivers, gushing from my eyes, down my face.

I'm hours away from being convicted as a felon and being sentenced to jail time, and there is no one here to tell me I'll be okay. No one to hold my hand and tell me they'll be waiting on the other side for me. Maybe I deserve to go to jail. It's not like I'll be missed. I think of all the people that go to prison but have families. The anguish they must go through. At least I won't have to put anyone through that kind of worry. Any pain I might encounter in there will be my own. If Lenny were still here, he would be beside himself. At least I don't have to worry about him and how he would deal with it. And Collette, she would go ballistic on Mother. At least with us not talking she won't feel that sisterly obligation to pick sides in our family. She can stay in a neutral state, like Switzerland.

I wipe the tears away with the back of my hand. It would be a pity, though, to go to jail before making up with Collette. I mean, maybe I was a little hasty, leaving her there on the sidewalk, alone with Carl.

Carl, one more person I can add to the list of people who won't care if I get placed in the slammer or stay a free woman. How could I have been so naive as to think I could just waltz into his life and have him welcome me with open arms, no questions asked. God, I really screwed that one up. After I stormed off like a five-year-old throwing a fit, there is no chance he would want to invite me into his life. I made sure any chance of a relationship was squashed.

I pick up the phone to dial Collette one last time. I hit the speed dial but decide at the last minute to hang up. Why should I burden her with this mess when we aren't even speaking to each other? I lie back on the bed and let the phone drop from my hand.

I close my eyes and let the images of what I imagine jail will look like swim through my head. I'll probably have to wear an orange jumpsuit and eat off a cafeteria tray. I wonder if I'll get a job while I'm in there. Maybe they'll let me work in the library. Just as long as I don't have to work in the kitchen it could potentially be tolerable.

I continue my morbid little game of coming up with different scenarios of my life in jail while drifting in and out of sleep. Maybe it will look different in the morning. Perhaps I'll like the color orange by then.

Chapter 22

The vibration on my back starts as a tickle but quickly becomes a nuisance. Groggy and confused as to what's bothering me, I blink my eyes a few times but decide it's easier to just let them stay shut. My mouth feels like I've been lying in a dentist chair having work done for the last hour, and my eyes are covered in the kind of crud you get after crying in your sleep. I swallow several times, trying to rehydrate my tongue, and try opening my eyes again, squinting through the light, rubbing the sleep out until I can focus.

When I can finally see past the haze, the first thing I notice is the thin blanket of white covering Main Street, or at least the part of it I can just make out through the sliver of parted drapes covering my window. The gray that frequently accompanies snowfall has disintegrated into clear blue skies. The sun, just starting its rise over the city, casts a pinkish, orange glow, making the snow glisten and sparkle, like my now discarded engagement ring, the one sitting in a dish by the bathroom sink.

After fighting with the blanket that is wrapped around me, cocoon style, I finally locate my phone, the Caller ID indicating Violet is the culprit responsible for my early morning wake-up call.

"Good morning." My voice is hoarse even to my own ears. I clear my throat.

"Ireland, sorry to wake you."

"Don't worry, I was just getting up," I lie as I struggle to a sitting position.

"Look, I know it's early, but we have a problem."

It takes me only a split second to remember what she's referring to.

"I know."

"How soon can you get down here? We need to get a handle on this before the meeting. We only have a few hours, and the sooner you can get here the better. Honestly, it's not looking good for us."

The images from last night, of orange jumpsuits, pop back into my head. What could we possibly come up with in a matter of hours? She was kind in saying, "It's not looking good," when rather, "It's looking like a lost cause," seemed more appropriate.

"I just need to freshen up a bit, I'll be there in thirty minutes," I reply.

"I'll be waiting for you."

"Okay, I'm on my way."

****

In under ten minutes I've washed my face, gotten dressed, brushed my hair into a ponytail, and slathered some deodorant on my underarms.

Feeling remarkably empty-handed, I head out the door. Just as I fit the key into the lock, I hear the intercom buzzing inside the condo.

It's like a lightning bolt striking my body. The last time I heard that sound was the night Officer Coby showed up on my doorstep to relay the news about Lenny. Instantly my throat closes up as the memories sweep through me like flood water demolishing everything in its path. I tighten my grip on the key and try to push down the vomit that is starting to rise. It has been days since my last episode. I haven't even noticed the lack of nausea until this moment, sneaking up on me when I least expected it.

The buzzer sounds again, causing me to jump. I push the door open and with shaky fingers push the call button.

"Hello?" I ask cautiously, knowing full well it couldn't possibly be Officer Coby again but still unable to shake the fear coursing through my body.

"Ireland?" The voice sounds familiar, but I'm having a hard time placing it.

"Yes?"

"It's me, Carl."

My heart stops. Carl? As in my father Carl? As in the very same Carl I yelled at and left standing on a street corner Carl?

He's here? But why? How? A myriad of questions zoom through my head all at once, but I'm unable to verbalize any one of them.

"Carl?"

"Yes, it's me. Can I come up?"

"Yes, yes. Hold on, and I'll buzz you in." I press the door release button and wait a few minutes before Carl arrives in the hallway.

"Hi," I say awkwardly as he comes toward me rolling a suitcase behind him. For some unknown reason, I latch onto this detail, watching as the wheels roll across the floor. It takes me a moment before I notice Carl looks different. He's cut his hair. Not just his long locks but his facial hair is missing, too. He looks very handsome, and younger. Again, I find myself drawn into his face, intrigued by how it can look so similar to my own.

"Hello, dear." He comes to a stop in front of me, and we stand awkwardly for a moment.

"You look nice," he says, trying to break the silence between us.

"Ha!" I snort a laugh. "No, I don't. But thank you."

"How have you been?" he asks tentatively.

"Honestly, I've been better."

"Look—"

"Look—" we both say at the same time.

"You first."

"No, you go ahead," he says.

But before we can progress our conversation any further, there is a buzzing in my pocket, and I suddenly remember I'm supposed to be in Violet's office in less than twenty minutes. I look at the door of the condo and back to Carl.

"Oh, man." I pinch the bridge of my nose and rub my forehead. "Carl, I really have to be somewhere in a few minutes."

Carl looks defeated, and I realize he thinks I'm brushing him off.

"But I can probably spare a minute or two," I continue while I start toward the open door of my condo. "Why don't you come in for a bit."

Once inside, I send a quick text to Violet.

—*Delayed, be there asap!*—

To which a response appears immediately.

—*The sooner, the better!*—

I click the phone off and slip it back into my pocket.

"Can I offer you some coffee or tea?" I ask politely.

"No, I'm okay. Thanks."

"I'm so sorry—"

I am cut off again when Carl says, "You're probably wondering—"

I pause, and we both give an awkward laugh, which helps diffuse the tension between us.

"I just want to say I'm sorry," I start.

This time Carl remains silent, listening to what I have to say.

"I should never have left like that. I acted like a five-year-old. I had unrealistic expectations of you, and I realize that now. I hope you can forgive me."

"Of course I can. But you're not the only one who needs to apologize. I didn't handle myself or the situation very well either. I guess you could say we're both new to this game."

Really, he should be telling me off right now, not apologizing to me, focusing on me with his overly concerned eyes. The way I acted in Hawaii was abominable, and we both know it. But it doesn't stop the sense of relief that washes over me at his words.

"After you left, Collette was furious with you. We went to a nearby coffee shop and took the time for her to cool down. It also gave us a chance to talk some more. She did her best to fill me in on what it was like growing up with your mother."

I wince at the mention of Mother, like I'm dodging a blow. I glance at the clock again. Time is ticking by, and if she gets her way, I'll be staring down a jail sentence in a matter of minutes.

"Coupled with the loss of your fiancé, I can see why you got so upset. It was a natural reaction to all the stress you've been under."

He has no idea the kind of stress I've been under and what I am still going through, right this minute.

"I guess I was just hoping for one thing to go my way," I say honestly.

"Collette was able to help me see why," he answers, "but you're probably wondering why I'm here, sitting on your couch in your home." He gestures with his hand to the condo. "And not just calling you on the phone."

"The thought did cross my mind."

"I took the red-eye from Oahu last night and caught an Uber here to your place this morning. After Collette left, I spoke with Kayla, and we agreed to keep the lines of communication open. We've been talking with Collette on the rare occasion."

"Well, isn't that nice," I scoff, cutting him off. I'm sure I sound as bitter as I feel, but knowing I've been left out just emphasizes the desolation I've been feeling. "Collette hasn't spoken to me since we returned home," I elaborate, for clarity's sake.

"What, really? I thought she would have called you."

"Nope."

Carl pulls his phone out and pushes a button—I feel another surge of jealousy as I notice he has her on speed dial—apparently getting her voicemail.

"Collette, it's Carl. I'm at Ireland's. Call me when you get this. We all need to sit down and talk. You know why," he says cryptically, hanging up the phone.

I notice a flash of satisfaction cross his face, like a parent who's just enforced a rule. But just as soon as it's there, it's gone.

"So you've been talking to Collette? How about

Kayla? I thought she wasn't prepared for all of this in her life," I ask. I don't want to admit it, but my own personal green-eyed monster is rearing its ugly head. She's my sister, my twin. She's not supposed to be talking to Carl without me. We do everything together, make decisions together. Or at least we did. And now, here she was forging a whole new relationship with our father without even telling me. All while we've been staunchly ignoring each other. Maybe she didn't see our bond the same way I did? Perhaps she was ready to replace our relationship with the one she was busy building with Carl.

"Yes, well, it's just been the occasional conversation over the last few days," he backpedals. "Kayla, and I talked about some things after you both left, but I really think we should all sit down together. we still have a lot to go over."

The buzzing comes from my pocket again.

"Sure, but I really don't have the time to sit around and wait for Collette right now." I glance at the clock for the third time. Ten minutes have passed, and if I don't leave soon, I am going to be late for the meeting. "In fact, I really do have to go now."

"Oh, okay."

I realize how abrupt I must seem to him. He's traveled all this way, and I've only listened to him for ten minutes before kicking him out. This was right on par with leaving him on the corner in Hawaii.

I sigh. "Do you have a place you're staying?"

"At the Marriott in downtown Bellevue."

"Let me give you a ride. It's on the way. Look, I *do* want to have this conversation, it's just that I really can't miss this meeting I need to get to. Can we do it after I'm done? I can come to pick you up at your hotel, and we can go to dinner?"

To myself I wonder if Brandon will take me away right after the meeting. Surely they would let me leave and schedule a time to start my sentence of five years of jail time later. How does it all work? I don't even know.

Carl stands and starts to gather his belongings. "I'd like that, yes."

"Okay, great. Let's go, then." I attempt to hustle us out of the condo, but for the second time in a matter of minutes the buzzer for the intercom sounds.

How on earth can I have two visitors in ten minutes whereas the darn thing has remained silent for the past month?

I look at Carl, who just shrugs his shoulders.

"Hello?" I ask tentatively, pushing the button.

"Ireland, let me in! I have something for you." Jenna's voice rushes over the intercom.

"Jenna?"

"Of course it's me! Come on, it's freakin' cold out here. Let me in!"

I push the door release and turn back to Carl, who is looking at me with questioning eyes.

"My best friend," I say, like it explains everything. But in all honesty, I can't figure out why she would be here either.

Carl just nods and returns to his seat on the couch where he was situated a few seconds ago. My heart sinks along with Carl's descent, watching him make himself comfortable again. It is becoming more and more evident that I am never going to get out of here.

I dig my phone out of my pocket and send another text to Violet:

—Another delay, so sorry!—

I cringe when the ping-back is immediate.

—Your ass on the line, not mine!—

The bite I've seen in Violet is making its appearance. She's treating me like a client, and I can tell she isn't in the mood to take any crap. But she is right. I need to get out of this condo, pronto.

Carl and I both turn to the door as Jenna barges through.

My eyes narrow as I take in her appearance, trying to decipher what it is she is struggling with as she comes through the door.

A large silver box is tucked under her arm, and she seems to be exerting a considerable effort to carry it.

"What the—?"

At the same time Carl jumps off the couch exclaiming, "Let me help with that."

Carl grabs the box just as Jenna struggles not to lose her grip, almost dropping it on the floor.

"Jenna, what is that?" I exclaim.

Jenna takes her time straightening out and stretching her back.

"Thanks!" She throws gratitude to Carl while simultaneously shooting me a questioning look over his head, as if to say, "Who's this and why is he here?"

I shake my head to answer and mouth back, "Later."

Carl stands up. "A computer tower?" He looks from Jenna to me and back to Jenna.

A slow, devilish smile creeps across Jenna's lips. "I stole the hard drive!"

"Excuse me?" I say.

"From The Club."

"You what?"

"I snuck into your office early this morning, before anyone was at The Club, and took this. It's all there, right?" she thrusts her finger at the silver box sitting on my hardwood floor.

My eyes grow wide as I realize what she's talking about.

"Oh, my God, Jenna! Yes! But how?"

Jenna digs into her pocket and produces a set of keys, letting them dangle off her ring finger.

"She took the memory stick, but she didn't remember to take the keys back." She smiles triumphantly.

"Oh, my God!" I exclaim again.

Carl's head is ping-ponging back and forth. "Um, am I missing something here?"

Jenna, unable to stand it any longer, sticks her hand out. "I'm Jenna. And you are?"

Carl takes her hand in his. "I'm Carl, Carl Martin."

I can see Jenna's grip tighten on Carl's hand. "Carl? As in Carl, Carl?"

"I see you're familiar with our situation." Carl chuckles in a lighthearted way, ignoring Jenna's blatant aggression toward him.

"I am."

"I can't believe you did this!" I say, purposefully interrupting their exchange.

Jenna drops Carl's hand and walks over to me, giddy like a two-year-old who just took the chocolate out of the pantry without her parents knowing.

"I know, right? I was thinking last night, how can we get the data you need? And since I'm not a computer hacker, I had to come up with something else." She pauses. "I came up with this!" She spreads her hands out, indicating the tower. "Will it work?"

"You're brilliant! I think it just might." I hug her, and at the same time another vibration lights up in my pocket.

I snatch my phone out and read the text.

—You're late! If you don't show up, it's seen as an admission of guilt. I can't help you if you can't help yourself. Do it for me and Mom and Dad. Do it for Lenny if you don't want to do it for yourself. I was expecting more from you—

I look up at the clock and immediately the blood drains from my face.

"What? What is it?" Jenna asks.

"I'm late," I say.

"Shit," Jenna deadpans.

"What in the world is going on?" Carl asks again, clearly lost.

"What's going on is Ireland here is being dragged through another one of her mother's shit games."

"Jenna," I exclaim, but she is right, this is a shit game I am playing in.

"What? How else do you explain her trying to pass off her 'financial indiscretions' to you?" She puts her fingers up as quotation marks.

"What kind of financial indiscretions?" Carl interjects.

"Oh, you know, the kind that land you a hefty fine or, better yet"—she looks pointedly at me—"in jail. Oh, and let's not forget the lovely little nickname you get to wear as a badge of your dedication to your mother. Felony will look great on the resume you're sure to have to fill out after you get out of jail."

"Whoa there, are you talking about tax evasion?" Carl asks, putting his past skills to quick use.

Jenna nods her head in affirmation.

"How exactly is your mother able to pass this on to you?" Carl turns to me.

"She ran all her personal accounts through The Club. Which means, as the accountant, she ran them through me. My fingerprints are all over the books. I'm the only one who has password access. She must have used my password, when I sent it to her while I was in Hawaii, to get into the files and change dates and entries. I don't know, it's just a hunch." I point to the silver box sitting on the floor. "That has all my previous backups on it. If I can convince the IRS to review it, they'll see where the differences are. If I can somehow prove Mother was the one to change the entries, I might have a chance to get out of this."

"But now you're late!" Jenna hops up and starts struggling with the silver box again.

Carl catches on and easily lifts it out of her arms. "Come on, then, what are we waiting for?" He starts out the door.

"Wait, Carl. No," I say with as much force as I can muster.

He stops and looks back at me.

"I know we're working on something here." I indicate him and me with my index finger. "But you made it very clear, in Hawaii, you didn't want to get in the middle of all this or to put your own family in harm's way." I let my breath out. I wasn't even aware I was holding it. "It's not your place. I have to do this on my own."

Carl sets down the tower and digs his hand into his

pocket.

"Actually, that's where you're wrong." He pulls out a neatly folded paper and starts unfolding it, but my phone rings, and I snatch it out of my pocket.

"Violet, I know I'm late, but I just received something that is going to help our case. Can you stall them?" I say breathlessly as I hurry to help Jenna with the tower, pushing Carl out of the way.

A cruel laugh comes through the line. "Violet? You have that little pipsqueak doing your bidding for you now? That's rich. I should have known you'd reduce yourself to groveling to your fiancé's family. Again, you're unwilling to take responsibility for your own actions. Anyway, I do believe you have something of mine. I want it back. Oh and you can tell your little yoga friend there she no longer works at The Club. In fact, she won't be working at any club as long as I'm in town."

"I have no idea what you're talking about, Mother," I say, trying to play dumb even though I know she's not going to fall for it.

"When are you going to learn, Ireland? I know everything that happens in my club. Jenna took the hard drive this morning, probably thinking you could somehow save yourself with it. But let me tell you a little secret." She pauses. "It's not. I've wiped the hard drive clean. There isn't anything left for you to do."

She's bluffing. She has to be. Or is she telling the truth? What if I give it to Brandon and there's nothing there?

"I'm coming to get it. Don't move," Mother says, interrupting my thoughts.

"Why do you need it, if there's nothing on it?" I

say, impressed with my own ability to think quickly.

"Don't play games with me, young lady. We both know you won't win. You are in possession of stolen property. I am coming to retrieve it. You will give it back to me."

"Or else what? You'll call the cops on me?" I scoff at her. "I think you've already covered your bases with that one." I pause, contemplating my next move. "No, I think I'm going to keep it. In fact, I think I'm going to take it with me to my meeting and give it to Brandon."

"Don't you dare. I'm warning you, Ireland. Don't you move."

"Goodbye, Mother. I'll be seeing you."

I hang up the phone to her screaming my name through the other line.

I turn to Jenna and Carl, who both have eyes like an owl, large and unblinking. "That was Mother."

"We got that," Jenna says.

"She's coming here to get the tower and the hard drive, the one she says she's wiped clean."

Chapter 23

Time is taunting me as Jenna, Carl, and I search the courthouse for the right door. We've already found our way into two dead-end hallways. I'm about to cave and ask one of the not-so-friendly-looking guards which way we need to go when we finally find the correct room number.

Gently pushing the door open, I peek my head around it. Violet, who is standing at a table with Brandon Shelton and another man, one I don't recognize, looks up at the disturbance.

"Geez, Ireland. Where have you been?" Violet rushes toward me while simultaneously checking her watch. When she reaches me, she adds in a hushed voice, "I've delayed them twice, but if we don't get started right now, they're going to pack up and leave."

"I know, I'm sorry. It's a long story, but I made it."

I step fully into the room and immediately feel exposed, like in the middle of a dream where you show up to school wearing nothing but your underwear. I sense Brandon Shelton's eyes boring into me, and I instinctively wrap my jacket tighter around my body. My underarms feel sticky with sweat even though the temperature in the room rivals the weather going on outside. Its obvious no one has bothered to turn the heater on in this stark room, and I know without a doubt it's on purpose. A single steel desk sits in the middle of the room surrounded only by steel chairs, file cabinets, and fluorescent overhead lights. There isn't a single item of comfort in this room. The whole intent is to make me break down faster, to admit to whatever charges they are about to bring against me.

And it is working. I'm just about to plead guilty right here and now when the door behind me opens and smacks me on the back, causing me to take a step forward, closer to the table.

"Aww." I rub my backside.

"Sorry," Jenna says as she marches through the door with Carl, who is still holding the computer tower.

"What is that?" Violet indicates the silver box Carl is carrying under his arm, ignoring the fact that Jenna and Carl have just pushed their way into the room.

"It's the tower. From my office," I say .

"And it has your backups on it?" Violet asks.

"We don't know. Mother says she erased all the backups, and I haven't had a chance to look. It just recently came into my possession," I say as Jenna flashes me a proud smile.

"Well, let's hope she's lying." Violet finally acknowledges the two latecomers. "You can put that on the table," she says to Carl, "and then go sit over there." She motions to two chairs that are at the far end of the steel table, out of the direct vision of Brandon and his mystery guest.

Violet places her hand on the small of my back and gently guides me closer to the table. Once I reach the edge, Brandon raises out of his chair, greeting me.

"Hello, Ireland. I'm glad you could join us today." His snide comment is dripping with sarcasm, but I decide to ignore him by not responding. He shrugs slightly and extends his hand to me. I grasp it, making sure my grip has just the right strength to it. Too loose and he will think I'm weak, too tight, and he will think I'm coming off as combative.

"Hello, Brandon. I'm so sorry I kept you waiting."

"Yes, well…" Brandon dismisses my apology. "Let me introduce Daniel Lens. Daniel is the IRS Chief Counsel Criminal Tax Attorney. He and I will be working together on your case." Daniel, wearing a suit almost identical to Brandon's only with a red-and-brown tie instead of blue like Brandon's, rises from his chair, and I repeat my previous handshake with him.

"Nice to meet you, Mr. Lens," I say.

"Right, well, let's get down to business then, shall we?" Daniel says, promptly dropping my hand, without correctly returning my greeting or meeting my eyes.

Brandon and Daniel return to their seats and wait for Violet and me to take ours.

Once we are settled, Daniel reaches out to the middle of the table and presses the start button on the recording device that has been placed there, waiting to document today's proceedings.

"Today's meeting is to discuss the findings of Agent Brandon and to gather more information regarding the case being brought against Ireland Jacobson. This is not a courtroom, and so it does not need to be treated as such." Daniel clears his throat and keeps reciting. "We are here to discuss the conspiracy of defendant Ireland Jacobson from in or about December 2013 through in or about November 2017, in the District of King County.

"The charges to be discussed are of the defendant and the fact she did knowingly and intentionally conspire and agree with Cynthia Jacobson and others to devise a scheme and artifice to defraud and commit perjury against the United States Government by means of false representation of earned income and expenses."

"Shouldn't you say something? Like, tell them I'm not the one responsible for all of this?" I whisper to Violet.

She shushes me with a wave of her hand. "You have to be patient. Our turn will come."

I glance down the table at Carl and Jenna sitting stiffly on the folding chairs. Jenna is staring at the floor, seemingly engrossed in the carpet in front of her, but when I look at Carl, he catches my eye. He mouths, "Be strong," and I try to reward him with a tilt of my head before turning my attention back to the two men sitting across from me.

Strong is not how I would describe myself at this exact instant. I look down at my hands that are shaking as though I'm freezing, and in an attempt to stop the tremors, I place them flat on the surface of the table. I feel like a caged animal in this small room. The walls seem to be closing in on me, and I can feel the confinement of the four walls. Just like how it will be in my jail cell if I don't find my way out of this. Can I stand to be in prison for months and months? How will I handle it?

Just as I am envisioning myself the target of some inmates looking to prove something, another image pops into my head. One of Mother. Only she is the one in an orange jumpsuit. If I don't take the blame for this, then Mother will surely be found guilty. Does she deserve to spend time in prison? Can I do that to my own mother? The person who gave me life? Am I the kind of person who could turn her back and take another person's life away? Is what she said right? Do the employees at The Club need her more than anyone needs me? I mean, what would it matter if I went to jail for a little while? There isn't anyone relying on me. Nobody needs me home. I don't even have a dog. Lenny is gone, Collette isn't returning my phone calls, and by all indications, I don't even have a job to return to. Maybe this is the best option. Maybe I should just take responsibility for it, even if I didn't do it. How bad can it be?

Daniel has continued with his diatribe and is now on to the description of my alleged wrongdoings. "The falsification of documents, overstatement of deductions and exemptions, and willful underreporting income, all designed to facilitate the stealing of more than one million dollars. The consequences for these charges are sentencing of thirty months' imprisonment and a fine of eighty-one thousand eight hundred dollars."

Violet opens her mouth to speak, and I immediately reach out and grab her arm, halting her progress. She looks at me quizzically. I glance across the table and motion for her to lean in. She does so, and I whisper, "I'm not sure I can do this."

"Do what, exactly?"

"You know, throw my own mother under the bus." I make a sliding motion on the table with my hand and immediately regret it when I see the sweat stain left behind. I make a lame attempt to rub out the streak with my shirt sleeve.

Violet pretends she doesn't notice. "Throw her under the bus? You mean like she's doing to you right now?"

"I know, but all those people at The Club, the employees—they depend on their jobs. Some of them have worked there for years. They're like family to me. I can't let them suffer because of me."

Violet stares at me like I've grown two heads. "Suffer because of you? But you've done nothing wrong. If anything, it was Cynthia who put them right smack dab in harm's way. She was careless with her business methods, and she was deceptive in how she chose to deal with it. Ireland, think about this. Think about what it would mean for you. Not just now, but in the future."

I look down at my hands, thinking about what Violet was saying.

The ping from my phone slices through the silence in the room.

"Sorry, so sorry," I whisper and drag my phone out of my purse.

I see Brandon and Daniel shooting evil looks my way. I fumble with my phone with the intent to turn it off, but the incoming text catches my eye.

—*Need you to call me immediately, 911. There's been an accident*—

I look for the sender of the message and am frozen in place when I see Greg's name at the top of the screen.

"Ireland? Ireland, you need to put that away." Violet is furiously whispering at me.

I glance up, and I can tell the blood has drained from my face because I'm feeling lightheaded from the slightest motion of moving my head.

"What is it?" Violet senses the sudden shift in my demeanor and leans in to see what is on the phone.

She looks up, and her eyes meet mine. "You can't leave. If you leave, this will be all over."

"Can't we take a break? I need to find out what's happened," I whisper to her.

"No, you just got here. They've been waiting on you already." She whispers back.

Daniel clears his throat. "I'm sorry, are we boring you over there?"

Violet makes a split-second decision and grabs my phone out of my hand and slides it across the table to Carl, who luckily has quick reflexes. "No, I'm sorry. We're ready. But I do believe Ireland's guests will be excusing themselves from the proceedings."

Carl looks confused for a minute before glancing down at the phone. I watch as his eyes grow in size and his face turns red.

There is a scratching sound as he stands up, rapidly pushing his chair back. "Yes, please excuse us." He turns to Jenna, who is clearly confused but stands obediently and follows Carl out the door.

I feel helpless as I watch the two of them leave, taking my only source of outside information with them into the hallway.

"Great. Now that we have your undivided attention, can we continue?" Daniel says, shuffling some papers in front of him, looking impatient.

I snap my eyes back to the two men sitting across from me and do my best to focus only on what is in front of me, but my mind keeps swirling back to the text from Greg and what it could possibly mean. There was an accident, but he didn't say who was involved in it? Was it Collette? The girls? Oh, God, please don't let it be the girls.

The touch of Violet's hand on my arm brings me back again. "What do you want to do? It has to be your decision. It's up to you if you want to present a defense."

I think about Collette and Molly and Maggie. I have to be there for them. Even if Collette is mad at me right now, I can't imagine my life without her in it. If she is hurt, I need her to fight for her life. And she needs me to fight for mine. Life is so fleeting. We never know when it might to be taken from us. I would have thought Lenny's death had taught me that, but I was too numb to realize what I should have seen all along. I can't waste another minute of my time alive. I'm the only one to blame for not taking charge of my own life. I can't keep bowing down to people or circumstances. I have to fight. Fight for my freedom, fight for my rights, fight for my life. My life is mine, and mine alone. I can make it what I want it to be. And right now, I want it to be cleared of these damn charges so I can leave this God-awful room and go see my sister.

The breath I didn't know I was holding rushes out of my lungs. I nod my head at Violet and turn to face Daniel and Brandon. I open my mouth to speak but am stopped when Violet places her hand over mine. She leans into me and whispers, "It's best if I do the talking now." She sits back in her chair and pulls herself up to her tallest form. "We request an opportunity to counter the charges brought forth by the IRS regarding defendant Ireland Jacobson."

I nod my head. I had momentarily forgotten I wasn't alone in this. This is why Violet was here in the first place. This is her moment. I need to let her do what she does best and thank my lucky stars she's willing to do it for me.

"Which is why we are meeting here today and not proceeding directly to the courtroom," Daniel counters. "We are open to hearing Ireland's defense on these charges."

"In the dispute of the charges brought forth on Ms. Jacobson, we would like to offer evidence that we believe will show her innocence."

"What do you have?" Brandon asks.

Violet stands up from her chair and walks over to the side table, where Carl has left the tower. As she reaches the table, there is a knock at the door.

"Oh, for heaven's sake." Daniel turns to the door. "Can't we just get through this?"

The door opens a crack, and Carl sticks his head around the opening.

"Come in," Daniel barks.

Carl takes a step through the door and hands Violet a note. "Ireland needs to read this."

"Now? Can't it wait?"

"I believe she needs to be informed of a situation. I am leaving now and want to make sure she has everything she needs before I go."

Violet brings the note over to me as Carl waits awkwardly at the door.

I unfold it and start reading.

Collette in a car accident, being rushed to the hospital. Jenna to watch Molly and Maggie. I'm leaving now to meet Greg. You finish here and come quickly. Not sure of the extent of the injuries.

Collette, my Collette, is being rushed to the hospital? No, I have to go to her. I can't stay here while she's hurt.

I stand up suddenly, scraping my own chair against the floor as it's pushed away.

Brandon and Daniel physically jump at my quick movements. "Excuse me, Ms. Jacobson, is everything all right?"

Carl senses my distress and quickly crosses the room, coming to a stop right in front of me, a physical wall blocking my escape. He leans in and whispers in my ear, "You have to stay. Ireland, finish this out. I know you want to go to her, but you can't risk this. She's going to need you. Fight this, finish this, and when you're done, come to the hospital. I'll go now, and I promise you, I'll call as soon as I find anything out." He grabs me and hugs me close to him.

I want to melt into his embrace, to stay there and have him *shush* me like a child, but I know he's right. I need to finish this, to stand up and own my life.

I pull back and nod quickly to Carl as he makes a hasty exit. I close my eyes, take a deep breath, and when I open them again, I turn back to Violet and take my seat next to hers.

Violet briefly covers my hand, in what I like to think is a moment of compassion but could just as easily be an attempt to stop my shaking, before removing her hand and continuing with her defense.

"Ireland has brought with her the computer tower that houses the hard drive that she does her backups on, backups dating back seven-plus years. We believe if you take the time to scan the backups you will find that the data was changed recently, at a time when Ireland was out of the state, leaving her without access to her computer. We are suggesting Cynthia Jacobson had access to the computer at this time, and that it was actually she who changed the data, trying to cover up the tax fraud in which Loraine and Cynthia were in collaboration."

"So you're saying that Ireland inputted the data, but it was Loraine and Cynthia who changed the numbers when they filed the tax returns. And that to cover their tracks they broke into Ms. Jacobson's computer, the one that Cynthia Jacobson does, in fact own, and changed the data to reflect what was shown on the tax returns," Daniel clarifies, with a questioning voice.

"Well, yes, that's correct," Violet states.

"That's a little farfetched, isn't it? I mean a mother framing her own daughter to get out of tax evasion? I guess I've heard of crazier things, but this one is slightly facetious sounding. Why would I believe it?" Daniel asks.

I notice Brandon looking at me with a tilted chin like he was trying to solve a puzzle.

"Because it's true!" I blurt out. Violet places her hand on my arm again, to quiet me.

"We are merely asking you to use the tools I know are available to the IRS. We ask that you use the subpoenaed bank records and off-site backups of Cynthia Jacobson and compare them to the backups on the hard drive we are providing. I'm well aware of the sophisticated technology available to your department. You should be able to see the changes as well as track the date the changes were made. This is all we are asking you to do."

Brandon tilts his head to me. "You were gone the first time I came to the office and spoke to Cynthia."

"Yes, I was. I was in Hawaii."

"Can you prove it?"

"Yes, of course! I still have the ticket stubs and the hotel receipt."

"Is your computer password protected?"

"Yes."

Brandon's mouth turns down in a frown.

"But…"

Brandon nods. "But?"

"But I sent Mother the password when I was in Hawaii. I texted it to her."

"Do you still have the text?"

"It's on my sister's phone. I'm not sure if she erased it or not."

"Can you find out?"

"Yes, of course. Only—" I pause.

"What?"

"Well, that was my brother-in-law, the message I just got. He was telling me there was an accident." I can feel the heat start to rise in my checks again at the thought of Collette hurt somewhere, while I was here, arguing with these men. "Carl and Jenna went into the hallway. They took my phone with them. I can't find out if she has the text without my phone."

Brandon's eyes widen. "An accident? Why didn't you say something?"

"We didn't want to risk the proceedings," Violet answers for me.

Brandon looks at Daniel and leans in to whisper something into his ear.

Daniel nods his head and sits back up. "It is the IRS's intent to always conduct a thorough investigation when dealing with these issues. We will take the hard drive into our custody and review the information you have provided us. If what you say is indeed on the hard drive, I believe we will be focusing our efforts on Ms. Cynthia Jacobson and Ms. Loraine Bolt."

I feel my body literally sag with relief at his words.

"We will need you to provide us with a copy of the airline ticket and hotel receipt as well as a copy of the text message that was sent to Ms. Jacobson."

"Yes, we can do that," Violet says.

"Then we are done here, for the time being." Brandon turns to me. "I believe you have somewhere you need to be." He extends his hand to me again, and this time when I take it, it's warm, and his fingers are soft around my own. "Take care, Ireland."

"Thank you," I say, meaning it.

Chapter 24

As I step into the quiet and serene emergency room of the Overlake Hospital, I do a double take to make sure I'm in the right place. The space I'm standing in bears no resemblance to emergency rooms depicted in TV shows or movies. No nurses are rushing by with gurneys, there are no mobs of people sitting in the waiting room with bandages around their heads. Instead, the polished hardwood floors are sparkling clean, and the receptionist, sitting in front of the pea-green wall with the sign boasting EMERGENCY in silver letters, looks refined and businesslike.

Although there are a scattering of patrons in the waiting area, they all seem to be content, sipping coffee out of paper cups or whispering quietly amongst themselves.

Feeling like I've walked into some alternate universe, I hesitantly approach the intake receptionist sitting at the desk.

"Excuse me?"

She looks up from her computer with a brilliant smile, and I'm momentarily pulled off track by her blindly white teeth. "Hi, how can I help you? Are you checking in today?"

"Um, no, sorry." I pause, feeling flustered and start again. "I'm Ireland Jacobson. I'm looking for—" but before I can even finish my sentence, the receptionist has snapped to attention.

"Ireland, yes. I have strict instructions to take you back right away," she says, rising out of her chair with a flourish and starting around the desk. "Please follow me." She snaps her fingers, grabbing the attention of another woman dressed in identical blue scrubs who magically manifests from around the corner and takes the seat the first receptionist has just vacated.

Without turning to make sure I'm following, she heads down one of the many hallways.

Obediently, I scurry after her, feeling more anxious with every step we take. We walk down the hallway until the nurse stops abruptly in front of one of the doors. The curtain that separates it from the hall is slightly pulled back, and I don't wait for the receptionist to tell me I can go in, I just brush past her in my haste to see Collette.

Before I even see her, I'm babbling like an idiot.

"Are you okay?" The words tumble out of my mouth as I get closer to the bed. I can hear the monitors beeping, counting the rhythm of her heartbeat. And as I get closer, I can see her leg is suspended above the bed and is encased in a full cast reaching from her toe all the way to her thigh.

The angle of her leg obscures my view of her face, which is why I stop dead in my tracks when I hear, "What are you doing here?"

The voice speaking to me from the other side of the bandages is not Collette's.

"Mother?"

"Of course it's me. Who were you expecting? The Pope?"

"Wait, what are you doing here?"

"Are you kidding me?" She asks rhetorically. "What do you think I'm doing here?"

I walk closer so I can finally see her face. Unconsciously I take a step back. The scratches covering her profile are gruesome and swollen, haphazardly placed there like someone had gathered shards of glass in their hand and blown them straight into her face.

"What happened?" I ask without thinking and take a step closer.

"What do you think happened? I was in a car accident." I notice her words are slightly slurred, and it dawns on me that she must be on some pretty heavy pain medication.

"Wait here just a minute." I turn on my heel and walk back out the door into the hallway.

"Like I can go anywhere," she calls snidely after me.

I look right and left, searching for someone to help me. I see a nurse walking away from me and hurry to catch up to her.

"Excuse me," I call out.

"Yes?" She turns around all smiles, but her expression changes when she reads my face. "How can I help you?"

"I'm Ireland Jacobson—" Again I'm interrupted before I can complete my sentence.

"Oh, dear! I'm so glad they got hold of you. You must have been beside yourself with worry, having both your mother and sister involved in the accident."

"Oh, yes, I have been," I lie. "I'm sorry, I'm just having a hard time understanding the whole story. Would you mind filling me in on what happened again?"

"Of course. It's a lot to take in, I'm sure."

I nod my head silently, hoping to come across as solemn, waiting for her to continue.

"The EMT called in a transfer for a vehicular accident this morning at ten o'clock. The driver of the first car, I believe that was the one with your mother in it, had been driving down Main Street when the light turned red at the intersection of Main and 100th Avenue. With all the snow and ice on the road, she wasn't able to stop the car in time. She ran right through the red light, hitting the driver's side of the car crossing the intersection, the one containing your sister."

"So you're saying my mother caused the accident?"

The nurse leans her head in and lowers her voice in confidence. "She must have been going really fast, but don't tell anyone I said that. The airbags deployed in both cars. Your mom sustained injuries to her leg, a broken femur. The windshield shattered on impact and she also sustained some cuts from the glass and the deployed airbag. She got lucky, if you ask me."

I cross my arms in front of me, and the nurse leans back a bit. "And my sister? Did she get lucky?"

She looks down at her clipboard and runs her finger down a list. I try to see what she's looking at but am unable to decipher the words.

She sees me looking at her paper and moves it slightly farther from my view. "They were transferring her from the operating room. Let me just go and check where they are having her recover."

"The operating room?" I can feel my heart rate

increase at her words. Please let Collette be okay, I pray for the umpteenth time today. "What happened to her? Can I see her? Is she okay?"

The nurse reaches out and touches my arm, but I barely feel the contact. "Why don't you go back and check on your mom. I'll get the information on your sister and come to get you soon as I know something."

Before I can protest, she is hurrying down the hall in the direction of the nursing station.

I turn and go back into Mother's room as directed. I pause in the doorway, really seeing her for the first time. It's a different version of the same person I've always known. Here in the hospital bed with only the thin sheet covering her petite frame, she looks small and fragile. Her usual presence, which normally takes up an entire room, has shifted. She is simply an injured woman lying in a hospital bed. Her phone, the one I thought was permanently attached to her hand, is nowhere in sight. She's not barking orders at anyone; instead, she's lying on her back with her eyes closed. Even among all the beeping of the surrounding machines, there is a peacefulness I've never experienced in her presence.

I take a few cautious steps forward, reminding myself where I just came from. It's like approaching a sleeping tiger. I know full well the image in front of me is an illusion. She is capable of turning at any moment. She has bitten me, and she is fully capable of doing it again.

"So you decided to come back?" She slurs as her voice cuts through my thoughts. I walk closer. Her eyes are still closed.

"The nurse said she was going to meet me in here

and tell me where Collette is," I say, realizing I still feel the need to explain my actions to Mother.

"Why would the nurse know where Collette is? Isn't your unappreciative sister on her way here? You two have always taken me for granted. It takes me being in a car accident for you to finally appreciate me? How did I end up with such spoiled children?" Her eyes flash open and sear into me. Any peace I felt just seconds ago evaporates with her gaze.

"Wait, do you not know?"

"Oh, for heaven's sake, stop speaking in riddles. Know what?"

"Who you hit when you went speeding through the intersection?"

"Don't go making me sound like some common criminal. I wouldn't even have been out in this God-awful weather if you and your sinister little sidekick hadn't snuck into The Club and stolen my property. If you were an adult of any kind, you would understand your responsibility for all of this nonsense. None of this would have happened if it weren't for you." She gestures with a sloppy hand to her leg.

I grip my hands into fists at my side to keep from striking an already injured person.

"Not this time, Mother."

"What do you mean, *not this time*? Of course this is your doing."

"No. It's not. I did not put you into your car. I did not push your foot down on the accelerator or make you speed through that light. Really, Mother, you are the one being selfish. Did you once think how your actions could possibly affect another person? And as far as taking the hard drive, which is now in IRS possession, by the way—" She starts to say something, but I hold up my hand to stop her. "If you hadn't set me up to take the fall for your corruption, I would never have had to take it in the first place. You were willing to let your own daughter take the blame for something you knowingly did. You were going to let me serve time in prison. And all for what? So you could sit on your throne at The Club? So your crown wouldn't be tarnished? You were more worried about saving face than saving your own daughter? Well, I'll tell you what. I'm no longer going to be your sacrificial lamb. You're going to have to find someone else to do your bidding for you. All my life I've lived in your shadow, or the shadow of The Club. You've never put Collette and me above your own desires. Isn't that the definition of parenthood? Placing the needs of your children above your own? You certainly did not." I'm on a roll now, and I'm having a hard time stopping.

"The amount of selfishness it takes to keep the truth from your daughters that their own father is actually alive, and not some dead guy you created in your head, not only baffles me, it disgusts me. So no, I will not let you blame me anymore. If Collette is—" My voice catches on Collette's name, but I keep going before Mother can speak. "If she's hurt in any way, you will not blame me for it. That I won't let you do. Your days of controlling me are officially over."

"What do you mean if Collette is hurt?"

I'm momentarily halted by her question about Collette and then remember that she still doesn't know.

"Oh, that's right, you still don't know," I scoff at her. "In your rush to secure the hard drive and ensure my demise, you managed to put your other daughter in the hospital. The car you T-boned? It was Collette's."

She narrows her eyes at me. "No, it wasn't."

"Yes, it was."

"How do you know?"

"They just told me. You and Collette were transported here in separate emergency vehicles after the accident. Collette was admitted to surgery."

"For what?"

"I don't know. They're finding out where she is now."

Her eyes leave mine, and her gaze drifts to the corner of the room. She's silent, lost in thought. When she does speak, it's slow and controlled. "Let me ask you something."

"What?"

She slides her eyes lazily across the wall to find mine again. "Are you happy with yourself? You've managed to create a situation in which you've not only put your mother in the hospital but your sister too. I must say that takes real talent."

I hear my teeth grinding together and make an effort to relax my jaw enough to get my next words out. "This is not my fault. I knew you were going to try and pin this on me. Like you do everything else." I pause to collect myself. "Not this time, and not anymore."

Before she can say anything else, I walk to the door, pausing just long enough to say, "Goodbye, Mother," before stepping through and closing the curtain behind me. I lean against the cool wood panel next to the door and close my eyes, willing my breathing to return to normal, along with my heart rate.

"Ireland?"

My head snaps up at my name.

"Carl!" I leave my post by Mother's door and rush to meet him as he comes down the hallway toward me.

"We've been waiting for you. What took you so long? What are you doing way over here?"

I glance back at the closed curtain and envision Mother, all alone in the room with her leg suspended in the air. "Nothing, I wasn't doing anything." I turn back to Carl who is looking at me quizzically.

"Where's Collette?" I ask.

"Come, follow me."

I glance one more time over my shoulder as I follow Carl down the hallway in search of my sister.

Chapter 25

"Just a little farther," Carl says as we continue down one hallway after another, leaving the emergency room and Mother on the other side of the hospital.

"They transferred her to the east wing for recovery. She has to stay there for the next forty-eight hours for monitoring before she can be released home."

I nod my head at Carl, feeling like this information is just incessant chatter. I know that, until I see Collette with my own eyes, I won't be able to hear what anyone has to say.

Mutely I follow Carl, keeping my eyes cast down toward the linoleum floors until we finally come to a stop in front of a door identical to all the others we have just passed. I look up, and Carl nods to the room, indicating this is the one we are looking for. With a sense of urgency, I reach for the door handle. But before I can grasp the knob, Carl places his hand over mine, halting my process.

I could cut glass with the comment I'm about to hurl at Carl, but when I turn and look into his eyes, it's the concern that's etched across his brow that makes me bite my tongue.

"Is it that bad?" I whisper, afraid of his answer.

"She's been beaten up pretty bad. I know she has a fractured rib and a broken arm. There was internal bleeding. She was rushed into surgery as soon as she arrived. From what I understand, they were able to stop the bleeding. She was just coming out of the recovery room when I left to find you. I haven't seen her yet either. I just know what the doctors have told Greg."

I can feel my throat closing at the thought of Collette being in pain. My sister, lying in a hospital bed on the other side of this door, with nothing I can do to make it better. A sense of humiliation washes over me as I remember this will be the first time I've seen her since I left her alone on the street in Hawaii. That could have been the last time I saw her alive. My sister, the person who is the entire world to me, could have been lost to me forever. I vow to never treat her like that again, while simultaneously sending a prayer of thanks that she is still here.

The touch of Carl's finger reaching up and brushing a tear off my check sends my thoughts crashing back to the door in front of me.

"Go on," Carl encourages as he steps behind me. "Go in."

Mustering up my courage, I gently open the door to the room and take a few steps in. It's dark inside, even though there is a window in the room. The curtains have been drawn shut, and just a corner floor lamp is illuminating the room in an orange glow. The same beeping that was in Mother's room comes from the machines scattered around this one. I notice an IV drip in addition to all the monitors. My gaze follows the tube from the IV down to the hospital bed, where Greg is sitting on the edge, bent over Collette, whispering softly to her. I look closer and see that Collette's eyes are closed.

His head lifts up at the sound of Carl and me

approaching, and he attempts a weak smile. He stands to greet us, and I notice he looks like he's aged ten years in a matter of hours. His eyes are bloodshot, and his hair is disheveled like he's raked his hand through it countless times.

Without so much as a word, I rush into his arms and we hug like a life depends on it. A single sob racks through Greg's body, and I tighten my grip on him, waiting for him to compose himself before loosening my hold. He takes a shaky breath and holds onto my arms like he's afraid to let me go.

"How is she?" I dare to ask. Turning from Greg to look at Collette, I'm shocked when I do finally look down at her. It takes me a minute before I can process all that has happened to her body. Carl had put it lightly. Collette was indeed beaten up. Bruises are present above both of her cheekbones and across her nose. Tiny cuts mar the side of her once-beautiful face. Her left arm is in a cast, and she has a wrap of some kind around her torso. The rest of her body is covered by the hospital blanket, so it's hard to discern what damages are hidden underneath.

"She suffered a compound fracture of her radius—it punctured right through her skin. They did a CT and an MRI scan, which is what caught the internal bleeding in her abdomen. She just got out of surgery. They fixed her arm and they stopped the bleeding. The doctor says we were lucky because they caught the bleeding early. It could have been a lot worse. She doesn't have any spinal cord injuries or head trauma. The cuts on her face and body are from the front and side airbags deploying, but those are minor compared to what happened on the inside. She was wearing her seatbelt, so she has a pretty nasty bruise across her chest, but the EMT said it's what kept her from being ejected from the vehicle."

As Greg talks, the image of Collette being thrown around her vehicle plays through my mind, and I feel sick to my stomach. I silently praise her for being the responsible one yet again.

Greg moves from the side of the bed, and I walk closer to Collette. I bend down and gently take her hand in mine, the one not wrapped in the cast, careful not to disturb the IV that is attached to the back of it.

Her eyes are closed, and she is breathing softly. The beeps of the monitor tell me her heart rate is steady.

"Thank God you're still here," I whisper. "I don't know what I would do without you."

"Of course I'm still here. They won't let me out of this place," comes her hoarse voice.

My head snaps up, and even though her eyes are still closed, she is attempting to grin at me. Dropping her hand, I lean in to hug her, but in my haste to envelop her I forget about the other arm in the cast.

"Oh!" Collette lets out a soft moan.

"Oh, no! Oh, I'm so sorry! I didn't mean to do that."

Collette lets out a pained laugh. "It's okay. Come on. Get in here." She motions for me to hug her again, and I lean down, gently this time, mindful of her injuries.

"I'm so sorry," I whisper into her hair.

"Me too," she says in the faintest of voices, obviously struggling just to speak.

I stand back up and notice Greg and Carl have

retired to the back of the room, murmuring between themselves. Carl with his arm around Greg, offering silent support. I'm momentarily fascinated by how comfortable they seem together for having just met.

I look back down at my sister. "What are you sorry for? Please don't be sorry. I'm the only one who should be apologizing. I'm so ashamed about how I acted in Hawaii. I left you standing on a street corner!"

The sides of Collette's lips turn up in an attempt at a smile, but the effort is too great, so she just says, "Don't forget stranded on an island."

"Right, and stranded on an island, with a virtual stranger." I smile at her. "I was such a jerk. I don't know what I was thinking."

"Mm-hm," Collette says before drifting off to sleep again, the pain meds kicking in.

I sit this way for a few minutes, holding her hand while she sleeps, listening to her breathing in and out.

I notice the chatting in the back of the room has stopped, and I turn to see Greg and Carl watching me.

When they see that Collette has drifted back to sleep, they come closer to the bed.

Greg puts his hand on my shoulder. "She's going to be okay, you know?"

I wipe the tears from my eyes with the hand not gripping Collette's. "I know," I manage to get out through a hiccup of breath.

I look at the men standing next to me. "I don't know what I would do without her."

They both nod solemnly, seeming to understand perfectly what I'm saying.

"She's my everything," Greg says and bends down to kiss her forehead. "I couldn't have her leave me either." He straightens up but doesn't let go of her hand that he's taken from my grasp.

"We should probably let her sleep," Carl says. "She's going to need her rest, if we want her to get better."

There is a moment of silence from Greg and me, and I can tell he's thinking the same thing I am. That I don't want to leave her. Not now that I've just seen her.

I look at Greg, waiting for his direction.

"How about you stay with her while I go check on the girls?" Greg suggests. "I need to let them know Mommy is going to be okay."

"Oh, the girls! Do they know what's happened?" I ask.

"I told them there was an accident, but I didn't tell them too much, I didn't want to worry them."

I nod my head in understanding while keeping my eyes on Collette's face.

"I'm happy to stay with her. You go check on the girls."

"You're sure you'll be okay?" Greg asks.

"I'll be perfect, as long as I can stay with Collette," I answer.

"I'll stay with her too," Carl offers. "That is, if you don't mind."

I look at Carl and feel a certain kinship with him that I don't know how to process or explain, so I just say, "I'd like that."

Greg gathers his things and heads out the door, but not before asking us to contact him the minute Collette is awake or if anything changes.

I assure him we will as he walks out the door, leaving Carl and me in compatible silence.

****

We stay that way for the next few hours, waiting patiently as Collette sleeps. I try not to focus on the long journey Collette is going to have to face to regain her normal life. I know she's going to curse every step of the way, but with her family and me by her side I know she'll make it through. I make a silent promise to her, to be there for her. I will never again leave her stranded and alone.

I'm finishing my solemn vow to Collette when Carl clears his throat and sits down in the chair opposite me, on the other side of the bed.

I look up, realizing he has something to say.

But instead of talking, Carl reaches into the back pocket of his jeans and pulls out a folded envelope, holding it between his hands. He turns it over a few times. I watch in silence before he starts talking,

"I know things have been a little crazy today," he starts.

That's the understatement of the century, I think to myself. But I just nod my head and wait for him to continue. "Anyway, you've probably been so preoccupied with everything that you didn't think to ask why I was here. In Bellevue, I mean."

I look at him and realize he's right, I've completely taken for granted Carl's presence here. I've used him as a support structure without even bothering to wonder how or why he was here in the first place.

"This is the reason why I came." He pauses to hold out the envelope to me. I reach out and take it gingerly from his fingers, like it might disintegrate from my touch. He doesn't have to tell me what's in the envelope, I already know.

"I've already looked at it," he says.

I stare at him intently, trying to place his emotions, to decipher what is inside the folded paper without having to read it.

Carl lifts his hand up and points to the envelope. "The results."

"Yes," I say, realizing I should say more, but lacking any intelligent words for this particular situation.

But it's Carl's next words that knock the wind out of me. "Collette knows already."

"How can you both know what this says?" I look at the sealed envelope in my hands.

"She didn't want to learn the results without you," Carl says, reading my mind.

"Then I really don't understand. How does Collette know?" I ask, trying and failing to hide my hurt feelings.

"I got the results first, and well, let's just say it's a bit more complicated than I was expecting. I called Collette yesterday to ask her advice. She was going to meet me at your condo to go over the results. We were going to do it together."

I'm beyond confused by what Carl is trying to say.

"What exactly do the results say?" I ask trying to figure out why he would need Collette's advice.

"Why don't you just open that." He points to the envelope. "I think it will all make sense after you read it."

I narrow my eyes and pull at the flap, releasing the seal. I reach in with my fingertips and gently pull out a two-page report.

It takes me a minute, reading it from top to bottom.

Only I can't really understand anything on the page. It's full of numbers and letters that don't make any sense.

I look over the top of the paper at Carl, who is looking at me with what I think is amusement in his eyes. "Need some help?" he says in a teacher's voice, his eyebrows raised.

"How do you know what it all means?" I ask in frustration.

"Look at the bottom left-hand paragraph," he offers.

I look closer, and sure enough below all the columns of what seems like random data there is a written paragraph:

The alleged father is not excluded as the biological father of the tested child/children. Based on testing results obtained from analyses of the DNA loci listed, the probability of paternity is 99.9998%. This probability of paternity is calculated by comparing to an untested, unrelated, random individual of the Caucasian population (assumes prior probability equals 0.05).

Under this in bold letters is:

Combined Paternity Index: 661,085

Probability of Paternity: 99.9998%

"So it is true. You really are our father." It takes me a few more seconds to let it all sink in, and when it finally does, I find myself propelled out of the chair, almost by a force of nature, and into Carl's arms.

"I feel the same way," Carl says soothingly, patting my back. "But I felt that way before I read that paper."

I peel myself off Carl and sit back down on the chair. "You could have fooled me."

Carl sighs. "I know. Look, it's not every day I get

that kind of information handed to me. I'm not perfect, and I probably didn't handle all this in an ideal manner. But Kayla and I have done a lot of talking, and she understands how I'm starting to feel about you and Collette. I'm so sorry I couldn't have been there for you all these years, and I feel terrible that all this time has been wasted, but I am letting you both know, right now, I'm going to make it my life's mission to be there for you from now on. If you feel lost, I want to help you find your way. If you feel alone, I want to be the one who stands by your side. I want to see you grow, accomplish, and finally enjoy all the things your life has to offer. And I want to be with you as you do it."

A chill runs down my spine, and I feel the most clear-headed I have in what seems like months. My face is dry, and my chest has lost the constant constriction I've been carrying around with me.

"You have no idea how much I'd like that," I say with the most confidence I've ever felt, save for the time Lenny asked me to marry him.

Carl squeezes my hand in his. "Ireland, I'd like you to remember what I just said as you read the next page of the report." He lets go of our hands and gently gives me the papers again.

I look at him with trepidation in my heart. I knew this was too good to be true. Is there more to the results that we didn't know? It says right here in black and white that he is our biological father, so what else can there be?

I take the papers and start scanning the second page.

The second page is different from the first one. It's a handwritten letter on the stationery of Dr. Collins. I start reading, and about halfway through the letter my stomach drops to the floor and I feel as though I might faint.

Dear Carl Martin,

I truly enjoyed meeting the girls when you brought them into the office the other day. I have enclosed the DNA results from the lab for you to go over. I am happy to answer any questions you might have on the results.

There is one additional piece of information that was brought to my attention that I feel I need to share in this report.

When Kayla originally booked the appointment, it was for DNA blood samples and an additional sample for an hCG test on Ireland.

When the lab processed the blood samples that we collected, they noticed Ireland's human chorionic gonadotropin, or hCG levels, were in 7,650-229,000 mIU/mL range. I'd say this places her around the seven- to eight-week mark of pregnancy. It is my recommendation she sees an ob-gyn for her first ultrasound and prenatal care if she has not already done so. I have attached a list of referrals in the Seattle/Bellevue area for her convenience.

Sincerely,

Dr. Collins MD

I look up and find myself staring into Carl's eyes. "It says I'm pregnant?!"

Chapter 26

"But how is that even possible?" I'm stunned, confused, and petrified all at once.

Carl looks at me like I've grown two heads.

"Oh, come on, I know how it *happens*. I just don't understand. I haven't even thought of anyone since Lenny died, let alone—"

"Well, how far along did Dr. Collins say you were?"

I recheck the letter, and sure enough, right there in black and white it says seven to eight weeks. I do a quick tally in my head and quickly realize it puts me right before the plane crash, the night Lenny and I made a mess of our kitchen.

I feel my cheeks flush hot at the memory.

"I see you've put it together," Carl says, a cocky grin across his face.

I bow my head slightly and mutter, "I do seem to remember something."

A small laugh escapes Carl's lips. He quickly regains his composure and sits patiently, waiting for my response.

"I'm going to be a mother," I say slowly and place my hand tentatively over my stomach, looking down to see if by some miracle I've gotten bigger in the last few seconds since I found out.

"Yes, you're going to be a mother," Carl repeats

for me.

"You're going to be a what?"

I'm thrown off by the sudden interruption, looking up and seeing Violet standing wide-eyed in the doorway.

"Did I just hear that right?" She makes her way into the room, heading straight for me. When she's just inches away, she pulls me to my feet and envelops me in a hug, wrapping me with her petite frame.

I let her hug me until she tires of our embrace, pulling away and holding me at arm's length. "Ireland, is it…? I mean, could it be…?"

"Lenny's? Yes, it has to be."

Tears instantly flow from Violet's eyes. She doesn't even bother to wipe them away, just lets them flow down her face while she keeps holding onto my arm. "Ireland, are you going to keep it?"

If I was shocked to find out I was pregnant just moments before, her question feels like a punch to the gut now. The thought of losing any part of Lenny again is unfathomable. "Of course I'm keeping it," I say without hesitation, even though I haven't even had time to process this yet.

"Oh, Ireland." Violet pulls me in for another hug, mumbling into my hair, "I'm going to be an auntie." When she pulls back, she catches sight of Collette over my shoulder, and she seems to remember her reason for coming here in the first place. She covers her mouth with a hand and whispers through her fingers, "Collette."

"She looks pretty bad, but the doctors say she's going to be okay."

"Really?"

"Yes, really. It'll take a few months of rehabilitation, but they say she's going to make a full recovery."

"Thank God." Violet turns away from me and touches Collette's hand, careful not to wake her. She stands, gives Carl a nod, and looks back to me. "After you left, I talked with Brandon and Daniel. They are going to review all the information on the hard drive against the off-site backups, and if it all checks out, they are going to focus the case purely on Cynthia."

"Thank you, Violet. I don't know what I would have done without you."

"Ireland, when are you going to understand? You are my family. If you need me, I'm there, now and always. And now, you're not going to be able to get rid of me. I'm going to be an auntie!"

I laugh at her unabashed enthusiasm, feeling myself starting to get caught up in it. "Yes, you're going to be the best auntie ever!"

My focus is broken yet again by a loud commotion outside Collette's door.

I listen for a few seconds, trying to discern what the noise is all about, before two pint-sized princesses clad in tiaras and sequins come barreling through the door. "Mommy!" they call, looking around the room for their mother.

Greg and Jenna come quickly through the door after them, whisper-yelling, "You have to be quiet in here!"

"Girls!" I exclaim, jumping into action just in time, stepping into their line of destruction before they can make it to their mother's bedside.

"Auntie Ireland!" I bend down and grab a girl in

each arm, hugging their little bodies to me.

I can see Carl in my peripheral vision, standing now, looking slightly bewildered by the sudden disturbance.

"Auntie Ireland, where's Mommy? I want to see Mommy," Molly whines at me, trying to peer over my shoulder.

I hold fast to my position, kneeling on the ground with a girl in each arm. "And you can, sweet girl, in just a minute." I look each of them in the eye with what I think is a solemn face, so they understand this is going to be a serious conversation. "First, I want to tell you that your mommy got a great big ow-ie. She's going to be okay, but I'm going to need you both to be very gentle with her. Can you do that for me?"

Both girls nod their heads, eyes big and sincere.

"Okay, very slowly, let's go see her."

I take a hand in each of mine, and we walk over, slowly, to where their mother lies on the bed. I notice they both look at Carl but don't say anything to him.

When we are at Collette's side, Molly reaches out a hand to touch her mom's arm. "Mommy?"

Molly turns to me. "Is she taking a nap?" She seems nonplussed by her mother's condition, and I'm silently grateful she isn't howling with sorrow.

"Yes, she's just resting right now, but you can sit here and hold her hand. She'll be waking up soon, and I know she'd love to see you when she does."

Molly nods her head and scoots into the chair, pushing to the side so Maggie can climb up with her. They both reach out and hold onto Collette's arm with their little hands. I watch them and smile, knowing that Collette is going to be okay, that she is going to be able to hold those little hands again and kiss their little faces again.

I glance over my shoulder, and Greg gives me a thankful smile. "I wasn't sure about bringing them here. I think in the end I caved because this one here"—he sticks his thumb in Jenna's direction—"wanted to come to check on you."

Jenna just smiles and shrugs her shoulders. "I wanted to see how everyone is, for myself."

"No, it's good. I think Collette will like seeing them when she wakes up. I know I would if I were her."

"Speaking of waking up." Greg motions to the bed where Collette is opening her eyes, blinking.

We all move to crowd around her bed, waiting patiently for her to focus.

"Well, this is quite a reception." She smiles, taking in each of us, one at a time.

"How are you feeling?" Greg reaches for her cheek and rubs it with his thumb.

"Like I've been hit by a car." She smiles.

"Mommy! You were hit by a car!" Maggie protests, and we all laugh.

"You're right, sweetie, I guess I was."

"I brought you my favorite Band-Aids. You can have them all." We laugh again, pleased with Maggie and her generosity.

Collette smiles at her girls and pats the bed next to her. Molly and Maggie both look up to Greg for approval. The second he nods his head yes, they are out of their chair and clambering up to snuggle into their mother.

I watch as the three of them become reunited and am impressed with Collette's natural motherly instinct.

But my admiration is cut short by a ringing from Violet's purse.

"Sorry, so sorry." She rushes across the small hospital room to where she left her handbag, muttering to herself, "I swear I turned the darn thing off."

I turn back to Collette. "Hey there."

"Hi."

"Do you need anything? Want us to call the nurse?"

"No, I'm okay, but maybe just…" She struggles to sit up more. "Just a hand." Greg and Carl jump into action, lifting and propping pillows behind her.

"That's better." She smiles her gratitude at the men and settles back into the bed, taking in each face smiling back at her, finally locking eyes with Carl.

"All I remember is your phone call and driving over to Ireland's. After that, well, it's all blank."

"It's probably better that way," Greg says.

I nod my head in agreement and make a conscious decision to tell Collette at another time who was driving the other vehicle, after she's recovered a bit and isn't so fragile. "We'll give you the details later. It's really not that important."

"Right. What's important is that you're here," Carl chimes in.

Collette looks from Carl to me and back to Carl. "Did you guys talk?"

"We might have had a conversation or two," Carl confirms.

She looks back to me. "So you know?"

"That Carl is our father, yes, I know."

She nods her head and looks at Carl. "And?"

"And that I'm going to be a mom? Yes, I know that

too!"

"Ireland!" Jenna shrieks from the side of the bed. She had been keeping quiet this whole time, letting us have our moment, but this news must have been too much for her. "You're pregnant? Oh, my god! That's, that's…" her enthusiasm wanes as she keeps talking. "Well, is it good?" she finally asks me.

I smile at her. "Yes." I move my hand to my stomach. "It's good. Shocking, but good."

Jenna gives me a hug. "Oh, I'm so happy for you!"

I smile again. "Yup, it looks like I'm going to be a mom!"

Molly and Maggie perk up at what I just said and start squealing and bouncing up and down. Collette laughs and tries unsuccessfully to calm them down. "Welcome to the club!"

"Ha! The chaos club!" Greg says, putting a hand on each girl's shoulder to keep them from jostling their mother.

"I have another club for you," Violet calls from the back of the room, stowing her phone back into her purse. "How does the free women club sound?"

I look at her expectantly, waiting for her to continue.

"That was Brandon. They were able to get into the hard drive and pull up your old backups. He said once they had the backups, it was obvious to them the data was changed on the dates you were out of town. You are no longer part of their investigation."

There is a chorus of "congratulations," and "thank God that's over," from around the room.

Suddenly drained from the day's events, I sit on the foot of Collette's bed and look around at the chattering people surrounding me. I think about Mother, just down the hall but all alone. How the decisions she made shaped how she ended up there and how even though I know who she is and how she operates, I'll still forgive her. I will always hold out hope that one day the ice around her heart will melt and she will want to be a part of her own family.

I think about Collette and Greg and how the little arguments we have don't really matter in the big scheme of things. What matters is that we have our health and our love for one another.

I think about Violet and Mel and Sheila and am grateful for them and their unconditional love and support, something I wasn't used to but now find myself relying on.

And finally I think about life and how fleeting and precious it is. I place my hand on my stomach and think of Lenny and the child that is ours growing inside me, and I know, without a doubt, that this child is his gift to me, to all of us.

Epilogue

"Hey! How's the boss doing?" Jenna's ever-chipper voice proceeds her as she bounds through the door of my office. It has only been recently that I've developed the acute ability to tell who has had a decent night's sleep and not been woken up umpteen times during one eight-hour period. And right now I know, without hesitation, Jenna is one of those infuriating people.

"Oh, stop being so bouncy. I'm exhausted!" I rake a hand through my hair and pull it up into a high ponytail, hoping it draws attention up and away from the bags under my eyes.

"I wasn't talking about you." Jenna keeps walking right past me, ignoring my obvious dismay, to the Lucite crib taking up the place of honor next to my new desk. "I was talking about this little guy right here," Jenna bends down and picks up the little ball of chunkiness that has been peacefully sleeping until this very minute. "Yes, I was. I was talking to you. Hello, Handsome." Jenna coos at the baby while expertly tucking him into her arm, bouncing up and down to soothe him from being woken. She bends her head down and takes in a deep breath right above his head. "Oh, I love that new baby smell. Who knew I'd be so baby crazy? Good thing you went and got knocked up so I could ravish this little guy."

I smile in spite of myself and push away from the desk, abandoning all the tasks screaming for my attention for a few minutes longer.

These little midmorning breaks with Jenna have become my favorite time of day. It's our ritual now, her stopping by on her way from the yoga studio, typically for just a few minutes' chat before running off again. But today was going to be different. We had plans to discuss.

Jenna adjusts her arms so she can stare at the precious package she is holding. "So, Mr. Leo Evans-Jacobson, how are you today? Hmm? What's that? You think Santa is going to give you a great big teddy bear for Christmas? Well, I don't see why not."

"Hey, now, don't you go getting any crazy ideas. I don't have room for a gigantic teddy bear right now."

"But you will when you're finished moving into your new place."

"You're right, and just as soon as we're all settled you can go get all the teddy bears you can carry, but right now, not so much."

"Oh, fine, you're such a spoilsport." Jenna redirects her attention to Leo. "Yes, isn't that right? Your mommy doesn't let us have any fun, does she?"

Right on cue, Leo lets out an ear-shattering wail. On instinct, I rise from my chair and reach out my arms to Jenna. She hands him over reluctantly. "Sorry but I got the goods. You can't compete with these lovelies," I say and squeeze my engorged chest together.

"Ew, gross. Those things are huge! Seriously, that's got to be uncomfortable."

"It's one of those 'miracles of motherhood,'" I say as I place a coverup around my neck and situate Leo so he can latch on, relieving me of the pressure that was starting to build up.

"Hey, just who I wanted to see!" Collette says, catching sight of Jenna as she enters the office. There is a quick embrace between the two of them before Collette comes to sit behind the matching new desk in the room. I'm pleased to see Collette no longer protects her arm while hugging Jenna.

"Have I told you guys I love what you've done with the place?" Jenna says as she lies down on the couch and kicks her feet up.

"Only about a million times." I laugh.

"Right, well let me just say it again. I love what you've done with the place."

I look around the room, and I'm pretty pleased with what I see as well. It only took Collette and me a week to completely transform Mother's top floor office into a partners' office, one that is warm and inviting. Gone are the stark white walls and functional furniture, and in its place are soft blues accented with warm golds. Potted plants dot the perimeter of the room, and the tufted robin's-egg-blue couch is the perfect final touch, as well as the ideal place to take a much-needed nap.

"I still can't believe how it all turned out," Jenna muses.

I look at Collette and match her identical smile. "Like it was meant to be."

"I know, but I still can't believe your mother, after everything, would still hand The Club over to you."

"She might be cruel and conniving, but above all that, she's a shrewd businesswoman. She knew it was her only option if she ever wanted to get a piece of her club back after she got out of jail."

"And Ireland and I are the two people who know this club inside and out. We were the obvious choice for stepping in and making sure The Club keeps running without any pauses," Collette adds.

"But you gave up your job at the foundation. You had just gotten that job, hadn't you?" Jenna asks.

"I had, but when family needs you"—she smiles at me—"you do what you can to help them. And, honestly, this was the best decision I've ever made. I love working with you."

"And I with you, I couldn't do all this"—I indicate the bundle of joy under my cover sheet—"without you."

"And if I'm completely honest, it's probably saved my marriage too. Greg was tired of staying at home with the girls. This way we're able to share the duties. He's much happier now."

"Say, how's he doing with the project, by the way?" I ask as I snap my bra back together and remove the cover to unveil a sleeping baby.

There is a brief pause in our conversation as Jenna and Collette ooh and aah over Leo before I place him back in the crib.

After the initial shock of being pregnant wore off, I spent endless hours worrying. Worrying about the self-medication I had done and how that might affect the baby growing inside me. Worrying about how I was going to provide for a child with no job and no foreseeable prospects and worrying about how I was going to raise a child on my own, without a partner to lean on. But in the end, everything worked out. My ob-gyn assured me that women have found themselves in the same position as myself, unaware of being pregnant and having a drink or two. And while she didn't encourage me to continue an alternative lifestyle, she didn't think I had caused any damage by my past indiscretions.

Now watching over my son with my sister and friend by my side, I can see just how right the doctor was. Leo is the most perfect baby I could have asked for. Chubby and healthy, he resembles his father in ways that make my heart ache. But also, in ways that make me smile with pride when I look at him. He is Lenny's last and best accomplishment here on earth, and I am a part of it.

"He's making great progress. He's waiting for some of the permits to come back from the city, and then we can start demo," Collette said, bringing me back to our conversation.

"You guys are crazy for starting a project so big. You know that, right?" Jenna says under the arm she has flung across her forehead, Grace Kelly style.

I look to Collette again, and we both just shrug our shoulders. "It's a big project, but it's our legacy with The Club. And besides, we have the whole family working on it."

"Well, that's the truth." Jenna laughs. "Mel's doing the construction, Violet is acting as the realtor, you've got Greg operating the whole project, and the two of you doing all the behind-the-scenes work, all while keeping this place running smoothly. I've got to hand it to you both. You really did pay attention all those years. I've never seen things go so smooth at The Club."

I smile. "I know, and the expansion project is bringing in even more memberships, too. I think the media campaign we ran helped to counteract all the bad press we were getting from the trial."

There is a brief moment of silence as we all reflect on the chaos of the last few months.

After Collette was released to go home, it became apparent that she was going to need to take time off work for her recovery. At the same time she was moping around the house, the trial for Mother started to heat up. What Violet had predicted indeed came to pass. The media took hold of the case, and the IRS didn't let up, sentencing Mother with imprisonment of five years and a fine of $250,000. When word got out that she was being tried for reckless driving resulting in bodily injury, tacking on an additional thirty days to her jail sentence and another couple thousand dollars to her fine, there was no end of it on the news.

Knowing there was only one way to save The Club, I called a family meeting. With Collette, Greg, Mel, Sheila, and Violet all in attendance, we devised a plan to divert the media attention away from Mother by coming up with an expansion project that was, in all respects, entirely over the top. In addition to the new childcare center, The Club would now house a complete overnight suite service for the nearby plastic surgery clinic, offering twenty-four-hour concierge services to those recovering from any surgeries.

With all the bungalows crafted after the ones Collette and I had stayed in at the Kahala Resort, Mel mapped out the details, leaving Mother no choice but to hand over the reins to Collette and me. And it has worked so far. With Mother already serving her time in jail, and construction underway, the media did an about face and started painting The Club and its new CEO duo as heroes of sorts, touting the accomplishment of the twin sisters who, against all the odds, were turning The Club around.

Collette and I have worked tirelessly to make sure the turnover has been done smoothly and without drama. With Mel and Greg spearheading the construction, it seems like the whole family is working nonstop.

But not tonight. Tonight Carl, Kayla, and Kai are flying into Seattle. After picking them up from the airport, we are all headed over to the Evans' home for Christmas Eve dinner.

"I can't believe you're breaking Club tradition and closing for a holiday." Jenna says, pulling us out of our thoughts.

"Some traditions are meant to be changed. That is how progress is made," Collette responds.

"And there is definitely progress being made here." Jenna answers.

I look around the office at the new furniture, at my son sleeping peacefully in his crib, right by my side, at Collette sitting at her desk, looking like she belonged there all along, and at Jenna, still perfectly perfect just being herself, and I smile. One thing I've learned this last year is that life will have its ups and downs. They will manifest themselves in ways that are inconceivable. They can challenge you, cause you heartbreak and heartache, or they can build you up, enlighten your soul, and broaden your horizons, but the thing that must be constant is that there must always be progress. And Jenna is right. There is progress being made here.

A word about the author...

When not spending her time creating make-believe people and places, Jacquline Kang lives in Kirkland, Washington with her very real family of one husband, three children, and two nephews.

In her past life, Jacquline has held jobs as a personal trainer, a spa manager, a dental assistant, and an office manager, but her true love is writing and sharing a well-crafted story.

Thank you for purchasing
this publication of The Wild Rose Press, Inc.

For questions or more information
contact us at
info@thewildrosepress.com.

The Wild Rose Press, Inc.
www.thewildrosepress.com

CPSIA information can be obtained
at www.ICGtesting.com
Printed in the USA
LVHW032038300320
651616LV00001B/43